SLEEP OF THE INNOCENT

SLEEP OF THE INNOCENT

MEDORA SALE

Charles Scribner's Sons • New York

Maxwell Macmillan International
New York • Oxford • Singapore • Sydney

Charles Scribner's Sons
Macmillan Publishing Company
866 Third Avenue
New York, NY 10022

Macmillan Publishing Company is part of the Maxwell Communication Group of Companies.

This is a work of fiction. Names characters, places, and incidents either are the product of the author's imagination or are used fictitiously. Any resemblance to events or persons, living or dead, is entirely coincidental.

Library of Congress Cataloging-in-Publication Data
Sale, Medora.
    Sleep of the innocent / Medora Sale.
       p. cm.
    ISBN 0-684-19305-1
    I. Title.
PR9199.3.S165S54   1991
813'.54—dc20   91-255

10 9 8 7 6 5 4 3 2 1

Printed in the United States of America

For
Dina Fayerman
and
Jacqueline Shaver,
whose patience and encouragement helped
to make all of this possible

SLEEP OF THE INNOCENT

CHAPTER 1

The call came in at 3:02 on a quiet Thursday afternoon in March. A north wind, blowing straight down from Baffin Island, was keeping the streets free of troublemakers; the dispatcher, working with purely mechanical efficiency, drowsed in the bright sunshine and thought of all the places where he would rather be. Warm places. Places where spring had already arrived. Places like . . .

The hysteria in the voice on the other end of the line had elicited his usual calm response without seriously interrupting his daydream, but the message he had taken down more or less automatically jolted him awake. The hysteria was routine; the tale was not. Wounding by gunshot is rare in expensive midtown hotels. "Please don't hang up, miss," the dispatcher was saying as a click signaled the broken connection. "Damn," he muttered philosophically, unsurprised, and set about dealing with the problem.

The Karlsbad Hotel was a scant two blocks from the corner of Bloor and Yonge, the midtown center of Toronto; there was a patrol car idling along James Street, fifty yards away, when the call went out. In seconds the constable in it had double parked in the no-parking area in front of the hotel, blocking a green Mercedes being tagged by an earnest-looking police cadet. "Here, you," said the constable. "Give us a hand. Fast."

The reply was indistinct. The constable took it as assent

and hustled in through the heavy brass doors, dragging the cadet after him.

"Third floor, apartment three-seventeen. Gunshot wound." He looked around the small, very quiet lobby. The elevator stood open. "Up the stairs. I'll take the elevator. And hang on to any witnesses you run into."

The cadet flew up the stairs two at a time, intent on arriving before that arrogant lazy bastard stepped out of the elevator. He paused at the second floor landing for a quick glance through the glass panel set in the door and looked down the corridor. Nothing. But the swish of a fire door opening as he rounded the corner to the next flight made him stop and look up.

A woman was clattering down the cement steps headed straight for him. His still-inexperienced eye took in a set of keys in her hand and a very tight and very short leather skirt; at the same time his nostrils were assailed by a heavy perfume that set off warning bells in his head. No girl he knew would wear perfume like that. Her eyes were on the steps as she rushed down them; her first intimation of his existence was a view of his boots. She stopped, her hand on the banister, and let her eyes travel upward. Her white face, under its white makeup, turned ashen, and the keys dropped out of her hand. He stooped to pick them up.

"Excuse me, miss," he said awkwardly. "I'd, uh—" He took a deep breath and started again. "I have to ask you to return to the third floor with me. If you don't mind."

"I do mind," she said sharply. "I'm late and I'm in a hurry. And I haven't been anywhere near the third floor, so I can't return to it. I've come down from the fifth. So, if I could have my keys back—"

The cadet hesitated for a moment. Lectures on the rights of citizens battled in his conscience with the curt injunction from the constable to grab anyone he could find. He looked at the skirt and the bizarre makeup, and his resolve strengthened. "Look here—someone opened that door to the third floor corridor, and I never heard you coming down those stairs all the way from the fifth. You'd better come along with me," he said firmly, "and give a statement to the other officer." He still held her keys clutched tightly in one large hand. He stepped forward, taking her black-clad arm in his other hand, and began to steer her up toward apartment 317, nervous perspiration pouring down between his shoulder blades.

Sergeant Rob Lucas dropped the telephone receiver back on its cradle and swore. Loudly. If he had not stopped to tidy off his desk, if he had not been a softhearted ass and agreed to stick around while Eric had one of his late, long, boozy, and erotic lunches, he would have been out of there before this call came in. Out and away, and it would have taken them hours to find him. He shoved the piece of paper across his desk. "When Patterson gets back, tell him to get his ass over to the hotel right away. The only reason I'm going now is to keep him out of trouble. Make sure he understands that."

As soon as he walked into the lobby of the hotel Lucas was almost drowned in an unwelcome wave of nostalgia. He had known the place from his school days. It was a quietly expensive apartment hotel, respectable enough that a man walking in there could equally well be seeking the sleep of the innocent after a late night at the office, or be paying a discreet visit to his mistress. It was also the place where his father used to take him for lunch on half holidays from school. The dining room was small, expensive, and good at what it did. It knew its clientele only too well; fads came and fads went, but at the Karlsbad one could be assured of properly smoked salmon, or Dover sole, or delicately pink roast lamb and an array of pastries for dessert that would soften the harsher moods of a mistress or delight a schoolboy at lunch. Not a place, he thought as he waited for the elevator, where people got themselves murdered. Not until now, anyway. But then, it had changed ownership since his days at private school. Perhaps the clientele was rowdier.

Having achieved the third floor, he pushed his way through the crowd in the corridor into apartment 317, stepped carefully over a cordless telephone lying on the floor of the entrance hall, and then stopped in the doorway to see what he was up against. The living room facing him was large and insipid, a model of middle-class restraint, enlivened only by the presence of the corpse lying supine on the floor. Lucas bent over to have a closer look. He had been a big man, somewhat plump, and expensively dressed. His face was clean-shaven and undamaged, its muscles slackened in death, in unpleasant contrast to the shattered skull visible through his thin, pale hair. You didn't need a medical degree to figure out that he was dead. Forty? Forty-five? He didn't look as though he'd ever been particularly pleasant. "He's been bleeding on the nice new carpet," said Lucas. "That'll irritate the management. Who is he?"

"Dunno," said the constable standing beside him, and shrugged his shoulders. "I just checked his pockets. No wallet—nothing like that. Someone's gone down to see the manager. He should know."

I wouldn't count on that, thought Lucas cynically, and glanced around at the bare room: pale blue walls, two large glass coffee tables with nothing on them but a half glass of red wine, side tables empty even of a magazine, no shoes or socks on the floor, no clutter at all, in fact. Except for the corpse. "What else is there?" he asked finally, and yawned. He should have been home in bed hours ago.

"Small kitchen, bedroom, bathroom. Nothing much in the kitchen except the other wineglass—bedroom and bathroom might be a bit more interesting."

Lucas walked around the corpse, glancing into the kitchen as he went, and went into the bedroom. The bed looked

like the aftermath of a demolition derby. Lucas picked up
a pillow and sniffed at it. "Perfume," he said. "Disgusting
stuff." He shook his head. "Recent activity in this bed, I'd
say. Wouldn't you, Constable?"

"I would," he answered briefly. "Look in there, sir."

Lucas walked over and opened the door. It led to a large
and luxurious-looking bathroom that reeked of the heavy,
musky odor that had permeated the sheets and pillows of
the bed. "Christ—it stinks in here."

The constable leaned in beside him and pointed to a bottle of perfume on the counter. Beside it sat a rumpled hand
towel. "She must have spilled some. The towel's soaked
with it. It's called Cobra, according to the bottle," he added
in bemused tones.

"I can smell, Constable," said Lucas irritably. The bathroom was even untidier than the bedroom. Towels spilled
out of a large linen cupboard, whose slatted door was hanging open; a couple of wet bath towels and an even wetter
bath mat were hanging over the edge of the tub and droop-
ing onto the floor. There were tubes and sticks and boxes
and bottles of makeup lying on the counter. He picked up
an uncovered lipstick lying in a pool of water on the edge
of the basin. It looked black to him, or maybe dark brown.
"Jesus," he muttered, "who would wear a color like this?
It's sick."

"That girl out in the hall," said the constable, as if
Lucas's question had been a serious inquiry.

"You mean they've got her?" said Lucas, yawning. "I'll
see her in a minute." He turned back to the bedroom.
"What's in these drawers?"

"I haven't had time to check yet," said the constable
defensively.

"Then get a move on. I'll search, you write," said Lucas
irritably, stuffing his notebook back into his pocket and
opening the top drawer. "In the top left-hand drawer," he
muttered, his fingers moving rapidly through the contents,

"women's underpants, white cotton, and black tights.
Count them later. Right below," he went on, closing one
drawer and opening the next, "there is one large white
sweater—wool—one pair of jeans, and three pairs of wool
socks. Below that," he went on, throwing open the bottom
drawer, "a black garter belt, black stockings, and black lace
pants. That's it. In the top right-hand drawer," he said,
slamming one closed with his knee as he opened the next,
"shirts, socks, shorts, and handkerchiefs, men's. Oh—and
just a minute—Jesus Christ!" he spluttered, digging farther
back behind the handkerchiefs. "Look at that."

"Either this guy had one hell of a sex life," said the constable, who was peering over his shoulder, torn between
laughter and admiration, "or he wore 'em six at a time!"

Lucas spilled two fistfuls of packages of condoms back
into the drawer. "Cautious, anyway," he said, grinning. "I
better talk to that woman. Get her for me, and then check
the closet," he added, walking into the living room and
almost stumbling over the corpse. "Do you think one of
you guys might manage to cover him up? I need this room
to talk to a witness." Someone drifted in the direction of
the bedroom to get a sheet. "And for Christ's sake, not
those sheets, you fool! They're evidence. What have you
gotten from her so far?"

"She says that her name is Stormi Knight," began the
constable.

"Come off it," said Lucas. "You've got to be kidding."

The constable's face reddened. "That's what she says,"
he repeated doggedly. "I just took a statement from her and
wrote it all down. I never questioned what she said. I reckoned you guys could sort it all out. She sings in a band;
she knows nothing about anything. She was visiting a friend
in the hotel—"

"Who?"

"A girlfriend. No name. Just a girl she met, when someone in uniform, actually it was that cadet over there," he

added, nodding out the door, "grabbed her for no reason and brought her up here and made her look at a dead man lying on the floor, and she's never seen the dead man before. And it made her feel sick, and she's thinking of suing us."

As they reached the hallway, the elevator door opened and disgorged a new crowd of people. "Thank God," said Lucas, rubbing his aching temple. "Here come the rest of them. I'm not even supposed to be here. This is Eric Patterson's case." He turned to the constable. "Look, tell Patterson when he gets here I'm talking to the girl, and he owes me. But not in there," he muttered, suddenly reluctant to return to that icy blue room. "What else did you get from her?"

"Not much—but when the cadet grabbed her, she dropped a set of keys. I tried them in the door," he added modestly.

"And?"

"One of them fits. The door of this room."

"Good. Where is she?"

"Over there, leaning on the wall."

In the discreet light of the corridor, Robert Lucas got the distinct impression of something dead propped up against the red-and-gold wallpaper. Stormi Knight was dressed in black: a black leather skirt that revealed too much skinny, black diamond-patterned leg; a black minuscule cardigan; a mop of curly shoulder-length hair dyed a flat, dead black. At least, he assumed it had been dyed. He didn't believe nature had ever been cruel enough to give anyone hair that color. When he got closer, he could see that her face was caked with white powder, except around the eyes, where her mascara and whatever had run and smeared into black rings. Her lips were bare of makeup, although surely the tube in the bathroom had been lipstick. That fat, dead mouth in there had probably eaten it off. He felt slightly sick. Closer still, and he could smell the heavy, cloying perfume, although it was less noticeable out here than it had been in the apartment. On her right cheekbone was the broad yellow smudge of an old bruise, barely concealed by the heavy makeup; on her right shoulder, close to the neck, an angry red mark spoke of a nasty bruise to come.

Lucas had seen them all before. He snapped open his notebook and said, "Name?" almost before she had registered his presence.

"Stormi—" she began sulkily.

"Real name, this time. If you don't mind."

"Jennifer Wilson," she said, and raised her chin stubbornly. "Stormi Knight's my stage name. So it is a real name."

"Who is the man in the apartment?"

"Which man?" she asked innocently.

"The corpse. The one the constable took you in to look at. How many corpses do you run across in one day?"

"I have no idea," she said steadily. "I don't know why you should think—"

"Why? Because you were carrying a key chain with the key to apartment three-seventeen on it when the cadet spotted you on the stairway, that's why. If you don't know him, how do you explain the key to his apartment?"

"Shit," she muttered, and paused, chewing her lower lip nervously. "I guess I should have told you, but I was scared I'd get mixed up in it—"

"Listen, lady," he said. "You are mixed up in it."

She shrugged her shoulders and then winced. "Uh, it's like this," she said. Her eyes flickered nervously. "I was out of town—the band was, the one I sing with—and when I got back, my landlady had rented my apartment to someone else. I was behind with the rent or something. Anyway, they hadn't paid us for this last job yet, and I was real broke, and this girl I met last night said she had this huge apartment she lived in, and I could sleep on the couch if I wanted. And so that's what I did."

"And what's this girl's name?"

"Krystal. And I don't know what her last name is," she

snapped. "We don't expect our friends to show us ID. And probably her first name isn't Krystal, either. It's probably Mary, or Lesley, or Susan, but she wanted something snappy that would help her career."

Lucas speculated for a second about the nature of the career and abandoned the line of thought. "So where's this Krystal now?"

"How should I know? She told me I had to clear up all my stuff and get out by eleven, just in case, and not to come back before three. Because she had a friend coming by. I figured it was the guy who was paying for the apartment, because Krystal sure as hell didn't have that kind of money. So I got out. I mean, I didn't want to run into him."

"If this Krystal was entertaining someone this afternoon, how come the sheets and everything stink of that perfume you're wearing?"

She blinked in a flash of amazement, and for the first time he noticed that behind the gooey black mess she possessed a pair of large, sharp gray eyes. "Oh, dear," she said, for a second sounding oddly sweet and innocent. "How embarrassing. I borrowed a couple of splashes of it. And I'm afraid I spilled it while I was opening the bottle. I'm such a klutz. It's kind of overpowering, isn't it? It's terribly expensive," she added, and almost smiled. "It's Cobra."

"Yeah—we got that. Now maybe you could give us—" He stopped and looked at three people stepping out of the elevator, two constables with another man in tow. That dark suit and polished exterior could only belong to the hotel manager. "Here—you," he said to the cadet, who was still standing around, looking curious and unsure of himself, "keep an eye on Miss Wilson. I'll be back in a minute."

He followed the small crowd into the living room and pushed his way up to the manager's shoulder. Someone pulled back the sheet that had been draped over the body. There was a dignified pause. "I certainly do know him," said the manager somberly.

"Who is he?" asked Lucas. "The person who rents this apartment?"

"He's the chairman of the corporation that owns this hotel," said the manager. "NorthSea/Baltic Enterprises. Apartment three-seventeen is the apartment reserved for the corporation, which means, in effect, for Mr. Neilson. That's his name. Carl Neilson. He lives—he lived out of town, near Thornhill; he used this apartment a great deal."

"Did he ever have company while he stayed here?" asked Lucas. "Female company?"

"Female company?" He paused. Lucas could see the battle raging within him. Between honesty and loyalty? Between discretion and disapproval? More likely the latter. "You understand, gentlemen, it is not my job to monitor the actions of the chairman of the corporation. And in addition, all the apartments are on the second and third floors, so that the residents, if they wish, may come and go as they please. Without taking the elevator. The stairs, as you no doubt have observed already, take you directly outside or to a section of the lobby that is not particularly visible from the desk. Deliberately. All that aside, however," he said even more gravely than before, "from time to time I believe that Mr. Neilson may have had female companions staying with him. I would not be able to swear to that," he added with emphasis. "But it has come to my attention now and again."

"Ah," said Lucas in tones of triumph. "Wait right there." And he dashed out of the apartment, returning seconds later with a protesting Jennifer Wilson. "This one?"

The manager shook his head. "I wouldn't know," he said. His tone expressed disapproval. She obviously did not live up to hotel standards in female companions. "I don't believe I've seen this young lady before. But she could have been going in and out by the side exit if she had a key—a privilege we extend to monthly tenants—and of course, Mr. Neilson could supply one to any guest he chose." He gave her one more searching look. The next time he ran into her, he would know who she was, thought Lucas. And he didn't give much for her chances of getting into this hotel again. "The maids might know her. But they went off duty at two-thirty."

Irritated, Lucas pushed her out of the apartment again and back into the care of the cadet. Before he could return to the manager, however, the elevator door opened once again, and the errant Eric Patterson stepped out. Lucas stepped in his way, blocking his entrance to the apartment. "Christ almighty, you sure as hell took your time, Eric. Where have you been?"

"So what's going on?" said Eric with cheerful insouciance. "I get back from lunch and there's this pile of urgent messages, including one kind of nasty one from you." He looked around appreciatively. "This is a nice plush place to find a body in. Who is it?"

"The chairman of the corporation that owns the hotel, Carl Neilson. A very big guy, every which way you look." Lucas yawned. "You want to take over here, Eric?"

"What have you done?" he asked, dropping the frivolity.

"Not a whole lot. The crew just arrived. The guys who got here first picked up a witness probably coming from the scene. I was just going to take her down and fingerprint her and have them run a residue test—"

"He was shot?"

Lucas suppressed the sarcastic response. "Yes."

"I'll do that," said Patterson. "You don't have to—"

"The hell you will. I'm taking her in, running her through, and then going home. If anyone stays up all night tonight, it isn't going to be me. I haven't slept in"—he paused to calculate—"thirty-two hours, and it's beginning to show."

"Okay, okay. And look, I appreciate what you did. That lunch was—words fail me, Rob, old pal. But anytime you need a return favor—"

"All I need right now is some sleep. I'm going. Oh, and

get the girl's keys from that cadet or whoever still has them, and find out if one of them fits the side door of the hotel."

"What?"

"Don't ask. Just do it. Or talk to the manager."

Lucas propelled Jennifer Wilson across the lobby, holding her by one thin arm, toward his car, which had been abandoned in front of the hotel. As he handed her in on the passenger side, he suddenly noticed what else was odd about her. The coat. Or rather, the absence of it. She wasn't wearing a coat on a day in March so vicious that it made January seem temperate. And he had been able to feel her tremble with the cold. "Where's your coat?" he said curtly as soon as she got into the car.

"My coat?"

"Yes, your coat. Why aren't you wearing it?"

"It's not that bad out," she said, still shivering.

"For chrissake, the dogs are sticking to the sidewalks out there, and you're trying to tell me you don't need a coat?"

"I came over here in a cab," she said hastily. "I was just carrying it on my arm, and I left it in the cab, I think."

"What kind of cab?" he said, turning the heat up full and unzipping his down jacket.

"How in hell should I know? I don't go around writing everything down, like you guys." She slouched down in her seat and lapsed into sulky silence.

And the sulky silence remained as she wiped ink off her fingers and glowered at the floor.

"So," he said coolly, "your name is Jennifer Wilson, and you sing in a band, and you have nothing to do with that apartment except that you spent last night there. And you never saw that guy before in your life. You know what I think? I think when that apartment is dusted for prints, we're going to find Neilson's, yours, and the maid's. Period. And most of all we're going to find yours. Because I think Krystal is a figment of your imagination. Couldn't you have come up with a better name?"

"It's not my fault that Krystal has no imagination," she replied, her gray eyes flickering at him from their smudgy sockets. "And if that's what you think, why not go ahead and fingerprint everything?"

Her confidence shook him a little. "Okay. Let's run through the whole thing from when you left the apartment this morning. Or better still, when you met Krystal last night."

"Sure," she said, sounding bored. She yawned, and once more he realized how hideously tired he was. "I went to my apartment and couldn't get in, so I put my suitcase in a locker at the bus station—"

"Why there?"

"Why not? It's central and open all night." She paused to see if he wanted to say something else. He leaned back, yawning. "I'm sorry if it's boring," she said. "But you asked for it. Anyway, I went to the pub—which pub, I know, the Pocket, on Queen Street—because I figured at least a few people I knew would be there. Well there weren't, really, but I sat at a table with one guy I'd met a couple of times before—"

"Name?" said Lucas. His eyes were closed.

"Doug. Just Doug. And some other people, and one of them was this girl, Krystal. Anyway, I put my purse down on the floor and had a couple of beers, and when I reached down to get it because I was going to the washroom, it was gone. So now I had no purse, no ID, no credit card—yeah, I have a credit card—and no money. I got real upset, and Krystal said I could sleep at her place. Is this what you want?" she asked, looking at the apparently sleeping sergeant.

He had been barely listening to her words; what his mind

was playing with was the sense of familiarity induced by
her manner of speech. Suddenly it came to him, and he sat
up, eyes open. It was the continual slipping up and down
in the social scale—from the tough-guy illiteracy of half her
explanations up to snatches of cool elegance and intelli-
gence. And it was familiar because he did it himself. It was
one of the things that alienated him from the people he
worked with. His inability to find a level and stick to it. It
made people suspicious.

"Sure," he said, lapsing back into somnolence once he
had settled that.

"Anyway, this morning Krystal told me I had to go out
because her friend was coming over, and she loaned me
some money and gave me her keys. So I went out for lunch
and did some shopping—"

"What did you buy?"

"Nothing. I went downtown and looked around at a lot
of stuff. Killing time, that's all. Anyway, I took a cab and
left my coat in the cab, like I said, and got back to the
hotel. I came in the side door and went up to the apartment.
When I opened the door, I heard someone make this awful
noise—a groan or something like that. At first I thought it
was—well, anyway, I realized someone was hurt, and I
looked in the living room and saw this man lying there,
bleeding, and I panicked because he looked as if someone
had just shot him, and I didn't want whoever it was to
shoot me, so I called the police and ran."

"You thought the assailant was still in the apartment,
and you stopped long enough to telephone before you panicked and ran? You're a brave person, Miss Wilson."

"Well, I didn't. I grabbed the cordless phone off the hall
table and ran out in the corridor and phoned."

"And how did the phone get in the front hall again?"

"I opened the door and threw it back in. I didn't want
to be accused of stealing a telephone."

"Well," he said, yawning again. "They say truth is

stranger than fiction. You just make yourself comfortable there while we check some of these wild notions out, Miss Wilson. I'll get someone to bring you some coffee. You want a muffin? It's the best thing you're likely to get around here right now."

She looked as if she were considering a protest, shrugged her shoulders and huddled down in her chair.

Lucas's faint hope of catching a half-hour nap—while the mills of justice ground up Miss Wilson's statement and processed it—dried up as soon as he hit the corridor. The reason was walking rapidly toward him, a vision of expensive tailoring and more expensive shoe leather. Inspector Matt Baldwin, who for the past three uncomfortable weeks had replaced Inspector John Sanders as his superior officer, with a look on his face that meant more work. More work for Robert Lucas, that is, not for Baldy.

"Patterson finally get down there?" he snapped. Hostility electrified the corridor.

So the puss had clawed its way out of the sack. "Yeah. He's there now. I was just clearing up one or two things before going home."

"Not until someone goes out to talk to the widow," said Baldwin. "I just found out who it is, so be tactful, eh? This ain't Ma Jones whose old man got knifed in a brawl. It's Lydia Neilson."

"Isn't she just a mile or two out of our jurisdiction?" asked Lucas with heavy irony. "Why not let the locals tell her she's a widow?"

"She may be a witness. And I've cleared it. Now get the hell over there, Lucas."

Common sense told Lucas to shut up and get out; exhaustion prodded him into one last flicker of insubordination. "Do we have an address? More precise than Mrs. Neilson, somewhere near Thornhill?"

Lucas's bad temper remained through an hour of rush-hour traffic, past the exit off the expressway, down two secondary roads, and into the play farms of exurbia. Everything looked bright and cold and dirty with the detritus of winter. But familiar. Once upon a time, in a time and a world far from this one, he had lived out here on one of these little gemlike farms, until his father had tired of country life and his mother had tired of his father. And of him. And the farm was sold—at a handsome profit, no doubt, since everything his father did was at a handsome profit. Except raise a son. And he grinned at that thought, slowed down, and signaled for a right.

The broad acres belonging to Carl Neilson were protected from the highway by a stone wall and wrought-iron gates. On one of the pillars a polished brass plaque said FREY-FIELDS. The gates were open, and Lucas pulled in. The house was pseudo-Georgian; the white fencing said horses, and the whole setup screamed money. As he mounted the steps, he wondered why Baldy hadn't chosen to come out himself. Clearly Mrs. Neilson would be right up his alley. It must have been an epic struggle between lethargy and upward mobility while he was deciding to send Robert Lucas instead. The chimes rang faintly, as though muffled by miles of carpets and tapestries and draperies and other expensive things. The door opened with a sigh; its place was taken by a square middle-aged woman in a white uniform and apron, who looked like something between a practical nurse and a short-order cook. She tried to size him up, failed, and addressed him in a manner in which courtesy mingled uneasily with contempt.

"May I help you?" The words were meek enough, but the tone was one of crossed arms and heavily planted feet.

"I'd like to speak to Mrs. Neilson," he said briskly.

"I'm afraid she isn't here at the moment. Is she expecting you?"

With a sigh he pulled out his ID and set it squarely under

the woman's nose. "Sergeant Robert Lucas. Metropolitan Toronto Police. It is most important that I talk to Mrs. Neilson as soon as possible. Do you know where she is?" This was the point at which the housekeeper should have screamed and fainted in alarm. She didn't.

"She's down at the stable," she said, in the same tones she might reserve for describing the whereabouts of the man who looked after the septic tank.

"In that case, I'll wait," said Lucas, prepared, if necessary, to sit on the front steps. Because if he left without seeing her, bloody Baldwin would send him out again. He wondered grimly how long he was going to be on special duty, stuck with Baldwin.

"You'll have a long wait, then," she remarked sourly. "If it's that important, you'd better go and speak to her yourself. It's in back—you can't miss it," she said, pointing to the gravel walk that circled the house.

If the neat white building hadn't looked very like a stable to him, he would have been drawn to it by the small warm noises—the stamps and snorts and nickering—that ooze out of all stables. The wide door was open, giving onto a clean cement floor, and he stepped inside. There were six box stalls, three on each side, but only three of them had tenants. The first on the left had been fitted up as a tack room, its walls bright with ribbons, and the first on the right as an office, with a desk, two chairs, and a camp bed all crowded into it. The stall next to it was stacked neatly with feed and straw. Mozart bubbled gently from a cassette player on the desk.

Two heads emerged over their doors to look at him; a third horse, a chestnut mare, was standing facing him with a faraway look on her face as her legs were being vigorously rubbed down. "Mrs. Neilson?" said Lucas to the crouching back in front of him. "Could I have a word with you?" The chestnut tossed her head in warning, and Mrs. Neilson rose quickly to her feet. She looked to be in her mid-twenties—startlingly young to be Neilson's wife. She had long shiny hair the same color as the mare's glossy coat, and dark eyes that regarded him acutely, wondering no doubt what in hell he was doing there. She was dressed in worn, mud-splashed corduroy breeches, a beige turtleneck sweater, and a gray tweed jacket with scuffed leather patches and a tear on the sleeve, but her riding boots were as clean and well cared for as the tack in the room to his left and as the coat of the chestnut mare. What man could possibly have traded—even temporarily—this magnificent creature for that thin, messy little slut in the hotel? Maybe he hadn't. Maybe Jennifer's story was true, then.

"Yes, certainly," said Mrs. Neilson at last, since he seemed to be without anything to say. "What did you want a word about?"

He gritted his teeth. This was the bad part, the part he had been avoiding by thinking irrelevant thoughts about her clothes. "I'm with the Metropolitan Toronto Police—Sergeant Lucas." He held out his card, as before. "You're Mrs. Carl Neilson? Your husband is Carl Neilson?" It was, he knew, a stupid thing to say, but it gave the widow the chance to realize that something was wrong.

It worked. She laid a hand on the mare's withers, as if to steady herself. "Something has happened," she said. "That's why you're here, isn't it?"

"I'm afraid so, Mrs. Neilson. There's been a—something has happened at your husband's hotel, at the Karlsbad. He's been shot."

"He's dead?" she asked, her voice flat. Lucas nodded, bracing himself. This was when the reaction started. Sometimes. Sometimes it didn't start until much later, and what you got was this cool stunned acceptance. Not as good for the widow, maybe, but a hell of a lot easier on him. "You're sure?" she asked again. "Dead? Not just hurt?"

"No—I'm afraid there's no question of that," he said gently. "He was dead when we found him."

"Did he . . ." She hesitated and stopped, taking a deep breath. The mare snorted and bent her head around to find out what was going on. "Did he do it himself? Was it suicide?"

Lucas shook his head. "It doesn't appear to have been suicide. No."

"Then that means that someone killed him."

"It looks like that."

"Who would—when did it happen?" she asked.

"This afternoon. I'm sorry someone didn't come earlier, but he had no wallet on him, and it took us a while to find out—"

"You're sure it *is* Carl?" she said quickly.

"The hotel manager identified him."

"Bent? Bent Sigurdson?"

That sounded familiar. Lucas nodded.

"He would know." She sounded oddly reassured, as though the certainty of the identification comforted her. "Poor Carl," she said. She stood absolutely still, leaning slightly against the mare. "He was so afraid of dying. More than most people, I think. Do I have to identify him? I will if it's necessary." She patted the mare, who was stamping restlessly and turned to nudge her pockets.

"She's expecting something," said Lucas, nodding at the mare.

"There's a carrot on the desk, if you don't mind," said Mrs. Neilson. "She'd kill for carrots."

He stepped into the office, grabbed the carrot, broke it in half and fed one piece to the impatient animal; then, with a friendly pat, he caught her firmly by the halter and led her into the empty box.

"You've done that before," said Lydia Neilson.

"That I have," said Lucas. "Did your husband ride? Is one of the horses his?"

"Well, in a manner of speaking, I suppose." She spoke hesitantly, as if she felt her comments could be construed as a betrayal of marital trust. "The mare is my hacking pony—actually, I guess she's a bit big to be called a pony, but"—she gave him a pale smile—"she's a pet. Well, they're all pets, in a way. Too much so. That was Jasmine. This is Hector—eh, baby, come here," she cooed, and a big bay stuck his head farther over the door. She opened it and led him out. "Isn't he a beauty?" she said. "Most of the ribbons in there are his. He's very neat and intelligent—he can tell exactly what I'm thinking before I think it." She raised his head to show him off. "You should see him over a fence. Poetry. Restrained poetry. But Carl's horse—I suppose he was Carl's horse, although he didn't ride him very often— is over here." Lucas held out the other half of the carrot for Hector, who took it with restraint and dignity and then paced elegantly back into his stall. "Achilles," she said, opening the last door, and an enormous gray gelding stepped out and then shook his head impatiently. "Isn't he a fine size? That's how they described him. He's Irish."

"Did you get him here?" asked Lucas.

She shook her head. "I went over to the spring sales and fell in love with him. Then they told me his name, and I knew it was fate. You should see him move. He's young yet, though. He's from Tipperary—the finest bloodstock in the country, they say. I paid a bundle for him by the time I had him shipped over. He was a birthday present for Carl—I wouldn't spend that much on a horse for myself— but Carl never appreciated him. He was threatening to sell him this spring; it broke my heart to think of it. Eh, baby?" she murmured. "Do you think you could find another car-rot? There should be one in my bag—it's on the chair. Everyone else got a carrot, didn't they?" she went on softly, rubbing his nose.

Lucas went back into the little office and found her hand-bag sitting on a chair. He unzipped it. Inside was chaos; everything you might expect to find in a woman's purse: wallet, keys, lipstick, comb, tissues, pens, pencils, notebook;

and, in addition, two large dirty carrots, a plastic bag with sugar lumps in it, and a hoof-pick. "There you go," he said, and handed her one of the carrots. "Who looks after the stable for you and exercises the horses?" he asked in real curiosity.

"Who looks after it? I do," she said, surprised, sending Achilles back into his stall with a nudge of the halter and a slap on the rump, and then reaching her hand with the carrot on it over the door to him. "I do everything. Clean it out every morning, give each one a good gallop, work with Hector a bit, groom them, everything. I love it. It gives me something to do. The house is filled already with people tripping over each other to do the work. They don't need me. Anyway, it means I have an excuse for not traveling all over the place with Carl on business trips. My God! What's the matter with me?" She sat down on a couple of bales of straw piled up outside Achilles' stall. "What am I saying? Carl's dead, and I'm bitching about going on business trips with him. I mean, I could have. Joe down at the riding stable will always look after the beasts for me if I need him." She shook her head and looked blankly up at Lucas.

"Don't worry about it," he said. "It's the shock. It takes a while to get used to it."

"I suppose," she said, standing up. She walked around the stable and fastened all the doors, picked up her purse, turned off the cassette player, flicked off the light, and headed toward the door. "Come back to the house and we'll have some tea," she said. "Mrs. Howard will have it ready."

She took him in through a small back door and along a short tiled hallway. The room she led him into was as seductive as the stable. It was relatively small, but a set of three windows looked out over the paddock and the stable. The windowsill was deep, with a couple of cushions lying on it:

someplace to sit and drowse away an afternoon, he thought. A fire burned in the fireplace, and the comfortable chairs and sofa were covered with dark, countrified material. There was a desk, audio equipment, a small piano, and some book space. The housekeeper stalked in with tea, followed closely by a thin, dark-haired little boy with worried blue eyes, who ran over to his mother's side and whispered urgently in her ear.

"I don't know, sweetheart," she said, gently shaking her head. "He's around somewhere. Ask Mrs. Howard. Maybe she put him away." He snatched up a chocolate-covered biscuit and left as quickly as he had come.

"That's Mark," she said simply. "He's eight. I'll tell him later. When we're alone."

"Do you have other children?" asked Lucas, looking down at the tea in his hand as if he had never seen such a thing before.

She shook her head.

He stared at the fire, mesmerized, relaxed. He could sit in this room for hours, beside this elegant, slightly muddy woman, except that he was not here on a social call. He pulled himself together. "Do you mind if I ask you a few questions?" he said.

"Not at all," she said readily. "What do you want to know?"

"Where you were this afternoon?" The cozy atmosphere came apart with a jerk.

"Oh. Of course. It's the obvious question, isn't it? Well— I was out on Jasmine. We went for a long ride—all through the woods. Didn't get back until after four. That's why I was still rubbing her down when you came in."

"Do you ride alone?"

"Usually. Very awkward, I suppose." She smiled and offered him a piece of shortbread. "From your point of view, I mean."

"Mrs. Neilson," he began, and hesitated.

"Yes?" She looked entirely composed and unafraid.

"Is there any reason that you know of why a girl, a singer, would have a key to your husband's apartment?"

"Reason? Do you mean a printable reason? An excuse? Not that I can think of. I mean, only the usual reason—and that seems quite likely." She seemed to ruminate for a while. "A singer, you said?"

"Mmm. A singer—with a band."

"With a band?" She seemed surprised. "What's her name?"

"Jennifer Wilson," said Lucas without thinking. Oh, Christ, he said to himself. That was bright. "Look, I shouldn't have given out her name like that," he said. "I'd appreciate it if you'd forget it, if you can."

"Oh, that's all right. I won't do anything to her, don't worry. I'm just surprised. I thought that Carl—well—you can't tell, can you?" She stared into the fire, apparently considering the oddities of life. "May I ask you a question?"

"That depends," he said. "Actually, you can ask it, but I don't promise to be able to answer it."

"Do you know when I can get possession of his private papers—his account books, I mean—and things like that? Not the business ones—they're the property of the corporation, I assume—just the private ones. I'm afraid that there are bills to pay and that sort of thing, and he was in the habit of locking everything up in his safe unless he was out of town. Then, of course, I looked after the household money."

"Don't you have the combination?"

"No." She shook her head.

"I don't know. But surely you can have access to anything in the house. Why don't you call his lawyer?"

"Maybe," she said unhappily. "I suppose I have to call him anyway."

"Did your husband have any enemies that you know of?"

"Enemies? What kind of enemies do you mean?" she asked sharply.

"Any kind," he said.

"Not that I know of. He might have, I suppose. Business enemies. I don't know anything about his business." She shook her head and turned to look out the window toward the stable.

Lucas stifled a yawn and couldn't think of anything else to ask her. "Thank you for your help," he said lamely. "And for showing me the horses. It's a long time since I've seen such magnificent animals. Do you have someone to stay with you?" he added. "I should be going."

"Don't worry, Sergeant. There are enough people in this house to guard me. Anyway, my sister will always come over if I need her." She sounded very tired now. "I'm all right, really. It was a shock, but Carl and I hadn't been what you would call close for some time. I'm not surprised about the singer in his apartment. I have Mark and the horses—I guess he needed something, too. Poor Carl."

With those words Lucas felt that Carl Neilson had all the obituary that he deserved, and he took his leave.

CHAPTER 2

By the time Rob Lucas was back downtown, it was dark—dark, late, cold—and even people who were supposed to have been working that day were home tucked up cozily in front of their television sets.

"Anything come in on the girl's fingerprints?" he asked, and sat down to tackle the clutter on his desk.

Patrick Kelleher glanced up. "Yeah. They're all over the apartment, including on that phone. She was the last person to have used it. And in my book that makes her the one who called in."

Kelleher's words were lost in the rustle of paper. "Where in hell are my reports?" said Lucas, sorting rapidly through the mess.

"Baldy came in and got everything," said Kelleher.

"Why?"

Kelleher shrugged.

"Anybody get anything else from the girl?"

Kelleher shook his head. "Don't think so. You going to let her go?"

"What do I hold her for? Lying to a cadet?" he said wearily. "Look, I'm leaving as soon as I talk to her again. Tell Baldy if he comes by."

"Oh," said Kelleher. His voice turned mock-official. "Inspector Baldwin has requested that you report to him as soon as possible. If you step into the hall, you might bump into him. He's kind of upset."

"Thanks," said Lucas, "a helluva lot," and headed out the door.

He collided with him as he rounded the corner. "Ah, Lucas. Good. A word with you," said Baldwin, leading him away from his office. "I'm assuming control of this case. Not anything against you, understand—"

"No need to apologize, sir. It's not my case. I was supposed to be off this afternoon."

"Whatever," he said irritably. "Anyway, you and Patterson—you understand, Neilson was influential. And Mrs. Neilson is very involved—charities, fund-raising, horses, opera, you know what I'm talking about. Anyway, you and Patterson just don't have the clout, or maybe even the tact, to deal with them."

"I don't mind, sir." Lucas yawned. "Patterson might be annoyed, though. He has lots of tact when he needs it."

Baldwin grunted. "That may be—but he has trouble remembering when to use it. Look, I've got Marty Fielding sitting in my office right now, bitching about police harassment of Neilson's widow. What in hell did you say to her?"

"Not much. We chatted about her horses, I asked her where she was during the relevant time period—"

"You asked Mrs. Neilson where she was?" said Baldwin. He looked incredulous. And then, in spite of himself, he added, "Where was she?"

"Out riding. Alone. She does it all the time." He paused to let that sink in. "Do you think someone would kill someone to prevent him from getting rid of a favorite horse, sir? Because if that's possible—"

"Oh, for chrissake, Lucas, leave Neilson's widow to me. And I want you to check in with me personally before you do anything; and I want reports—detailed reports—on everything you do, say, or find out. Have you got that? I'm going over to the hotel, and I'll pass the word on to Patterson. What are you doing now?"

"Releasing the witness we found at the hotel—and then going home."

"Oh—right," he said vaguely. "Don't lose track of her."

"I won't," Lucas said and yawned.

Jennifer Wilson was sitting at a table, flipping through the pages of a magazine, when Lucas opened the door of the room she had been stashed in. "Miss Wilson?" he said, and yawned again.

She continued to stare at the page in front of her. Maybe singing in a rock band had deafened her.

"Hey—you," he said louder. "Jennifer. You can go home now."

She whirled around. "Sorry—I didn't hear you. It's not often you get a chance to read last year's news. Did you say I could go? Really?"

"Sure. You want a ride home?"

"That'd be nice," she said. "If I had a home to go to. Maybe you could drive me to a motel. How far out do you go?"

"How far out do you want to go?" he asked. "This time of night, it doesn't take that long to get anywhere, really."

"How about around the airport, then?"

He had asked for that one. "Sure. What the hell. I guess you could say it's on my way—sort of. Get your stuff." He stopped to think for a second or two. "Right, you don't have any stuff, do you? Well, then let's go." He went first, followed by the quick clicking of her little black half-boots, paused to grab his parka, and headed out to the parking lot.

"Around here is okay," said the girl suddenly. They had been traveling for twenty minutes or so through light traffic and had reached an area of plazas, parking lots, cheap family restaurants, and motels.

"This is quite a ways from the airport, lady," said Lucas.

"It's not as though I was catching a plane. I just want a place to stay for a few days that's off the beaten track. Off my beaten track, anyway."

"Have you eaten?" asked Lucas suddenly. "Because I haven't, and I'm hungry."

"Not since breakfast," she said. "Except for that stale muffin."

A stab of guilt pierced his fatigue. "How about there?" he said, waving to their right. "Italian, with lots of parking." She made a small sound that might have been assent, and he pulled into the lot.

The waitress stood over them, balancing on one foot, as though the other one hurt too much to use, and waited. "You want something to start with?" she asked. "A cocktail or anything?"

He looked up from the oversize plastic-covered menu. "I'll have a Blue and she'll have—what would you like? Beer? Wine? Something?"

"I thought you weren't supposed to drink—"

"I'm not on duty. What'll you have?"

"The same," she said, turning to the waitress.

"And bring us a whole lot of garlic bread to start with," added Lucas, "unless it's going to take too long. We're starving."

"Won't take long at all," she said comfortingly. "I'll be right back."

He put the menu down and looked across the table at Jennifer, puzzled. "You look different," he said.

"They let me use the washroom down at the police station," she said. "I washed my face."

That was it. Those great black smudges, the caked white quality of the skin, they were all gone. Now she looked pale and tired, but human. "The bruise looks worse now," he said, touching the discolored patch on her cheek. Its center was still dark. "It must have been a good one. And this one doesn't look too healthy, either," he added, touching her shoulder, where the angry red mark was turning to a purple stain. She winced. "You have a left-handed friend, I take it?" he asked.

"What makes you say that?"

"Because your visible bruises are on your right side. I suspect that's where the others are, too."

"What others?"

"I doubt if he only marks you where the world can see. Look, Jennifer, I don't know who it is you're mixed up with, but has it ever occurred to you you'd be better off without him? I've seen what guys like that can do to a woman, you know, and it isn't very pretty. Why don't you get out while you still have some teeth?"

She turned her head back from her study of the parking lot and fixed her eyes steadily on him. "You really know how to make a girl feel good, don't you? Well, maybe I already know that. Maybe that's why I'm out here and not downtown," she said, and shivered.

"You're shaking," said Lucas, touching her arm.

"I'm freezing," she said. "This sweater isn't very warm, I'm afraid. Neither is the skirt."

"Jesus," he said. "I forgot you don't have a coat. Just a minute."

When he got back from the car, he was carrying a heavy dark-blue-and-white-patterned sweater in his hand. The beer had arrived and so had the garlic bread. She ripped a piece in two and ate most of the first half as he walked to their booth. "Have some," she said. "It's heavenly."

"Put this on first," he said. She wiped the butter off her fingers, slipped out of the booth, and dived into the sweater. It covered her skirt almost completely. She carefully folded up the cuffs until her wrists were visible and looked down at the effect.

"It's beautiful," she said. "A bit large, but very warm and beautiful. It must look good on you." She slipped back into the booth.

"So my stepmother says. She knit it, she claims, and the color is supposed to be the same as my eyes." He picked up a piece of garlic bread and realized just how hungry he was.

"I ordered lasagna and salad for both of us. She said it was the best thing on the menu." She looked over at him, holding up her arm in the direction of her face. "Your stepmother's right. It is the same color as your eyes. Wow. A beautiful cop. It doesn't seem fair, somehow. How did you break your nose? And why didn't you have it fixed?"

To his horror, he felt himself blushing. "Playing rugger. And I felt it improved my face. You've never been a blue-eyed blond male with a cute little nose in a men's washroom, or you wouldn't ask me that."

"I can't say I have been. You poor lamb," she said with a grin of mock sympathy.

He shrugged, as if her tone didn't matter. "Anyway, life got a bit easier for me after the nose was smashed a couple of times."

"At your size?" she asked, and then answered herself. "But of course—you weren't always that size, were you?" She paused to tackle the beer and garlic bread again. "What's your name? Besides Sergeant Lucas, that is. Since we're having dinner together."

"Robert," he said uncomfortably.

"But people don't call you that," she said. "Robert's much too formal for someone who looks like you. And Bob is too casual. I bet they called you Robin at home. I shall call you Robin—unless you object violently."

He stared at her in amazement. "And how about you?" he countered with a flash of anger. "Why do you do this to yourself?" He picked up a lock of her hair. "And wear those clothes?"

"Oh, that's nothing. Just part of my professional disguise, that's all. People expect it. Here comes the lasagna. I hope it's good."

＊   ＊   ＊

He pulled up in front of a reasonable-looking motel a few blocks farther on. "I guess that'll do," she said. "I can look after myself from here. Thanks for the ride. And dinner."

"I'm coming in with you," he said, abruptly remembering that he was supposed to be keeping an eye on her. "Just to make sure they've got a room. Besides, what about money? If you really did lose your purse—"

"You still think I'm lying, don't you?" She laughed. "I did lose my purse, but I borrowed some money. Remember? I've got plenty." She patted an area in the vicinity of the hipbone.

"Plenty? I figured she lent you a ten."

"Oh, no. Her friend was pretty generous, I reckon, and she's easygoing about money. She must have thought there was more where that came from. Poor thing."

"Okay," he said in a voice heavy with doubt. "I'm coming in anyway, though. Just in case. But I'll stay in the background."

"Oh, good," she said dryly. "I wouldn't want you to sully my reputation. Let's go."

He concealed himself tactfully behind a rack of postcards on the other side of the lobby while she checked in. "Right," said the man behind the desk, as a key hit the desk with a muted clang. "Room one-sixteen. Right along the corridor over there. You sure you don't want something on the top floor? It's quieter." Lucas strolled over to the desk.

She picked up her key and shook her head. "I like to be near the ground," she said. "We all have our little oddities. Oh, hello, Robin. Thank you. It was a lousy start to a friendship, but dinner was great."

He tried to think of something to say, nodded, and left.

Lucas walked into his apartment, dropping his parka on a chair. It was a long drive from Finch to Adelaide Street.

And on one beer and a glass of wine he felt as if he'd been up all night boozing. Sleep, said his tired brain. He started for the loft that served as his bedroom, shedding clothes as he went; by the time he was up the short flight of stairs, he was down to his shorts. The ringing of the telephone came as a hideous jolt. "Shit," he muttered, and picked up the receiver.

"Lucas. It's Baldwin. Where in the hell have you been?"

"Stashing the witness in a motel and getting myself something to eat. Sir." Odd that he had instinctively reversed the order. "What's wrong?"

"Wrong?" he roared. "Marty Fielding's on my back. Wants to know what's being done, who killed his client, everything." In the ensuing pause, Lucas could see him pacing fretfully back and forth. "Everyone else in the city wants to know, too. What did you get from the girl?"

"Nothing much," said Lucas, yawning. "Calls herself a singer, but she's probably a hooker with a pretty mean-tempered pimp. Lots of bruises. I think she was in the apartment when Neilson got killed—didn't kill him but can identify the person who did. She's scared."

"What makes you think she was there?"

"I just don't believe in this mysterious girl, Krystal, who lends her an apartment on fifteen minutes' worth of friendship. And she was wearing the perfume the bed stank of, and her fingerprints were all over. It stands to reason. Neilson brought her in for the day—or whatever—and when he was killed, she was under the bed or behind the couch or something like that. And besides, she doesn't have a coat. No one goes out without a coat on a day like this. I'll bet there was a woman's coat in the apartment. Was there? You got a list there of the stuff they found?"

"What kind of coat?"

"How the hell should I know? Probably black and not very big."

"Just a minute."

Lucas sat down on the edge of the bed and stared at the wall. Come on, Baldy. Get a move on.

"Yeah. A black leather coat, size eight, woman's, made by—"

"She was there. And so scared, she forgot her coat."

"It was in the living room closet. She couldn't have got the door open without moving the body. So, don't lose track of her, eh? Where did you put her?"

"The Blue Star Motel. No one's likely to find her there. Good night, Inspector. I've had it." And he dropped down the phone and climbed under the bedclothes in the same motion, sinking almost instantly into oblivion.

CHAPTER 3

Lucas walked into the noise and activity around his desk with his eyes clamped half-shut and his mouth dry and foul-tasting. He wasn't sure how much sleep he had finally managed the night before, but it hadn't been enough. Not nearly enough. He put down his coffee, carefully removed the lid, and with equal care set his almost-cold Danish beside it. So far this morning he had successfully avoided speech. Even the woman at the bakery where he picked up his breakfast had said, as she always did, "Black? And you want your Danish warmed up?" and he had nodded. Gratefully. And so, when Kelleher said, "Morning, Robert," all he got in return was a croak.

He took a mouthful of coffee. That was better. "Anything new?" he said in a voice passably like his own.

"Not so's you'd notice."

"Nothing?" he asked incredulously. "What's everyone been doing?"

"Tripping over each other's feet. Whatever you do, duck when the phone rings. Ten to one it'll be Baldwin screaming at you to do the exact opposite of what you were supposed to do five minutes ago. If you follow me. I've only been here an hour, and he's phoned at least four times, screwing everything up. Eric's not here—he'll be in later. He went off to get some sleep. Been chasing around most of the night, I think, trying to avoid Baldy. He has this big list of people he's not supposed to question, and he's looking pretty grim."

"That's going to look great when it hits the papers, isn't it?"

"Yeah," said Kelleher, with a certain amount of relish. "Won't it? Tempting thought. I want to be here when Sanders hears about it, too. Not that Baldwin's his favorite person anyway."

"Where in hell is Inspector Sanders?" asked Lucas forlornly. "If he doesn't come back, I'll never get away from Baldy."

"Somewhere in the States with his girlfriend," said Kelleher. "Having a hell of a lot more fun than we are and screwing up everyone's schedule. I wish to hell people didn't just take off on holidays anytime they felt like it," he added, in a low-voiced mutter. "Leaving other people stuck with assholes like Baldwin to deal with. Anyway, relax. It's safe around here for a while. Baldy's coming in late, thank God. Did you know him when he spent all his time bending paper clips and worrying about politics? I never realized what a pain in the ass he could be when he started taking his job seriously." He paused to pick up his coffee. "So help me God, I'll never complain about someone not working again. I swear. By the bones of my sainted Aunt Mary."

Lucas grunted and pulled the telephone closer to him.

"Room one-sixteen," he said, when he reached the desk at the Blue Star Motel. During the ensuing pause, he started in on the Danish. It was cheese. He varied the kind from day to day, depending on his mood. Cheese meant exhausted. And grim.

"Who do you want to talk to?" The voice on the other end was a suspicious voice. A cautious voice.

"Jennifer Wilson."

You could almost hear the head shake. "Miss Wilson left last night."

"Last night? She only checked in last night." There was an icy pause. "Damn," muttered Lucas. And then something else occurred to him. That little bitch had gone sneaking off with— "You didn't find a blue sweater in the room, did you?" he asked. "Men's, large, hand-knit?"

"Who is this?" Now the voice was heavy with suspicion.

"I'm a police officer," he started in his usual bored sing-song, "and I've been—"

"We made a damage report on the room to the officer who came by this morning," he said coldly. "There wasn't any sweater."

"Damage? What damage?" The world had gone mad on him this morning.

"The damage caused by the people who broke into the room," he said carefully, as if he suspected that Lucas was not very bright.

"What in hell are you talking about? Someone broke into her room? Why didn't you tell me that in the first place? Was she hurt?"

"I don't believe so. I think Miss, uh, Wilson—if that's her name—had already left by the time they entered."

"Let me speak to the clerk on duty last night."

"He's asleep," said the voice. It sounded shocked.

"Then wake him up. No—I'll be out there as soon as I can. I'll see him then. Just leave everything as it was."

There was a significant pause. "I'm sorry, sir. But the constable said we could repair the damage. The workmen are already in the room."

"Damn, damn, damn," muttered Lucas. "Never mind. I'll be out sometime this morning."

He dropped the phone back down and cursed the girl, the motel, the phone, everything. "Something wrong?" asked Kelleher, amused.

"I've lost the witness," said Lucas. "I stashed her in a

motel last night, showing touching faith in her word that she was going to stay there for a few days, and she took off in the middle of the night." He omitted the complication, the strange people who came to visit her and apparently destroyed her room, because explaining them was going to be beyond him at the moment.

"Baldy's going to be pleased, isn't he?"

Inspector Baldwin was not pleased. His face became unnaturally still, then reddened slightly, and then paled to white again. There was silence—ominous silence—for at least a minute.

"Let me see if I understand this," said Baldwin at last. "First of all, you find someone outside the murdered man's apartment who has come out of it very recently, but you decide, even though this is a very sensitive investigation, that she is not important enough to hold. You drop her off in an out-of-the-way motel of her choice—"

"Not exactly, sir," said Lucas. "She chose the direction; I found the motel."

"Some motel in her part of town, then. You still think she's relatively unimportant. And then you decide when you're talking to me that she must be an eyewitness to Carl Neilson's murder, and on that comforting thought you go to bed. Leaving her to skip out in the middle of the night with a couple of accomplices. What made you think she hadn't killed the man? Do we have a better suspect?"

"Her hands were clean. She hadn't fired a gun. And we got her right after the phone call went in. For God's sake, the guy was still bleeding when the constable got there," said Lucas defensively.

"Gloves? Rubber gloves?" snapped Baldwin.

"There weren't any," said Eric Patterson, who had walked into the office without knocking—or any other ceremony—as was his habit. "We've combed through the entire apartment. And there's no place to stash them between the apartment and where the cadet grabbed her. And before you ask—no one's opened the windows since they were last painted, a year ago, but just in case, we searched every inch of land under them anyway."

"Did you search her?"

Patterson looked at Lucas, who shook his head uneasily. "I didn't. But she wasn't wearing very much, and it was pretty tight."

"So," said Baldwin. "She could have slipped a pair of surgeon's gloves in her underwear."

"There's something else," said Patterson, yawning. "She might have hidden the gloves, but we didn't find a weapon, either. Harder to miss. Did she look strange to you, Robert? Like she had a Beretta in her bra?"

"Listen, she couldn't have hidden a hairpin in the outfit she was wearing."

"Or a Colt in—"

"Watch it, Eric," said Baldwin. "Well, if you're right, and she didn't shoot him, then she must know something about the person who did. I want her found. Soon. Today. How far can she have gotten since the middle of last night?" Lucas looked at Patterson and shrugged his shoulders. The answer, of course, was that she could be landing in Paris right now. "And as soon as you get any sort of lead on her, I want to know. I'm under great pressure to find out who killed Neilson. Fielding has already called a couple of times this morning. We need results, and fast."

"I sure as hell screwed that up," said Lucas gloomily as they walked back down the corridor.

"Don't worry about it. She's probably not that hard to find. You want me to get onto it?"

"Don't bother. How many people can it take to find one girl? What I can't figure out is what's gotten into Baldwin. You'd think Marty Fielding was the goddamn mayor. Or the prime minister."

"Jesus—where have you been for the last year?" said Patterson.

"Out of it, obviously. Who's Fielding? Besides being a rich lawyer. I know that."

"Fielding is the membership secretary of the Yacht Club. No, it's not even *The* Yacht Club. Baldwin doesn't aspire— yet—to *The* Yacht Club. It's the Sandy Cove Yacht Club. You know. Number two. We try harder."

"I see. And Baldwin wants to join—"

"Right. And so he doesn't want Fielding annoyed at him."

"He's crazy. He should keep his boat at a marina. It's cheaper and less aggravating."

"Oh, he doesn't have a boat. If he gets in the Yacht Club, he's going to buy a boat and learn how to sail." Eric chuckled. "I wonder if Marianne gets seasick," he added softly.

"Marianne?"

"His wife. Last year it was horses, remember? He took riding lessons, the whole thing."

"Yeah, I remember."

"Only Marianne kept breaking out in some sort of rash, and they discovered she was allergic to horses. So he had to find something else."

Patterson's gossipy, malicious voice went on and on while Lucas tried to imagine Baldwin on a boat. He was a big man, used to getting his own way through sheer size and forcefulness. Lucas imagined him standing by the mast, roaring at the wind to blow from the right quarter and stop all this messing about. And then—wonderful thought— being swept overboard. Boats. His thoughts drifted away from Baldwin. Lucas's father belonged to *The* Yacht Club, all ties, blazers, white flannels, and quarts of gin. Those sails, at least twice a summer, in his father's *Nonesuch*, with his stepmother lying about chattering and oozing sex all over the place. His father, to give him credit, still regarded sailing from the point of view of the serious racer he once had been and preferred to stay quiet and sober on the water;

if Tricia hadn't been along, Lucas might have enjoyed himself. But there was no point in going sailing with someone who talked incessantly. On a boat, in the middle of the lake, was the only place around where you could get away from the interminable sound of voices and phones ringing and bloody internal combustion engines. He shrugged. Patterson's monologue seemed to have exhausted itself. He went back to finish his cold coffee and Danish before setting off for the motel.

The March sun poured down on the ferry dock as the *M/V Uncatena* edged gently away from Vineyard Haven. Inspector John Sanders, Metropolitan Toronto Police Department, Homicide, and Harriet Jeffries, free-lance architectural photographer, were up on deck, leaning companionably against the rail, staring down into the water. They were almost alone. Most of the people crossing were islanders, year-round residents of Martha's Vineyard, and for them the off-island trip was routine enough to make them consider hot coffee and a warm, comfortable seat inside more important than looking at late-winter scenery.

"It's beautiful, isn't it?" said Harriet, yawning and pulling her coat more tightly around her.

"The parking lot?" asked John, pointing to the broad expanse of asphalt where cars lined up to get on the ferry.

"No, you benighted idiot—the island. Now. In March. With lots of cold wind and no tourists. Except for us, of course." She turned to look at him. "Do you suppose that the locals saw us and groaned—here comes the tourist season all over again?"

"Maybe they took us for a sign of spring—like robins." He wrapped his arm tightly around her shoulders. "After all, the sun started to shine just as we pulled into the harbor on

Wednesday. We've given them three whole days of good weather."

"I still can't believe that we actually got here," said Harriet. "That you were willing to walk out and leave them all behind. How much vacation time did you say you had accumulated?"

John ignored the question. "Me? When did you last take a holiday?"

"I never take holidays," said Harriet smugly. "I merely change my working locale temporarily when I get sick of Toronto architecture." She giggled huskily. "And alter my working hours somewhat."

"To between eleven and eleven-thirty on Tuesdays and Wednesdays."

"Something like that." Harriet leaned forward over the rail and looked past her companion in the direction of the open water. "You know, you could be right. About our bringing good weather. Look at that."

The ferry was gliding tranquilly into a wall of fog. Somewhere close to their ears, a crew member loosed a melancholy, ear-splitting blast of the horn as the world disappeared behind a blanket of gray. Harriet jumped and then shivered in the cold dampness. "What a magnificent atmosphere," she said. "All we need is a ghost ship to come drifting past."

"If we're really lucky," said Sanders with a grin, "we'll have to put back into harbor and won't be able to get off the island for another week. Maybe I should have a word with the captain—"

"No chance of that," said a pleasant-looking man who had suddenly appeared next to them, also leaning on the rail. "No need to be nervous. That's my cousin in there," he added, nodding in the direction of the bridge. "And a little fog never bothered him."

"I wasn't nervous," said Sanders irritably. He felt that a

significant moment had fled, and he resented this man for chasing it away.

"We just don't want to go home, that's all," added Harriet. "Are you from the Vineyard?"

"Yes, just back for a few days. Visiting." Reluctantly, Sanders relinquished his hold on Harriet, and the three of them fell into the kind of inconsequential chatter that serves to pass the time on brief voyages such as this.

"What are you thinking about?" asked Harriet, when their newfound acquaintance had taken himself off for a final cup of coffee. "You look—I don't know—profound. Or maybe gloomy. Worrying about what's happening at home while you're not there? Or is this the effect of three days alone on an island with me?"

"Why should I worry about what's going on at home?" Sanders grinned at her. "What could possibly be going on that they can't handle without me? No one's indispensable, Harriet, my love. Not even me."

"I'm indispensable," said Harriet. "And don't you forget it." She ducked his mock attack and deftly caught his wrist as it went by. "And that looks very like Woods Hole up there. We should be thinking about getting the car—and then onward. To Boston."

"Backward, you mean," said Sanders sourly. "We're on our way back. And my gloom certainly isn't retrospective. It's the thought of next week that doesn't exactly fill me with joy right now." He released his wrist gently from her grasp and put his arm around her again. "What is there about us? We've never spent more than a week together since we met."

"But it has been the most gorgeous holiday, hasn't it? And we promised not to wreck it by getting into fights over what happens next," said Harriet lightly. Then she shook her head. She turned to face the wind, and her green eyes filled with tears. "Damn it. Why in hell am I trying to sound like Pollyanna? You're right. It is going backward. Come on. Let's get out of here." She twisted away from the solid comfort of his arm around her shoulders and headed for the companionway, following the small crowd down to the hold. Silently they climbed back into Harriet's car, ready to start the return journey.

It took Rob Lucas a lot longer to drive to the motel during the day, fighting his way through a newly sprouted forest of road construction, delivery vans, and pedestrians. The manager was not pleased to see him. He had already dealt with the situation, written off the damage, and wanted no more to do with the police or anyone else on the issue. On the other hand, he didn't want to stand around all day arguing with a policeman in his lobby, and he agreed, finally, to rout the night man out of bed and send him to the conference room.

In ten minutes the door opened and the desk clerk from the night before arrived with a tray. "Hi," he said. "I'm Bernie. I thought you might like some coffee. You brought that girl in last night, didn't you? I knew you were a cop. I can always tell. Here," he said, putting a cup and the cream and sugar in front of him. "Have some of this," he added, setting down a plate. "It's strudel. One of the maids makes it. It's better than the shit we serve in the coffee shop. Now, what can I do for you?"

Lucas tried the strudel. Bernie was right. He mumbled his thanks through a mouthful of crumbling pastry and plunged in. "Okay, what happened last night after I left?"

"To one-sixteen?" Lucas nodded. "Some guy comes to see her—asks for her by name, Jennifer Wilson, and says she's expecting him. Well, that happens, although I wouldn't have thought she was the type."

"You didn't tag her for a hooker?"

"Naw. Not her. Anyway, there's another guy sort of in the background, too, and that bothers me. Well, I tell him she's in one-sixteen, and he heads off to the corridor. It's the last unit in that wing, and I figure it'll take him a minute or so to get there. So I call the girl. I always do that. When they want to be surprised by some guy in the middle of the night, they give 'em their room numbers. She asks what he looks like, I tell her, she says thanks a lot, and that's it."

"What did he look like?"

"Kinda short, maybe a little bigger than me. And skinny. He had one of them blue caps like sailors wear, so I couldn't see his hair—but he had a dark mustache and a skinny face. Mean-looking bastard."

"You notice a lot."

"It's part of the business," said Bernie philosophically. "You meet a lot of strange people in hotels, and it's a good idea to recognize 'em when you run into them again. Just so's you know where you're at."

"What about the other guy?"

"The one in the background? I didn't get a good look at him—just his back when he was going through the door into the corridor where one-sixteen is. But he's probably over six feet and maybe one ninety, two hundred pounds."

"So what else happened?" he asked impatiently. "Anything?"

Bernie looked at him with bright and cynical eyes and went on. "In a couple of minutes I get a call from one-fourteen, something about a lot of noise next door. I go to look, the door's swinging open, and the lock's splintered; I check if the girl's there and call the cops from the room." He paused for a second. "Then I look at the door again. Someone's bust through the bolt and the chain. Not surprising—those door frames are pure crap. Anyway, the bathroom window's wide open. The screen's undone and been dropped outside. She must have left right after I called, because the room looked untouched except for the doors and the towels and the spot where she turned the bed down to get out. You know what I mean? She had used the room, but it was neat, and no one was pulled around in it."

"Did she walk on her bill?"

"Nope. When she asked for a room she pulled a huge wad of cash out of her pocket and peeled off two fifties to pay for it. Room was sixty-five dollars. You figure she stole the money? That why you're here?"

He shook his head. "I don't know. She's just a witness, mostly. Can I use that phone?"

"Sure. Dial nine."

It took a good five minutes to find someone who had a copy of the victim's possessions near to hand. "You got it there?" said Lucas impatiently. "Now, did Neilson have any cash on him?"

"Jesus, yes. Didn't you know? He had—let's see— $5,637.83 on him in cash. Mostly in fifties and twenties, a few hundreds."

Lucas dropped the phone down in amazement. If Jennifer Wilson was a thief, she was a pretty restrained one.

CHAPTER 4

She sat in her car, shivering uncontrollably in spite of her warm clothes, and told herself she had to leave before someone came to the apartment looking for her. It was only going to be a matter of time—not days but hours or even minutes. After all, it hadn't taken them more than two or three hours to find the motel room. If she got away, she might be safe; there was nothing of hers left in the apartment. She had collected every last scarf and pair of panty hose and stuffed them all into the trunk of the car. And now light from early dawn was oozing its way through the cracks between the buildings. She had to get going. She started the engine, but her foot trembled so wildly on the accelerator that she stalled it again. She could never control the car. Well, stupid, she said to herself, you don't have any other choice. Get out or stay and be killed. She slipped the lever into drive and pulled away from the curb.

She kept chewing over yesterday afternoon, her mind returning to it like a gerbil to its wheel. No, she thought, wrong image. More like a dog to its vomit. Trying to make sense of it. She had been lying in the bed with the sheet pulled up to her chin, dressed in the black bra and the hideous black stockings with the tacky garter belt. He had showered first. He always showered first, as if he suspected that she would befoul the bathroom for him. And he had locked her out, as he always did. What in hell did he do in the shower that could possibly be more embarrassing or disgusting than the things he did in bed? Play with her clothes? They were in the bathroom, as always. That was where he liked her to take them off, allowing her to prance into the bedroom half-undressed. That way he didn't have to look at her squirming out of her panty hose or dragging a sweater over her head. He had come out at last, red-faced, shiny, his little fringe of hair wet, and started to get dressed. She didn't move. He liked her to stay in bed, relaxed and happy-looking, until he left. Which was fine with her. Up until then the afternoon had seemed perfectly ordinary, although there was a tension in him, a kind of triumphant tension, as if he were about to make a killing on a deal.

As he adjusted the knot of his tie, whistling softly, there was knocking on the door, first hesitant, then firmer. He looked at his watch, grinned, reached for his suit jacket, and turned in her direction. He had been expecting someone.

"Come on," he said brusquely. He ripped off the sheet and grabbed her by the shoulder, digging his hand deep. "Out of bed, you lazy bitch," he said cheerfully, and yanked her over the side. "Into the bathroom—lose yourself. I don't want him to know there's anyone here, understand? It'll screw up my deal if he thinks someone's listening in. Don't come out until I tell you to, and don't run the goddamn water. Stay dressed like that." All this time his hand was digging into her shoulder, harder and harder, until, with a shove, he threw her in the direction of the bathroom.

She closed the door, reached automatically for the lock, and then took her hand away in fear. Nausea twisted her stomach; her shoulder throbbed. She knew what was coming. She wrapped an outsize bath towel around her and sat down on the edge of the tub. And thought. Once before, only last week, someone else had turned up. He had dragged her half-naked out of bed and, smiling cheerfully, had grasped her around the waist and thrust her in the direction of his friend. "Nice, isn't she?" he had said. "She'll keep you entertained while I get those papers."

She had been deeply offended. That had been the worst thing about it, she decided. It still made her squirm to remember that she had honestly believed that he would care how she felt. She told him with as much dignity as she could dredge up that she had no intention of entertaining his friends—that was no part of their deal. She could still see that look of momentary amazement on his face before he punched her. The blow landed on her cheekbone and sent her reeling across the room. His friend sat down, grinning drunkenly, and watched. Carl had picked her up with one hand around her upper arm, clenching it so hard that she thought the bone must break under the pressure, and dragged her over to the phone. He called the desk to send up his chauffeur, and when the man arrived, took the car keys from him and handed her over. "Hang on to her, Cassidy," he said. "Don't let her move. I'll be back."

And they had remained like that, except that his grinning friend had helped himself to another drink, staring at her until she thought she would scream from the pain and embarrassment. In twenty minutes or so he had returned with two more men and a bedraggled-looking whore. She would not forget that afternoon in a hurry. Her ideas on the role of a mistress had been drawn from misty, romantic, nineteenth-century portraits. She had seen herself as the lady of the camellias from *La Traviata*: all champagne, diamonds, and beautiful clothes, with a little elegantly passionate sex thrown in. Not a participant in disgusting little orgies with slimy businessmen. She swore she wasn't going to go through that again.

But when the chauffeur had turned up at her apartment that morning to drive her to the hotel, she had been alone. She stared at him, horribly conscious of how strong he was and how little he cared what his boss did. She had been too frightened to tell him she wouldn't come with him.

But this is the last time, she had thought, sitting in

Neilson's bathroom, with her feet on the damp bath mat. No more.

She had not been able to hear what was being said, but there were more than two people out there. Something had not worked out; he had been expecting only one. Then the low-pitched voices from the living room changed. Someone was yelling threats—Carl? She heard a high-pitched scream; someone yelled "Shut up." Then Carl, roaring that they'd never get away with it. There was pain and terror in his voice. It wasn't until that moment that it occurred to her that she, too, was in danger. There were at least two people out there threatening Carl, and she was trapped in this room, unable to yell for help and hope to be heard. These apartments were well built; noise did not travel well from unit to unit. She looked frantically around the bathroom, and finally opened the only door available to her. It was the linen closet, built to fill in the space between the head of the tub and the wall. It had generous, deep shelves that were piled with extra towels and bedding, more than anyone could need. She could just fit between the shelves, she thought, if she were desperate. And she was desperate. She removed some hand towels from the middle shelf and threw them up to the top, along with the extra blankets, and then pulled the bath towels forward, clearing a space behind them. She grabbed her clothes from the counter, knocking over a bottle of the hideous perfume Carl had bought her and splashing it all everywhere. On her, on her clothes, on the shiny fake marble. She hastily mopped it up, slung the clothes on the back of the shelf, pushed aside the piles of towels, and crawled in. As she eased the pile back to its position in front of her, she heard the first shot. Unmistakable, but surprisingly muted. She yanked the door shut as well as she could without a handle on the inside, and discovered that the louvered door gave her a perfect view of the bathroom. A voyeur's dream, she remembered thinking, with fine irrelevancy, as the second gunshot rang out. She began frantically arranging the towels in front of her and waited. If Carl were wounded or dead, she had a chance; they might not find her in here. But if Carl had the gun, and those people were dead, what would he do with her? There was no point in trying to hide from him. She was horrified to find herself praying that he was dead as she listened for his familiar roar.

There was silence, absolute and total.

She cowered behind her wall of towels, trying desperately hard not to make any sound in the stillness. When the noise came at last, her body twitched convulsively, and the towels skidded over an inch closer to the edge of the shelf. It was a voice from the bedroom, probably, an odd voice, hoarse and squeaky. "There's a girl in here somewhere. This room stinks like a whorehouse. Jesus, smell that lousy perfume."

"Don't be stupid," said the other voice. "Of course there was a girl—that's what he uses the place for. But she isn't here now. It stinks of that piece of crap on the floor. Sweat and terror—did you ever see anyone so damned scared in all your life? I loved it. Bastard."

"Shut up and look—there's someone here." The squeaky voice throbbed with panic. "I know what I can smell."

"Okay, okay." She crouched down lower. She heard the creak of the bedroom closet door. "Not here. Nobody. Try under the bed."

"Don't be stupid. There's no room under the bed."

At last the bathroom door opened. "This is where the smell comes from," said the second voice. "Someone's spilled perfume in here." She heard the rattle of rings as the shower curtain was jerked back and felt a rush of cool air past her ear as the door to the linen closet opened. She held her breath and concentrated on invisibility. "There's no one here."

"Well—she hasn't been gone long," said the first voice. The tone was grudging, irritated. "These sheets are still damp and sweaty. Do you think she saw us when we came in?"

"Don't be stupid. If she'd seen us, we'd have seen her, wouldn't we? I don't know about you, but I was looking, and I didn't see any hooker anywhere in this building. I didn't see any female. But I suggest we get the hell out of here anyway. Some of the deaf biddies on this floor might have heard us."

She heard a door slam. She waited, terrified, feeling her calf muscles seize up while she counted slowly to a hundred. Finally she pushed the towels over to one side again and crawled with difficulty out of the linen closet, landing face-first in a heap on the damp towels Carl had left behind. She was sore; her legs and arms were unwieldy and unwilling to do what she asked of them. She started to massage her leg and then shook her head with impatience. There was no time for anything like that. She hastily pulled on the skimpy leather skirt and tiny sweater she wore for these encounters and walked silently over to the door. She counted to three and turned the doorknob, convinced that two people with guns in their hands would be sitting on the bed, smiling, waiting for her to come out. She pushed the door open. The room was empty.

He was in the living room, lying on the pale blue rug, close to the archway that led to the hall, as if he had been trying to get to the front door when they killed him. She noted dispassionately that there wasn't much left of the back and top of his head, but that it had been enough to block the closet door from opening more than a few inches. Someone had tried. Looking for her, probably. She had always thought the living room was an odd place to have a coat closet in an apartment this expensive. For the briefest instant she contemplated trying to get close enough to the thing on the floor to reach in for her coat. She couldn't. She backed into the bedroom, and with panicky haste bent her mind to essentials. A pair of clean panties. Her boots, by incredible luck sitting in the bedroom closet. On her way through the living room, boots still in one hand, she snatched up the cordless telephone. Caught between the horror inside and the unknown terror that might be waiting for her in the dimly lit hallway, she cowered against the front door and dialed 911. When the impersonal voice asked for her name, she slid the button to "off" and let the instrument drop to the floor. She shoved her feet into her boots, and began doggedly to thread the laces around their metal cleats. Tears welled up in her eyes as she tried to control her trembling fingers. You can't leave with your laces undone, she screamed wordlessly to herself. They'll know where you've been if you do. It took a thousand echoing measures of time before her boots were laced and knotted and she could leave the apartment. She turned toward the elevator, changed her mind, and ran for the relative security of the stairs.

CHAPTER 5

Rob Lucas slammed open the door, walked into the room, and slumped down at his desk. Traffic arteries between the Blue Star Motel and downtown had been clogged with cars driven by irremediably pigheaded and stupid maniacs; his fatigue and irritability levels were reaching new heights, and he was beginning to wonder what he was doing here. He looked up at the mildly sympathetic features of Patrick Kelleher. "Hey, Kelleher," he said, "how in hell do you find one lost hooker in this whole goddamn city?"

"You could try Vice," said Kelleher. "But I suppose you thought of that already."

Lucas nodded gloomily. "Of course, it might be possible—naw—" He shook his head. "I keep this up, and I'll be looking for quarters from the tooth fairy."

"What in hell are you talking about?"

"She said she was a singer. But—"

"You could try it. It must be easier to find a singer in this town than a hooker. Sheer numbers—there can't be *that* many singers."

"I wouldn't be too sure," said Lucas, standing up.

"And where in hell are you going?" asked Eric Patterson as he walked in and slung his coat down on an extra chair. "In case someone asks me to find you?"

"Off to give Baldy his hourly report," said Lucas, "and to spend the afternoon trying to track down a band singer. How many bands do you figure there are in this town?"

"No more than two or three thousand," said Patterson, grinning. "Happy hunting."

Gloomily convinced that he was wasting his time, he decided to pretend that success was possible and started at the most obvious place—the Musicians' Union. He asked the voice at the other end of the line if a girl named Jennifer Wilson, who called herself Stormi Knight, was a member. There was a pause. "Yes," said the bored voice. "She's with a group called Sex Kitten." He was so startled, he had nothing to say.

"Do you have an address for her?" he asked at last.

"No," said the voice coldly. "We don't give out that information. You could try her agent. Al Hamilton represents her. He's in the phone book," she added, lest he tax her energy further by making her read out the agent's telephone number.

"Yeah, she's one of mine," said Al Hamilton when Lucas finally got through to him. "She doesn't like being called Jennifer, though," he said. "Claims it's too sweet a name, too innocent-sounding for a singer. I think Stormi's worse myself, but what can you do? The group started out modified punk, you know, and wanted real hard-driving names— but that stuff doesn't sell anymore, not for all the bread-and-butter jobs. They're into soft rock, easy listening. They get a lot of work; people like them. You know, weddings, dances, that sort of stuff. They're out of town right now, doing a week at a ski resort." He paused to take a breath. "You wanna hire them?"

"What do you mean, out of town?" protested Lucas. "I was talking to Jennifer—Stormi—last night."

"Just a minute." There was a pause and a muffled roar in the background. "You're right. The job ended Wednesday. But they haven't called in yet. Kevin always calls as soon as they're back in town."

"Kevin?"

"Yeah—it's his group, Sex Kitten is. Not Stormi's. Although you'd never know it to talk to her."

"How far away is that resort?"

"Who is this, anyway? You want to hire them, what difference does it make where the resort is?" Lucas identified himself once more, and the agent's voice lost most of its energy and enthusiasm. That level of excitement was reserved for paying customers. "I see. Well, it's not that far. It's the Pine Valley Lodge—about two hours away, unless you're driving on the weekend. Then it might as well be on the moon."

"You got an address on her?" asked Lucas.

"What's this all about?" he said, his voice crackling with suspicion.

"Homicide. Someone was killed, and we'd like to talk to her. Just as a witness, Mr. Hamilton. Look, you want to call me back? Look up the number in the phone book, ask for Homicide, then ask for me by name."

"You know, Sergeant, I think I will," said the agent and hung up.

He sounded relieved when he got through to Lucas again. "Sorry about that, but you wouldn't believe the sick guys out there trying to find out where the girls live. I gotta protect my musicians—they're an investment, you know," and he laughed to make sure Lucas realized he was being funny. "Anyway, she lives at four ninety-two Oak Street, downstairs, and I got her telephone number here, if you want it."

But the telephone rang at 492 Oak Street sixteen times without any answer, and Lucas finally gave up. He reported— yet again—on his progress, giving Baldy the address as proof he was still on the job, and went off to look at Oak Street.

It was a street that had gone from never having been elegant to being actively run-down. Here and there, a few hopeful people were trying to renovate, but for most of its short length it retained a forlorn air. A good place for a musician, he supposed. A rock band could rehearse all night, and it would never occur to the neighbors to complain. They might heave bricks through the window, but they wouldn't complain. At least, not to the police. The bell marked Ground Floor rang loud and empty through the rooms. He peered through a small window in the front door at a narrow vestibule holding a few coats and a pair of boots. He walked along the porch that spanned the front of the house and looked in the front window. A bedroom that without a doubt had once been the front parlor. Behind it, through an arch, he could see a dining room, with a round table and chairs in dark wood. Family castoffs, probably.

He walked to the right and up a paved path that followed around the house into the back garden. The view through these windows was just as unhelpful. The back room was also a bedroom, unoccupied at the moment. He shrugged and headed back to his car. It seemed fitting, somehow, that she wouldn't be easy to find. But just before he unlocked his car door, another thought occurred to him. He walked back to 490, up a neat concrete path, to a new porch with shiny black metal railings and rang the bell. No answer. No one lived on this street during the day. He went back to his car. This wasn't even his case.

It was too early to go home and too late to do anything useful. He had settled down at his desk to make up his final report for the day when Eric Patterson came in, looking haggard and exhausted. "How's it going?" Lucas asked lightly.

"It isn't," said Patterson. "I've been trying to get something on his recent business deals. That five grand he had in his pants pocket wasn't there to tip the doorman. He has to have been mixed up in some transaction that was purely cash."

"Blackmail?"

Patterson shook his head. "Not that I can see. Maybe. I think it's more likely to be a sweetener for someone. I mean, it's too much money and not enough. See? Not enough for a deal—his deals are two-, three-million-dollar babies. Buildings, hotels, that kind of shit. And it's too much just to carry."

"Maybe he was going to the track."

He paused, running his hand over his stubbly cheeks. "No, track hasn't opened yet, has it? Still, you're right. It's a logical amount for a gambling man to carry. I'll look into that." He yawned and stretched back in his chair. "You get anything on that mysterious witness of yours?"

"I've discovered that she exists. That's something. And she sings in a band and lives on Oak Street."

"You and Baldy are both demented, chasing after this bimbo. You're wasting your time." He slung his feet up on the desk and leaned his head back on his arms.

"Look, Eric. She was in that apartment when Neilson got shot. I'm sure of it. They found her coat in the closet, the closet he was leaning against. And she sure as hell didn't come in the apartment, find a corpse, move it, put away her coat, move it back again, and then call us. Did she?" Patterson grinned. "And she stank of that crummy perfume that was all over the apartment, too."

"Did she? I hadn't realized that. I never actually saw her, you know. From my personal experience, she could just be a figment of your imagination. But how do you know it was her coat?"

"It was black leather, and she was dressed in black leather, and it was her size, more or less."

"Well, maybe."

"What else did you find in the apartment?"

Patterson removed his feet from the desk, leaned forward,

opened a drawer, and took out a sheet of paper. "Photo-copy. Wonders of modern civilization. It's a nuisance having your reports snatched away from you as soon as you finish them. Anyway, we found—property of the hotel—"

"Skip that."

"Okay. We found, in the kitchen, a bottle of champagne, two apples, a quart of milk, a half bag of coffee and a glass container of orange juice. In the bathroom, besides the towels and stuff, we found one lipstick, Luscious Purple, one tube of mascara, one black pencil, one bottle of Ivory Princess liquid makeup, one container of white powder—it looked white to me, anyway—one bottle of Cobra perfume, almost empty, one jar of face cream, one bottle of moistur-izer, and one box of tampons. Some of these things were in a drawer—the face cream and the tampons—the rest were all over the counter. In the bedroom drawers—"

"Forget the bedroom drawers. That's my list."

"All the sexy underwear and stuff. Okay. In the bedroom closet was a suit, gray, pin-striped. Living room closet: one ladies' black leather coat, one men's gray topcoat. Missing: shaving things, toothbrushes, toothpaste, that sort of thing. No one lived there."

"It sounds as if she used to turn up early, get into that incredible outfit, including the makeup, and take it all off again before she left. Then she must have showered and put on clean underwear and left in her jeans again. Weird. I like the bottle of champagne. It's a nice touch for such a slob. I wonder if he always had a bottle."

Patterson shook his head. "No. He had put in an order for it in the morning. He didn't usually ask for champagne, apparently. He often ordered a bottle or two of wine, which he also kept in the refrigerator. Oh—I forgot. There is a bar in the living room, and it contained—"

"A lot of booze. Anything else?"

Patterson laughed. "No. Except why do you call him a slob? Did you know him?"

"Nope. I just took an unreasonable dislike to his face and his taste in women."

It was ten o'clock the next morning before Lucas managed to get an answer at the agency. A sleepy Hamilton said that he hadn't heard from Stormi as yet and suggested that he try calling the resort himself.

"I'll do that, Mr. Hamilton. Now, if I could trouble you for the addresses and the telephone numbers of the rest of the members of the band, maybe I won't have to bother you again."

Hamilton groaned. "Look, first of all, you'd better get her mother's address and phone number. That's the one she uses most of the time. And sure, you can have the others. Phyllis!" he yelled, just off the mouthpiece. "Give this nice man the addresses for Sex Kitten, will you? My wife will get them for you." He yawned, and Lucas was handed over to yet another person.

Lucas pulled up in front of a neat suburban two-story house and looked at it in surprise. He hadn't expected this kind of background, somehow. He had expected something against which a girl could rebel—poverty or ostentation. A small woman answered the bell, thin and pleasant-looking, with an open cheerful face.

"Do come in," she said when she was able to break through his explanations. "There's a terrible wind today. I was out in the garden, just trying to tidy it up a bit before the ground gets too sloppy, and my hands got frozen. Here," she said, leading him into a small room, "we'll sit in the den. It's nicer, really. And I'll get you some coffee. I'll bet you've come right from downtown if you got this address from Mr. Hamilton. That's a long drive just to turn around and drive back again." She disappeared and returned in seconds with a tray with mugs of coffee, cream and sugar, and a plate of cookies. "Nothing homemade, I'm afraid. Since Jennifer left—she's our youngest—I don't bake as much. Now—Jennifer. I'm sorry I don't know where she is at the moment. She was up at that ski resort, and she hasn't got back yet."

"I called the resort," said Lucas, and—"

"Oh, the job is over, but Jennifer's taken a couple of days off. She likes the country, and she was awfully tired. They've been working almost steadily since Christmas. She'll call me as soon as she's back in town, though. That's our arrangement. I never worry if she's been out of town and doesn't get back right away. Unless I knew she had another job, then I might worry, but she doesn't. Not right away. But she'll be by to get her mail and collect her phone calls. She uses this as her official address still. She was sharing the flat with a girl named Amanda or Annabel or something like that, and they have a phone, but she prefers not to let people have that number. This way we can act as an answering service. We bought her one of those machines for Christmas—not that we mind taking her calls, but we thought she might like the privacy, but she said, no, and made us keep the machine. She says there are too many weirdos, she calls them, out there, and she doesn't want to have to deal with them."

"Does she have a boyfriend who might know where she is?"

"I don't think so. She used to go out with Ryan—he was in the band—but they had a fight, and Ryan got another offer and he went off to the West Coast, I think. She hasn't really had a boyfriend recently."

Lucas smiled and drank his coffee. There was obviously a limit to what Jennifer told her mother. "Why does she dye her hair black, Mrs. Wilson?" he asked out of a sudden anxiety and desire to make sure they were talking about the same Jennifer Wilson.

"Oh, she hasn't gone and done that again, has she?" said her mother, with a look of half-amused distress on her face. "I knew we shouldn't have gone down to Florida. I thought I'd finally talked her out of doing things to her hair. She has such pretty hair, and it looks terrible like that. I keep telling her it'll all fall out if she keeps on dyeing it these awful colors every few months, and she just smiles and says it's part of the act and if she goes bald, she'll get herself a fancy wig. After all, she says, Dolly Parton wears wigs, and look at the money she makes. You just can't argue with her. She's that sharp. And funny when she wants to be."

Lucas put down his coffee mug and rose to his feet. "Thank you, Mrs. Wilson. You've been very helpful. And please let us know if you hear from Jennifer. Call me at this number," and he jotted down his name and the number, "and if I'm not there, ask for Sergeant Patterson, or failing that, Inspector Baldwin. They'll all know what you're talking about. Of course, you can always leave a message, and I'll get back to you." He hoped she had absorbed the fact that he really wanted to hear from her, although from the slightly distracted look in her eyes, he doubted it. "I don't think your daughter realizes how important her evidence is—she probably doesn't realize even what she was looking at when she witnessed the event. So she probably won't think to contact us." He would have been happier if he had thought she was listening to him; but she seemed to be one of those people who rarely give concentrated attention to any monologues but their own.

Eric Patterson was leaning back in his chair again, looking considerably livelier than he had the day before. "So—how's the mystery witness tour going?" he said, and put his feet up on the desk in the attitude of a man who expects to be amused.

"Not only does she exist, Patterson, you slob, but she has parents and a nice house in the suburbs. The only thing that puzzles me is that both her agent and her parents are under the impression that she is in the north woods right now and hasn't been near the big city in a week."

"Really?" said Patterson, removing his feet from the desk in honor of the occasion. "Maybe you're chasing the wrong chickadee."

"I thought about that, but you know, Pine Valley isn't far from here. She could have come down. Neilson was killed the day after they finished their stint up there. There's a big name group in there for the weekend now—they were just a filler."

"So she came down to see him, meaning to go back and loaf around with the boys in the band," said Eric, grinning, "only events intervened, and she got nabbed by us. So as soon as she can get away, she scoots off back to the woods to recover. And those sinister figures stalking the corridors of the motel whatever-it-was were just Joe and Ed from the band."

"Guys in rock bands aren't called Joe and Ed," said Lucas. "But if that's true, why would she duck out on them? And why would they rip the door off its hinges instead of just waiting for her to answer?"

Patterson ignored the question. "That means you'll have to wait until her ma or her agent calls you." Lucas nodded. "And that means you'll be available to canvass everyone on the second and third floors of the Karlsbad Hotel to find out if they heard anything."

"Come off it, Patterson. It's a hotel. You aren't going to find any witnesses still there from Thursday," said Lucas.

"Don't be stupid. Those floors are where the permanent residents live—or didn't you know that?"

"I suppose I did. No one has reported hearing a gunshot? What was he killed with, by the way?"

"A twenty-two. Understated—"

"And relatively quiet. A professional?"

"Possibly. Doesn't make things any easier, does it?"

Sanders stepped into his apartment at nine o'clock on Sunday night and was overwhelmed with a powerful sense of oppression. It had been his suggestion to end the holiday then, to make a swift break between love and work. Harriet had given him a look he had trouble interpreting and then agreed that it was a good idea, pointing out that it was going to take her the rest of the evening to sort out a week's worth of mail and telephone messages. It had been one of his crummier ideas. He wondered if she felt as alone and abandoned at this particular moment as he did. He rummaged around in the refrigerator for a beer, pushed a pile of books and newspapers off his most comfortable chair, and reached for the telephone.

"Ed," he said, with relief when he heard the voice on the other end. "How are things? What's been happening while I've been away?" His shoulders dropped in relaxation, and he raised the bottle to his lips.

"No," said Sanders. "Haven't heard a thing. We were in the States. You'd have to assassinate the Pope in Toronto for it to hit the news on Martha's Vineyard." He listened for a moment. "Yeah, I remember Carl Neilson. Didn't he try to buy the entire town council in King City or someplace like that three or four years ago? They almost got him for it, too. Thank God I was away. Let Baldwin screw it up." John Sanders listened for five more minutes without interrupting before saying good-bye and gently replacing the receiver. He stood up and walked over to the window; he stared thoughtfully at the forest of high rises silhouetted against the black night, shook his head, and reached for the telephone again.

CHAPTER 6

"He always was a stupid bastard," said Ed Dubinsky softly. The sergeant shoved the loose papers on his desk to one side to clear a space for his partner to sit on, close enough to hear him. "Well, maybe not stupid, exactly. Anyway, they should get him the hell out of this department."

"What's gone wrong with the case?" asked Sanders idly.

"Aside from the fact that Matt Baldwin's been running it? I'm not quite sure," said Dubinsky with uncharacteristic humility. "Maybe it's that the widow's lawyer is Marty Fielding. Baldwin's scared shitless of Fielding. Always has been."

"Wasn't there something about Carl Neilson and girls?" asked Sanders.

Dubinsky rocked his hand gently back and forth. "Who can tell? He owned that place down on Dundas, La Celestina—remember? Hooker was killed in the alley behind it. We sniffed around him a bit because it looked like she used to work out of the restaurant, but nothing came of it. That was Baldwin, too, wasn't it?" he said innocently. "And Patterson. They nailed the pimp for it, but he got off. He was a vicious bastard, that pimp. But that doesn't mean he killed the hooker."

"Christ, I feel like I never left the city," said Sanders gloomily. "What have you been working on?"

Forty-eight hours had passed by, forty-eight hours in which Lucas had knocked on doors and attempted to interview the residents of the Karlsbad Hotel, the shopkeepers on both sides of the street, the owners of the town houses behind the hotel. Nothing. He had collected a few reminiscences, several diatribes on the disintegration of society, and a great many baffled looks. Now he sat at his desk, meticulously fleshing out his report on the material he had collected. It was not difficult to write. No one had heard anything even remotely resembling gunfire. No one had noticed anyone behaving in a suspicious manner. In fact, no one had noticed anyone. People who had been home had been sleeping, or watching television, or listening to the radio; everyone else had been finishing late lunches, shopping, going to movies, even working. Those, of course, were the people who could remember what they were doing three days ago. Most hadn't the faintest idea.

Eric Patterson padded into the room, settled himself at his desk, and looked at his watch.

"What's up?" said Lucas, yawning. "You're looking pale and sinister, Patterson, like a tired wolf about to eat Red Riding Hood. You should get more sleep."

"Nothing the matter with me," said Eric, turning his chair half around so he could stretch his legs out past the desk. "I don't need ten hours a night in the sack to wrap up a simple case like this."

Lucas ignored the crack. "So what's up?"

"Not that much. Just a hunch, what you might call a twitch in the gut. I've been nosing around Neilson's phony corporation, and there's one bastard that looks like a rabbit smelling the stew pot every time you ask him a question. I think I'll have another go at him this afternoon."

"Who is he?"

"The treasurer." Patterson grinned cheerfully.

"Does he look like someone who owns an illegal twenty-two?"

"He doesn't have to. He could have connections somewhere. Everybody's got some kind of connections. Anyway,

I just want to bounce him a few times and see how high he jumps." He looked at his watch again. "Well, I'm off. Timing is everything." With that, he loped out of the office like a cynical wolfhound, his raincoat flying out behind him.

And that meant that it was Rob Lucas's hand reaching for the telephone when the call came through. "Four ninety-two Oak Street, lower apartment," droned the clear, businesslike voice. "Female, tentatively identified as Jennifer Wilson, age twenty-three, apparently bludgeoned to death sometime during the night." For a moment he sat absolutely still. He could see her standing in the restaurant, looking absurdly childlike in his blue sweater, observing him coolly; then waving her arm in the direction of his face and teasing him about his looks. His stomach twisted painfully and he got up. In the flurry that followed, he remembered to drop a note on Baldy's desk, grateful at least that he was not in the office to discover that their witness was now dead. He should have taken her midnight flight more seriously, done something more aggressive to protect her. "Christ almighty," he said to the walls of the elevator, "I might as well have killed her myself and been done with it," and punched hell out of the buttons.

Six or seven people were standing around that large front bedroom when Lucas got there, waiting for someone— him—to arrive and start more things happening. "How did he gain entry?" he snapped.

"Through this window," said a constable who was leaning against the frame of the bay window in the front of the room. "It was unlocked, maybe even open a crack. You can see pry marks in the wood of the sill. A crowbar or something like that. Rusty."

Reluctantly, he looked down at the girl on the floor and froze. She was facedown, dressed in a long flannelette nightgown with little flowers on it. One side of the nightgown was caught under her, revealing a stick-thin leg as far as a smooth pale thigh. There was no mystery about the cause of death. Someone had smashed in the back of her skull with tremendous force. Blood and tissue had congealed in a black and sickening mess, horribly visible against her pale blond hair. Straight, short, blond hair. "Is this the girl you called in about?" he snapped finally at the constable standing near the door.

"Yeah, this is the girl." He looked askance at Lucas, as if wondering if the man were entirely sane. "The neighbor rang the doorbell, and when no one answered, she looked in the window. She said the girl's name is Jennifer Wilson. She's out on the porch if you want to talk to her."

"This is Jennifer Wilson?" he repeated stupidly. "Have you guys finished taking pictures?" he asked. The photographer nodded. "Anyone mind if I turn her over for a second?" The photographer shrugged. No one else said a word. Lucas took her gently by the thinnest, narrowest shoulders he had ever touched on an adult and turned her stiffening body over. Blue eyes stared at him above a thin, slightly curving nose and a narrow mouth, all set in a slightly elongated face. She would have been a pretty girl, he thought, with life in that face, and probably spectacular when made up for the stage. But there was one thing that she certainly was not. She was not his Jennifer Wilson. She was five inches shorter and twenty or thirty pounds lighter, and although his Jennifer hadn't been particularly large, this girl was elfin in her tininess—a doll-like creature. She was also, he observed with dismay, the daughter of the nice woman in the suburbs. Every bone in her face told him that. "Damn," he said at last, and set her back the way she had been found.

"Has someone gone through her things?" he snapped. Silence. "I want to know if it's all hers. It shouldn't be too hard to tell. She must be size one, if there is such a thing. If you find anything that seems to belong to someone else, let me know."

"What about prints?" said an intrepid voice.

"After they've finished," he said. "After they've finished."

The murder weapon—a rusty and aged-looking crowbar—had been extracted from the leafless bushes in front of the house. No particular attempt had been made to conceal it, for the excellent reason that concealment was unnecessary. The chances of tracing it to anyone were very dim. It was covered with blood and hair, undoubtedly Jennifer Wilson's, and no doubt the pathologist would find corresponding rust marks in the wound, but it was one of thousands of rusty crowbars in the city, of exactly the same design, and there was not a recoverable fingerprint on any of its surfaces. Plastic-shrouded, it had made its futile trip to the lab shortly after Jennifer Wilson's body, also plastic-shrouded, had left for the morgue. Lucas headed for the back bedroom. The print crew had been through and was now at work on the front bedroom; he was in full possession. There were twin beds, each covered with a thin orange bedspread, both concealing naked mattresses. In the corner was an old chest of drawers, empty even of dust particles. The closet was bare, except for a handful of wire coat hangers; even the wicker wastepaper basket had nothing in it but a plastic tab from an adhesive bandage. He collected it carefully and put it away, forlorn hope though it was. The bedside table in between the two beds had a drawer with an old ballpoint pen inside it. No matchbook covers from favorite hangouts, no name on the pen. No revealing letters jammed carelessly under the drawers. Just a few curls of dust under the beds and a couple of darker patches on the walls where pictures had been. Posters, he supposed, judging by the size.

He was interrupted in his reverie by one of the constables who was working on the front room. "Hey, Sergeant," he said. "You want to talk to the neighbor? She says she's getting chilly out there."

"For chrissake, you mean she's still on the porch? Why didn't you tell her to go home?"

"I did," he said, with the look of a long-suffering and misunderstood man. "She didn't want to miss any of the excitement."

"Well, tell her again. I'll be over in a minute."

It was actually closer to five minutes later when he presented himself on the concrete porch and rang the bell. This time it was answered almost at once by a plump elderly lady with bright and curious eyes, who regarded him steadily as he introduced himself, and then picked up his ID suspiciously and stared at it long enough to memorize it. "Come in, Sergeant," she said finally. "You're the person who came a few days ago to see Jennifer, aren't you? I saw you crawling around her garden, trying to get in the back window. I thought police weren't supposed to do that. That's what they say on television, you know. But perhaps it's only in stories that police don't break into people's houses."

He sighed and braced himself for trouble. "You were in when I came out here before? When I stood here and rang your doorbell?"

"Oh, yes." She nodded vigorously. "I'm always in during the afternoon. That's when I take my rest. Very important, the doctor told me. That's why I didn't answer the door. Besides, you know, I couldn't tell who you were. And crawling around the garden like that, you could have been a burglar. Or a rapist." As she spoke, she led him slowly into a living room filled with dark, overstuffed furniture and a multitude of little tables. He picked his way carefully through the hazards and perched on the edge of a chair, taking out his notebook as he went down.

"Another policeman was out here looking for her yesterday as well," she observed brightly. "I suppose she must have been in some sort of difficulty." She waited a hopeful second or two for a response and then ploughed on. "Had something stolen, I expect. You never know—the people who live here these days—it gets worse and worse. Anyway, I was in the garden. It was in the morning, and I always work outside for a little while during the day unless the weather is too bad. It's very important to get out every day, you know. That's what the doctor says."

"Who was this policeman?" asked Lucas in the momentary pause while she caught her breath.

"Oh, I wouldn't know that. He didn't actually say he was a policeman, you know; he just looked like one."

"Did he show you any identification? Like that card I showed you?"

"Oh, no," she said, almost shocked. "Of course not. But he didn't want to come into my house, you see. I would never allow anyone in my house who didn't have proper identification—I'm very careful—but he just wanted to know about Jennifer. It's funny, he said the thin girl with black hair, and she is thin, too thin, but I told him no, she didn't, she had blond hair, and that black hair was just a wig. She had three wigs, you know. Very expensive they were. One all fluffy and curly and long, the same color as her own hair—a Dolly Parton wig, she called it. And the black wig he was talking about. And then a lovely dark red wig—that was my favorite. She was telling me all about them one day when she came over for tea. I wasn't feeling too good, and she was so excited about them that she went and got them and modeled them for me. She used them for her work. She was a singer, you know. For one of those rock bands. Such a lovely girl."

"Can you tell me anything more about this man who came around yesterday?" said Lucas with a sense of almost suffocating impatience.

"What else do you want to know?" she asked vaguely.

"I mean, he was a tall man, and he had a raincoat on, and one of those tweed hats."

"How old was he?"

"Not very old. No, not very old at all."

"My age?"

"How old are you? You don't have to answer that," she added archly. "He could have been your age, or older. Or maybe younger. It's so hard to tell what age a man is, don't you find? Women are easier, I think."

"What color was his hair?"

"He had a green hat on, I know that. I don't think I saw his hair color. He had blue eyes," she added, "or maybe brown."

Lucas tried another tack. "What did he want to know?"

"Oh, he just wanted to know if Jennifer was back yet from her job. I said she was, but she was out. She'd just come in yesterday morning about ten, and she'd popped over to see me—I keep a key to her flat when she's out of town, in case of emergencies, you see, because her roommate's never home and the girl on the top floor is out at work every day and goes away every weekend, and if you ask me, she doesn't spend every night at home during the week, either, but that makes her a nice quiet neighbor, so I'm not complaining."

"What roommate?" asked Lucas. "There doesn't seem to be—"

"Oh, well, then, maybe she's moved out. I thought I hadn't seen her for a while. Anyway, Jennifer had to run out and do some shopping, and that was when he came around. He said he was sorry he missed her, but he'd call back some other time. She said he was probably selling insurance, but he didn't look to me like a salesman. It was when she got back that she said that—she'd popped in again because I'd asked her to get me a pound of butter while she was out."

"What time did you say this man came around? Ten-thirty?"

For a brief miraculous moment, there was a pause. "Yes. Because I had just gone out into the garden, and I go out at ten-thirty, right after my tea, and he was just walking up the path between the houses."

When he got back to Jennifer Wilson's flat, his ears still ringing from the monologue, the front bedroom was clear for inspection. He stood in the center of the room and looked around him. The double bed was almost unrumpled. She must have climbed out of bed when she heard her attacker, leaving behind that slight hump in the bedclothes and a flash of visible sheet. Why hadn't she screamed? Or perhaps she had, and no one had heard her. Another question for the neighbors.

He started with the closet. It was small and jammed with clothes. On the left she kept her spangled, gaudy-looking stage costumes; next to them was an assortment of ordinary casual garments: skirts, sweaters, sweatshirts, and jeans. But every piece of clothing was tiny. As was all the underwear lying in the drawers. No one larger than Jennifer Wilson could have struggled into any of it. The walls were covered with posters and photographs of the real Jennifer as Stormi Knight, some of them alone, some with the five male members of the band surrounding her.

On the top shelf of the closet (how had she reached up that high? he wondered, and then saw a solid-looking stool pushed into a corner) were three hatboxes. He carried them over to the bed and looked inside. There were the wigs the neighbor had seen: the Dolly Parton; the black one—long and straight, designed to make her look ghoulish; and the dark red one. And this was the reason that little Jennifer Wilson was dead. For owning a black wig and, one gloomy day, modeling it as a joke for her neighbor, to cheer her up when she wasn't feeling well.

*   *   *

The sun, sulking behind some ineffectual clouds, had almost set before Lucas got back to his desk. His head ached, his hands were shaky, his stomach rebellious. Guilt and misery and total bafflement, that was why he felt this way. Guilt because it was his inefficiency that had caused a harmless girl to be killed, and guilt because his first reaction when he saw that silky blond hair and realized that the victim had not been *his* Jennifer Wilson was profound relief. After a moment's consideration he added hunger. There had never seemed to be a moment in this day when going off to eat lunch had been even a slight possibility.

The interview with Mrs. Wilson had been acutely painful and completely useless. She was confused and baffled, unable to understand why anyone could want to harm her Jennifer. As he listened, a nagging voice in his head was muttering, No one did want to kill her; he wanted to kill an over-made-up, perfumed little whore, who for some reason borrowed your daughter's name. For a horrified instant, he thought he had said the words aloud, but Mrs. Wilson had continued to stare helplessly at him, tears sliding down her cheeks unheeded, with no change in expression. It wasn't going to help the woman bear her grief to hear that Jennifer's death was just a mistake. And perhaps it wasn't. There are, after all, many painfully familiar reasons for pretty, fragile-looking, harmless girls getting themselves killed. He had ventured to ask her if her Jennifer had known another Jennifer Wilson, a girl with black hair, and Mrs. Wilson had silently shaken her head. She had no time for such irrelevant questions, she seemed to be saying. Not now.

She had come to the conclusion, finally, that Jennifer's death had been caused by a demented person, not responsible for his actions, and that, curiously enough, she did find comforting. Miserably, Rob Lucas agreed that this could very well be what had happened, and assuring her that they were doing everything in their power to find whoever it was, he fled from the scene.

He had sat in his car a block away from the Wilsons' house and thought. It was possible, of course, that the man in the green hat had had nothing to do with the Wilson girl's death. He hadn't believed it when he first heard about him; he didn't believe it now, but he still had to behave as though the possibility existed. So now it was time to look at the boys in the band.

Kevin was tiresome. He bounced between playing the aggrieved juvenile, defensive and hostile, and the horrified adult, ready to string sex murderers from the highest tree. For just as Mrs. Wilson had clung to the notion that Jennifer had been the victim of a poor demented creature, Kevin clung to an image of sex-crazed pervert. He did, however, provide a rational explanation for the band's disappearance. This had been the first time that they had had a full week off since before Christmas, and they had spent three days in a borrowed chalet, skiing and eating and drinking and sleeping. And which of them, Lucas had asked, had been sleeping with Jennifer? None of them, Kevin swore. Not since Ryan left. She had said she would never mix work and sex again. And she hadn't. What had happened with Ryan had almost broken the group up just when they were getting somewhere. Rob filed that away for future reference and left Kevin to cope with his grief and how to find another girl singer.

The rest of the group—Steve, Scott, and Brad—had all been huddled together in Scott's apartment, looking nervous, confused, and alike. Their only contribution was that Ryan was capable of smashing his ex-girlfriend's skull in if he hadn't been in San Francisco that week. But none of them, not Kevin, not his three interchangeable sidemen, had ever seen or heard of a girl with black curly hair who called herself Jennifer Wilson. Lucas yanked the keyboard closer to him and started to write up a report. Maybe he'd get something to eat later.

Lucas walked in the next morning to discover a major reorganization in work loads. Kelleher was now coordinating the investigation into the death of the Wilson girl. Lucas could feel the weight lifting from his shoulders. With luck, he might never have to face Mrs. Wilson again.

"Great," he said. "Just watch the woman next door. She'll strangle you in the world's longest sentence."

"She can't be worse than my mother," said Kelleher. "And I've survived thirty-five years of listening to her." He got up and reached for his jacket. "I think I'll be off and have a look at that rock band. I'd like to get them before they're awake. I read the stuff you wrote up last night—anything left out as not suitable for Baldy's tender ears?" Lucas opened his coffee and took out his Danish, shaking his head, and then stopped. "Yeah—there is one thing. I sent someone to check the prints in the Wilson girl's apartment against my missing witness. Any results?"

"You haven't seen them? Your witness's prints are all over the place. The back room, the victim's bedroom, everywhere. When you find her, I'd like a word. Like, where was she in the middle of the night?"

Lucas turned his back on the rest of the room, put his feet up on the window ledge and worked on his breakfast while he considered the problem of finding Miss X. The chances were pretty good that her name was nothing like either Jennifer Wilson or Stormi Knight, so he might as well stop thinking of her as Jennifer. That, of course, explained why she didn't react to being called by name. What had looked to him to be general contrariness and sulkiness had been simple unfamiliarity. So we call her X, he thought, taking a bite of Danish. And X is either a whore or a musi-

cian—or something else altogether. But let's start, he continued to himself, by assuming she is one of those two things.
Of course, he reflected, there is nothing to stop you from
being both a whore and a musician at the same time. And
where does that get us?

All I need is a picture and a visit to Vice. That will take
care of the prostitution end of things. Maybe. If she's
known to them. Or a picture and a lot of visits to places
where local musicians hang out. He thought with a sinking
heart of the hundreds of little bars and clubs in the city and
suburbs where rock musicians played, and groaned aloud.
"What's wrong?" asked a passing constable of Kevin's gen-
eration, and Lucas suddenly felt old. In the six years since
he had been twenty-two, he had lost touch with the world
of groups and teenage wonders.

"Where would you start looking if you wanted to find a
singer with a rock group?"

"Any singer? Or a particular one? I mean, if you want
to hire a band—"

"No, I'm trying to track down a girl. A witness."

"The witness you lost? I didn't know she was a rock
singer. I thought she was—"

"Yeah, well, let's assume she's a rock singer. I need a
name for her. And maybe even an address. But I'll take a
name, to start with."

"Try the record stores. Those guys that work there, they
know everybody. Here, start with the big ones—I'll write
them down for you," and muttering energetically to himself
the names of a host of establishments, he wrote furiously
for a minute or two. "I don't have the addresses, but they're
not hard to find. Besides, you might even know some of
them," he added with good-humoured contempt. "They sell
classical stuff, too." Lucas's reputation for having peculiar
tastes was well established.

"Would you believe I also listen to country and western? No, you wouldn't. Thanks. You're a pal." And he

reached for the phone to track down their sketch artist and plead for an instant drawing of X.

Two hours later he was heading for Vice, armed with a pile of copies of a sketch of X. On the whole, he thought it had come out a reasonable representation of her, although maybe it made her look a bit too pleasantly respectable. Vice did not greet him with enthusiasm. "Jesus, Lucas, do you know how many hookers there are in the city? What do you think we are?" said someone resentfully, tossing the picture back at him.

A sleepy-eyed detective in plain clothes picked up the sketch. "I don't know," he said. "Maybe. She looks vaguely familiar. But that doesn't mean a thing. You want to sit here and go through mug shots of every hooker we've booked in the past couple of years, be my guest. I don't think you'll find her, though. I haven't noticed her working downtown. How old is she "

"Early twenties?"

"Naw. I thought maybe she was one of those kids who come through for a couple of weeks and then get whisked off home again or somewhere by some social worker. There are so many of them, I can't tell them apart. No can do. Sorry." That was it. And off Lucas went in search of record stores.

Every store seemed to have at least one clerk with an amazing knowledge of the local scene. They all knew Sex Kitten—a group Lucas had never heard of before this week—and that gave him a certain confidence in their opinions. He started with the two largest stores. In the first he drew a complete blank. In the second, the clerk stared at the picture and then called to someone poring over a stack of computer printout in the office. She stared at it, too, and frowned. "I can't place her," she said. "But she looks familiar."

"Could you have run into her at a party?" suggested Lucas. "She's about your age."

The girl shook her head. "Not familiar that way. Familiar, like I saw her on a record jacket or something. Can I keep the sketch?" Lucas nodded. "Give me your name, and if it comes to me, I'll call you." She wrote his name down on the back of the picture and whisked off again.

He turned an inquiring eye back to the clerk. "Sorry. She looked, like, vaguely familiar, that's all. That's why I called Betsy over. But if Betsy can't come up with the name, no one can. She has a phenomenal memory. Still, if Betsy remembers her, like on a record jacket, the kid is probably a singer or something. Somewhere, for somebody."

"Betsy wouldn't have seen her hanging around on the street outside, or in the store looking at records, and remember her from that? Get the girl confused with someone else?"

"Definitely not. Betsy remembers faces, like, in context, you know? If a hundred people she'd seen before walked into this room, she could say, those ninety are customers, I saw those two on television once, that's a waitress somewhere, that's a politician, that's a hooker who works the street out there—she's good."

"Thanks. Betsy should join the police force." And he left the store feeling elated. Somewhere in this city someone had to know who X was.

Nineteen record stores later, his faith in the phenomenal Betsy began to fade. Nineteen clerks stared at the picture, consulted their friends, shook their heads, said they knew every singer in town, and she wasn't one of them. He walked into the twentieth tired, hungry, thirsty, and discouraged. The more discouraged because the lead had seemed to be so fertile in the beginning. If he'd been searching for a needle in a haystack right from the start, he wouldn't have objected so much. After all, he was used to that. It was the irrational rise that Betsy had given to his expectations that had caused this corresponding depression. That and hunger. The twentieth clerk looked at him and handed back the picture. "How the hell should I know? What do you think I am? This is just a part-time job I got, mister, not a goddamn career," he snarled. "I don't even like music. You wanna buy a record? Pick it out and give me the money."

Lucas walked out onto the pavement in a rage and looked around him. To the east were more record stores and some fast-food restaurants; to the west were two pleasant shops across from the University's Faculty of Music that carried a lot of hard-to-get classical music. There were also a couple of cheap, slow-paced, friendly restaurants, where one could spend hours over a meal, one Middle Eastern and one Italian. This late in the afternoon they'd be almost empty. Obviously he should head east, grab a quick lunch, and finish this damn thing up today. He headed west.

The Middle Eastern restaurant was about ten shop-fronts away to the west. To get to it he would have to pass the first record store. Perhaps he would slip in, show them his picture, just in case, and see what they had that was new and interesting. Then lunch. Then back east to the grind. The entrance was down a flight of concrete steps, and the shop itself was long and narrow. Bins filled with CDs lined the two side walls. The cash register, unattended as usual, was at the front; the only other human being in the place was sitting at the order desk in the back, working in a little pool of light, listening to a recording of *Pelléas et Mélisande* that Lucas particularly liked. The shop was dimly lit after the brightness of the afternoon, and it took a minute for his eyes to adjust. "Excuse me," he said, opening his small briefcase for the twenty-first time that day, and stopped dead.

There she was. Right in front of him, tacked to the wall behind the order desk. Boots, short black skirt, tiny black top, long black hair. Posed with her foot on a chair, looking bold and sluttish, with one hand on the backrest, the other on her hip.

"May I help you with something?" asked the young man at the order desk, who had by then risen to his feet.

"Yes," said Lucas. "You certainly may. Who is that?"

"Lulu?" he asked. "The main character in the opera. Berg's opera. The soprano," he added, as though talking to a mentally deficient.

"No, no," said Lucas. "I know that. But that girl in the poster. Is she the one who's singing Lulu? Or did they hire a model?"

"Oh, no," he said, shocked. "They don't do that. No, that's the Lulu. Annie Hunter. I was the tenor," he added. "That's why I still have the poster up. Can't bear to take it down. That's me, Peter Johnstone. I sang Alwa. My first big part."

"This is an old production then? I see it says it's on April eighteenth, nineteenth, and twentieth. Is that last year? Who put it on?"

He nodded. "Last year. It was a student production, really. We're all at the Faculty. Of Music," he added condescendingly. "Opera."

"You mean this Annie Hunter is a student?" His surprise must have been evident on his face as he spoke.

"Well, I don't know what she's doing now. Annie and I were in the performance program together—last year was our first year in the Opera School. I really haven't seen her this year at all. Once or twice on the street, maybe, but not to talk to."

"She had the lead?" Lucas's astonishment was palpable.

"Sure. She's pretty good. Actually, she was a terrific Lulu," he added generously. "Good voice and a great actress—that's why she got the part. There was no one else at the school who could have *been* Lulu. Sort of vicious and bitchy, yet seductive and pathetic, you know?"

Lucas did know, but had no intention of discussing the point with Mr. Johnstone. "You have no idea where I could find her now?"

"Why do you want to find her?" he asked, dragging himself from dreams of past glory to a present-day suspicious practicality.

He drew out his ID silently.

"Is she in trouble?" Lucas could feel the pull of fellowship, the closing of ranks in the face of the enemy in the tenor's every word.

"I certainly hope not," he said. "She may have witnessed a crime—a serious crime—and she could be of great help to us."

"I see. And what in hell do you mean by witness? Cops seem to mean some pretty funny things when they call someone a witness."

Lucas tried to sound nonthreatening. "Just that. We think she was an eyewitness to a serious crime. We think that the people who committed the crime knew she saw them. And are looking for her."

"Just a witness." Lucas could see the clerk wavering. "So if anyone else asks you about her, it'd be nice if you had a memory lapse."

"You mean, she may be in real trouble," he said flatly. "I see." He sat down to his order books again. "I don't actually know where she is myself. But if I were you, I'd check with the secretary at the Faculty. She knows everybody and everything." He swiveled around in his chair and looked back at the wall behind him. "And I think I'll just take this poster down for a while. It's time I replaced it anyway." As Lucas walked away, he saw the young man carefully removing the thumbtacks from his poster and rolling it up.

As he walked by the opera section, he paused at *B* for Berg and pulled out a copy of *Lulu*. "What the hell," he muttered, "I don't have it," and he walked back to the order desk to pay.

He looked at his watch as he left the record store and was startled to discover that it was almost five. If he ate now, the secretary at the music faculty would be gone by the time he got there. He could wait. He began dodging his way across four lanes of rush-hour traffic to the music school. But the administration offices were locked, lights out, silent as the grave. He knocked loudly, in case someone was working late. Not a sound. He rattled the doorknob vehemently. A pleasant-looking girl who was walking past tried to put him out of his misery.

"It's no good knocking," she said. "Even if they were hiding in there, they'd rather go out the window than answer. Believe me. You can get them at nine o'clock tomorrow."

"Thanks," he muttered. Then, inspired by sudden hope and her friendly face, he added, "You wouldn't know a girl named Annie Hunter, would you? She was here last year, I think."

She shook her head. "Sorry. I'm only in first year. What was she doing?"

"Opera," he said, hoping that was the right category of response.

"That's a graduate program," she said. "And anyway, I'm in strings," she added, and trotted on her way.

Only slightly discouraged, he headed for the restaurant and a telephone call to report to Baldy that his witness had a name—a real name, he thought, although not yet verified from other sources. He was beginning to feel cautious about things like that. Baldy wasn't around to hear the happy news; he left the message to be added to the pile on his desk.

He thought gleefully of the inspector spending his evening plowing through hours and hours of reports—every one of which he had summarily demanded, each one his own fault. It must be a shock to his system, thought Lucas, to be back to the routine of endless hours of actual work. He was probably out right now buttering up Marty Fielding over a martini, assuring him that all was well for his client, before heading back to the grind. Thank God. And that meant that instead of being hauled down to report in person, he was going to be able to eat and drink himself into a pleasant haze, go back to his apartment, take the phone off the hook, put up his aching feet, and listen to his new recording of *Lulu*.

CHAPTER 7

Lucas pushed aside his coffee and stared down at the soggy pastry on his desk. It had been 2:00 A.M. when he had given up trying to get to sleep. Neither books nor late-night television had been able to lull his jumpy brain, and he had prowled around the apartment until five-thirty or six, when he had slumped onto the couch and fallen into restless slumber for a couple of uneasy hours. A lousy way to start a lousy day. He had to get away from his desk. Maybe he should try the Faculty of Music. Not that inquiring there was likely to get him anywhere, he thought with more than his usual pessimism. Some sort of curse lay over this case. "I'm off," he muttered to the room in general. No one paid any attention.

The secretary at the Faculty of Music glowered at him across the counter. "Annie Hunter?" she said, her voice tight with suspicion and dislike. "I don't give out information about students to unauthorized people." He pulled out his ID. She glanced at it, and the atmosphere in the room chilled several more degrees. "Is this supposed to make a difference?" She walked back to her desk. A flash of stubborn anger kept Rob Lucas standing immobile where he was. After a lengthy pause, she vouchsafed him one more glance. "Is she in some sort of trouble?"

"No, she is not in trouble," he said, exasperated. "She's a witness. That's all. But we do have to talk to her."

She was not convinced. "I'm afraid I couldn't tell you where she is right now," said the secretary briskly. "She dropped out last spring."

He looked at the name plate propped up on the desk. "Mrs. Dubchek, I have to get in touch with her. She witnessed a crime. And the person—or persons—who committed it know she saw them. Can you understand that? And they're looking for her."

She studied him, pondering. "Well, she really did drop out last year. That is, she didn't reregister in the fall. Her father had died a few months before that, and I think she had financial problems. Of course there was no need for the little fool to leave," she added. "She could have applied for extra grant money. But Annie always worried about money. She may have been too discouraged to think of asking for help—or was afraid we'd turn her down. Students," she went on. "A fragile lot, some of them. Very hard on themselves."

"You have no idea where I might look for her? Who her friends are?"

"She hasn't seen any of her old friends. I asked around in the fall, trying to get an address for her. They won't be any help, I'm afraid. But, just let me look. Don't despair." She disappeared into another room, emerging very shortly waving a manila folder. "I haven't retired her file yet—there are advantages to sloth, you know. I don't have a valid address, but, as I remember, I do have a copy of an odd letter that we wrote to her lawyer when she was in first year—something about her official status at the Faculty. Don't ask me why. I think her father requested it. Wanted proof she really was a student before he would continue to send support money. Parents," she added sadly, shaking her head. "Unpleasant, some of them. No wonder she always thought she was on the edge of starvation. Anyway, the lawyer ought to know where she is if anyone does." As she spoke she flipped through the contents of the folder in front of her. "Here we are. This is the address. And she had a lot to do with those lawyers over her father's will, I know that. Because she was in here worrying about it a lot last year. The poor thing needed a mother figure in her life," she explained, and Lucas began to understand why he had received so hostile a reception. "She's an orphan now. Such a sad word, isn't it? Even for a girl of"—she looked down at the file in front of her—"twenty-three." She picked up another piece of paper. "In fact, I have that address here as well. She listed her next of kin as her lawyer. It made me want to cry. But then, I get sentimental over them. Some of them, anyway. Some of them are absolute—well, I won't go into that." She picked up her file and turned to go, and then changed her mind and turned back to him. "Look, Sergeant, if you see her, will you do me a favor?"

"Sure," he said.

"Tell her to come back. Not to worry about the money. Tell her we won't let her starve. Please?"

"Sure," he said. "And thanks for the help." He ran lightly down the steps of the music building. The morning sun warmed his forehead, the cold north wind that had been blowing for days had died down at last, and his spirits rocketed upward. It was spring. Luck was cartwheeling along the sidewalk in front of him; failure was an unthinkable proposition. He stood irresolute in front of the building, debating whether to drop in on the lawyer unannounced or to find a phone and make an appointment. He had left his car down at headquarters, and the law office was only a mile or so away. Fate murmured in his ear. Clearly, he should walk and chance that the lawyer could and would see him.

Either Mr. Hennessy, of Hennessy and Garside, had a miserable law practice, or he, too, had been infected by the shift in the weather. When Lucas arrived at his office, the receptionist had looked coldly at him, muttered about people arriving without notice and expecting to see people, and then, after a brief telephone conversation, said with a glare, "Mr. Hennessy will see you now."

The lawyer was short, rotund, florid, and cheerful-looking. He belonged at the head of a gleaming mahogany table with a snifter of his namesake's cognac in his hand, gently infusing the surrounding company with good fellowship. At the moment, however, he was leaning forward across his almost-bare desk; he tilted his head like a suspicious and potentially hostile bird when Lucas sat down in front of him. "You were asking about Annie Hunter, I believe," he said, mildly enough. "Yes, I know her. I think I might even add that she is a client. And now that I've told you that much, perhaps you'll tell me what your interest in her is."

"First of all," said Lucas, "is this Annie Hunter?" He put the artist's sketch down on the lawyer's desk.

Hennessy nodded. "I've seen better pictures, but this does seem to be Annie," he conceded. "And again, now that we know we're both talking about the same person, perhaps you could explain your interest."

Lucas took a breath and launched into a fairly straightforward and moderately complete version of the trouble that Annie Hunter was in. Mr. Hennessy looked at him intently, his fingers laced together somewhere near his chin, and nodded occasionally.

"Just let me see if I understand you," he said, widening his eyes innocently. "You say my client was stopped for questioning on a staircase in a public building some distance from where a murder had been committed, because you assumed that she had something to do with the murder?" He smiled and continued on in mild tones. "Did you hold everyone who happened to be in the building on their lawful occasions that afternoon?"

"Her fingerprints were found in the apartment," said

Lucas, grateful that he wasn't in court right then, trying to justify their actions. "And she did admit, uh, say that she found the body. I'm not accusing her of anything, Mr. Hennessy. I don't think she's done anything, but I think she saw more than she said she did. And I believe that my hunch is confirmed by some odd things that have happened since: her hotel room was broken into; she gave us a false name—and a girl of that name has been killed. Possibly in error for Miss Hunter."

"Aren't you assuming a great deal on very little evidence, Sergeant?"

"Look, I'm not trying to prove her guilty of anything. We simply need her evidence, and we'd like to make sure that she's safe. Anyway, I don't think so," he added. "That I'm jumping to conclusions. Or if I am, so is someone else, which amounts to the same thing. The victim, Mr. Neilson, was killed with a twenty-two pistol, very—"

"Professionally? Is that what you mean?"

"Exactly. Do you see now why we're concerned for her safety? Do you know—do you have any idea where she might be?"

Mr. Hennessy swiveled his chair around and looked out the window at the soft blue sky and hazy, trailing clouds for a perceptible length of time. "You put me in a difficult situation, Sergeant," he answered at last. "I have information that you might find useful, but I'm not sure that I'm being very wise in passing it on. However—" He leaned forward and picked up his telephone. "Mrs. Green? Could you bring in the Hunter files? Thanks." He looked back at Lucas. "It was her father, really, who was my client. I inherited Annie, so to speak. We were joint executors of her father's estate. Ah, thank you, my dear. You are a marvel," he said to his secretary as she dropped two files on his desk. He sounded as if he meant it. "A copy of his will," he said, opening the top file. "Mr. Hunter left his second wife— Annie is his daughter by his first wife—a large sum of money; the residue of the estate he left to Annie, making her, with me, his executor as well. Sounds fair on paper, doesn't it? Well, in order to settle debts and pay the second wife the amount named in the will, we had to sell almost everything. His house, a few next-to-worthless stocks, and some bonds. Annie was left—after legal fees, which I pared down to next to nothing—with about three thousand dollars, his car, and a little cabin. Not at all what he intended, I suppose, but there was little I could do about it short of going into court for relief and using up most of the estate's assets in the process. I suggested that she sell the cabin and the land it was on to finance her schooling, but she said that she preferred to keep it, arguing that she liked it and that it wasn't worth much. She was right about that. It lacks amenities, and it's not on a lake. Her father bought it as a hunting cabin. Anyway . . ."

Rob Lucas stirred impatiently in his chair, in a vain attempt to hurry him up.

"I have heard from my client, Sergeant. She discussed her position in this matter with me, and told me that she was considering spending a few weeks at the cabin until the situation resolved itself. She doesn't feel safe here in the city."

Under that steady, accusatory gaze, Lucas felt an upsurge of guilt. "We could assure—"

"I have the official description of the lot in the will," Hennessy went on, paying no attention at all to Lucas's protestation, "and that ought to be enough to get you there. It's miles from the nearest town, and there's no telephone— or much of anything else—so if you want to find her, you'll have to send someone in person." He closed the file with a snap and stood up. "I'll have my secretary photocopy that description for you."

"Just a minute," said Lucas, stubbornly retaining his seat. "How much did she tell you about what happened at the hotel?"

Hennessy shook his head. "Oh, no, Sergeant. My client may have let slip a few speculations under the stress of the moment, but it would be most improper for me to pass them along, even if I could remember them. Hearsay," he added gloomily. "Idle gossip, in fact. I'm not very happy that I've given you this much. However, if you do see Annie, could you tell her something for me?"

"Certainly," said Lucas.

"Tell her to give us a call when she gets back into town—we'd like to see her again. She and Karen—my wife—get on like a house on fire. Karen's batty about music." As he reached to open the door, he suddenly stopped and turned around. "There was one thing," he said. "I almost forgot. When she told me she wasn't selling the cabin, she said that she had been offered a very good part-time job. Well paid. Enough to let her finish up her degree. That's why I was startled to hear she'd dropped out of university. But she must be keeping up with her voice lessons. They meant an awful lot to her. I don't know what job it was that she was offered, but her coach was Renée LaBourdière. If you can't find Annie at the cabin, Renée might know where she is."

Lucas hesitated in front of the keyboard as he finished his account of the interview with Hennessy. It was a stark, pared-down outline of the conversation, limited to the barest facts. He could remember with unpleasant clarity the first report he had written for Inspector Baldwin. The sarcasm it had been greeted with still made him hot with anger every time he thought about it. "Impressions, Lucas?" he had said. "Impressions? What do you think you are, a printer? Since when did a sergeant have impressions? I look for evidence, Lucas, not impressions. Save the impressions for your girlfriend."

He had sworn that Baldwin would never get anything but the bare bones from now on. But if he didn't put down his conclusion that Hennessy already knew a great deal about the crime, and that his source was Annie Hunter, he would have little justification for driving up to the cabin to find her. And that was what he was determined to do. Of course, if she were still in town, it wouldn't matter. He reached for the telephone book and began to look for Renée LaBourdière.

It took Lucas four attempts to get past the busy signal; when he finally reached the vocal coach, he felt he'd been connected to a whirlwind. The voice at the other end crackled with impatience. "Of course I know Annie," she said. "And I'd like to know what she thinks she's doing. She hasn't been here since before Christmas. She canceled a couple of times because of a sore throat—we all know what that means."

"What does it mean?" he asked, curious.

"Sore throat be damned," the coach snapped. "It means she wasn't working and couldn't face me. Tried to tell me she was depressed. How could she be depressed? She was coming along magnificently. She has no business wasting her time with depression. She hasn't taken a practice room since November, and then she simply didn't turn up for her lesson and didn't call—and when I tried to reach her, her number was out of service. What could I do? I'm sorry I can't be more helpful. But if you see Annie, could you give her a message for me?"

"Sure," said Lucas. Why not? he thought. When I finally track her down, I'll just put an arm lock on her and make her listen to a half-hour list of messages from everyone she knows.

"Tell her to call me. At once. And let me know what's going on. You don't think she's found another coach, do you? And was too embarrassed to tell me?"

"Not as far as I know," said Lucas. "And I'll tell her." He put the telephone back down and began to type up his impressions of the interview with Hennessy.

"How's it going?" said a voice that could only have been Eric Patterson's. Lucas turned and nodded. Eric picked up a report from his desk and idly flipped over the pages, yawning heavily as he did it. He dropped the paper back down and sat down.

"Could be worse," said Lucas, to fill the ensuing silence. "How are you getting on with the grieving widow and friends?"

"Getting on? Are you kidding? Baldy hasn't let me within a hundred feet of her. Actually, that isn't true. I was allowed to accompany him out to her little shack in the country and take a few notes for her official statement. Her alibi stinks, doesn't it?" He yawned again and stretched his legs out beside his desk, where they could trip anyone walking by. "Of course, that's the difference between the rich and the merely prosperous. They're allowed to stink. Of horses, dogs, lies, you name it. It makes them authentic. You getting anywhere in finding that witness? Because we are getting nowhere at the moment, and we could use a break."

"I think she may have taken off for her cottage. I thought I'd drive up there tomorrow morning. It's not that far."

"Why not get the locals to do it for you?"

"Because I don't want her arrested—I just want to interview her. And I'd rather do that myself. She's the skittish type. You had lunch?"

"Nope. Let's go."

"I just have to give this to Baldy and let him know what I'm up to," said Lucas, picking up the report. "I'll be with you in a minute."

"And so that's precisely where we stand at the moment." The voice of Inspector John Sanders's superior officer was soft and controlled. The rage was only perceptible in his eyes and in a faint tension around his nostrils. "I have been considering Inspector Baldwin's request for leave on health grounds." He tapped his fingers irritably on a piece of paper that occupied the central position on his desk. "Very seriously. But we can't do it. Not when I know damn well it's bullshit. If I were as healthy as Baldwin, I'd be a happy man. On the other hand, he *is* acquainted with some of the principals in the investigation. And he *is* moving so discreetly, it could take him ten goddamn years to finish the preliminary work on the case. He's giving us an out, but we can't afford to take it. Not with our current work load." He sighed and pulled the top file off the stack of material near his right elbow. "Even though it's awkward and inefficient to change horses in midstream, you will take over the Neilson investigation. Considering how little Baldwin's done on it so far, you shouldn't run into too much duplication of labor," he added sourly. "Baldwin will continue with the Wilson—"

"Aren't they related?" Sanders raised his head from contemplation of a far corner of the broadloomed office and looked sharply across the desk.

"Only in the feverish imagination of one of the investigating officers. As far as I can tell. If they do turn out to be related, of course, you will coordinate your work with Inspector Baldwin. And John—"

"Yes?"

"Neilson was rich. And he had friends. But he wasn't the goddamn Prince of Wales or the premier's favorite nephew or anything like that. There is such a thing as treading too softly."

"When do I start?"

"This afternoon. I'm having lunch with Baldwin in about thirty minutes, and I'll straighten things out with him then."

The morning's euphoria had died away. Lucas almost envied Patterson, who could manage to come to terms with a pompous ass like Baldwin and was now so wrapped up in the Neilson case that he had been unable to concentrate on anything else. Talking to him had been like trying to have a reasonable conversation with someone who was hurtling down fifty stories in a broken elevator.

Lucas turned back to the document in front of him—Kelleher's report on the band members—and could only see a pair of wide gray eyes and a mass of tangled, dead-black hair. He gave up trying to read. Miss Hunter was alarmingly well cast for the part of Lulu, he reflected. If you considered Lulu's fondness for luring men to their deaths, for example. Had Annie done that to Carl Neilson? Set him up for a hit and then screwed up by not getting out in time? If she had, he probably deserved it. Lucas could still summon up the revulsion he had felt when his overvivid imagination had placed Neilson's plump and thick-lipped body into that bed with Annie Hunter, young enough to be his daughter. You're thinking again, Robert, he said to himself. Heroines in operas spend a great deal of time luring men to their deaths. And then, of course, said the little voice in his head, they die, too. That's how it all ends.

He shoved the report away and stood up. None of those sullen-faced kids in the band seemed to have had motive or opportunity for smashing Jennifer's head in with a crowbar, and that left him nothing to do that seemed important enough to tie him to this desk. For some inexplicable reason Baldy insisted on ignoring the relationship between the two cases, treating Jennifer Wilson's death as an unwarranted interruption in the investigation of Carl Neilson's. Baldy refused to consider the fact that Annie Hunter's fingerprints were liberally scattered over both apartments. All of this gave the investigation a curious lack of substance. Lucas was too tired, too restless to deal with phantom tasks on paper. He grabbed his coat and headed outside. He turned in the direction of excitement—strip joints, arcades, obscene underwear shops, panhandlers, and underage prostitutes. Amid all that petty crime and corruption, the only thing he saw that engaged his attention was a movie theater. That was what he needed. He would waste a couple of hours on something totally unrelated and let his scattered thoughts sort themselves out.

He lasted ten minutes. The film had promised to be a sophisticated comedy; every word of dialogue touched a nerve. The male lead was pompous and irritating; the female pretentious and silly. He had already run into too many posturing egos of both sexes in the last five days to watch another one here. He stalked furiously out of the theater, elbowing, glowering, and intimidating his way through the crowds on the street.

Lucas passed through them all without noticing their existence. The only sensible thing to do at that point, he concluded, was to throw some clothes in a bag and head up for the woods. He could find the girl, talk to her, get himself a room for the night, and be back by ten the following morning. No one would even notice he'd gone until he walked in again.

In twenty-five minutes he had the car and was back at his apartment, where he changed his suit for a pair of heavy corduroy pants, a wool shirt and a thick sweater—it was still winter up there—and then put on his hiking boots. He picked up his shoulder holster, considered leaving his weapon behind, shrugged, and slipped into it. He grabbed his bag, his down-filled parka, and the tape he had made of his new recording of *Lulu* the night before while he was listening to it. He slipped the photocopied description of the hunting cabin and the lot it was on from the jacket pocket of his suit coat to his parka and left the apartment.

CHAPTER 8

By three-fifteen Robert Lucas was on the expressway heading out of the city. The fact that he had not told anyone that he was leaving early impinged briefly on his conscience. But since the difference would be whether he was back at his desk before or after lunch tomorrow, who would give a damn about that? Unless, of course, said the little voice at the back of his head, all hell breaks loose tonight, and they're looking for you. "Frankly, my dear," he said to the ramshackle maroon van he was passing at the moment, "I don't give a damn."

He was fairly sure he knew where he was going. The cabin ought to be more or less in the center of a square formed by two highways and two connecting secondary roads. There were towns at the northwest and the southeast intersections; as he remembered it, the land in between was rocky bush, drained by several streams, most of which had been dammed by beaver to make a series of shallow, mucky lakes. Not a place he would have chosen to build a cabin, he thought. The center section appeared on his map to be crossed by a couple of gravel roads; otherwise the area was close to impassable. At least it was too early for black flies and mosquitoes. In June there'd be enough of them to carry off a cabin and everyone in it.

He chose the highway that cut through the woods on the far eastern side of the square, for no particular reason except that the one time he had traveled through the area, he had preferred the eastern town to the western one. It was not quite sunset when he arrived, and the main street was almost deserted. He stopped to have a careful look at the description Hennessy had given him, and real doubt began to creep in. What had seemed obvious in the bright light of morning in Hennessy's office might not be so simple out here in the fast advancing twilight. To start with, he had to find Township Road 23, which ought, according to this piece of paper, to branch off from the highway he was on now. But there was never any guarantee that these local roads would be marked. He started up again. Ahead, a gravel road branched off to the left, miraculously decorated by a small white signpost. He slowed almost to a standstill. There it was. In tiny lettering, black on white, TWNSHP 22. The next one should be—might be—TWNSHP 23. Of course, it was possible that it could turn out to be TWNSHP 21. Only there didn't seem to be a next one. For miles and miles, he drove at a snail's pace. At this rate, the sun would be long set before he found the turnoff, and he would be searching for his target by moonlight. The only thing on his left at the moment was an apparently endless beaver swamp filled with tall ragged stumps of dead birch and poplar. Maybe the beaver had drowned TWNSHP 23, he thought. Then what in hell would he do? The answer was simple. Wait till morning and ask the locals. So where was the problem? With that decided, he speeded up and passed by a gravel road on his left, unmarked.

He braked, reversed and swerved left, hoping like hell that this wasn't a driveway leading to someone's palatial summer estate. "But it can't be," he muttered. Not a chance. Who would build a palatial estate in the middle of a beaver swamp? It seemed worth a try. The car bounced and thudded over sharp ridges and down into bone-jarring potholes. The spring thaw had created its annual havoc with the roads, and it would be months before anyone tried to repair them. He stopped once more to look at the description. If

he was on TWNSHP 23, then five miles in he should come
across a private road heading south, which, after a mile or
so, would give him access to the property in question. He
started up again. Around the next curve the road began to
climb and to twist as it climbed. The swampy landscape
changed; the trees grew farther apart and were more likely
to be pines than poplars. There was considerably more snow
lying between them. He checked his odometer. One more
mile if his calculations were correct, and there should be a
road off to the left again. Darkness was closing in under
the shadow of the pines, and he began to worry about missing the turnoff. He slowed, switched off the tape, and rolled
down his window. The only noise except for his engine was
the muted roar coming from a stream on the left. The road
continued to climb up, rather more steeply now, twisting to
the right around an outcrop of rock dead ahead. When it
resumed its rightful line, it was in the middle of a tiny
meadow. At the meadow's edge was a small track running
off to the left and into the woods. This must be it.

He bounced and lurched another half mile through mud
and slush, trying to convince himself that this had to be the
road to Annie Hunter's cabin. If it weren't, and the car got
stuck, it was a long hike back to civilization. The track
turned sharply to the left and climbed, passing over a small
wooden bridge. A stream. As he came out of the curve,
Annie's retreat lay ahead of him.

The cabin was indeed small. It had been built out of logs
in the last century, he supposed, but recently someone had
carefully caulked and patched and shingled the aging structure. It sat in a small clearing that spread out, fan-shaped,
down the southwest face of the hill he had been climbing
to get there. The sun had just set, and the sky glowed deep
red; the streaks of snow in the meadowland burned scarlet
in the surrounding darkness. The stream was even more
turbulent than he had realized when driving over it; it
rushed past the cabin, skirted the meadow, and disappeared

into the woods again. Smoke was pouring out of the chimney of the cabin, and the smell of the wood fire mingled headily with the scent of pine and melting snow. But the sweetly pastoral scene made him uneasy. The cabin windows were dark, and when he pulled his car up in front of the door and killed the engine, the silence was profound and unnatural. Another car was parked over to the right, under a tree, dark in the shadows. He had taken it for a derelict, left there by someone too lazy or too cheap to have it junked. Its windows were smashed in, its tires flattened. But even in the fading light something about it looked wrong. He took his heavy-duty flashlight out of the trunk and played it over the car body. The paint was shiny, the trim unrusted, the roof clean. The interior was filled with pebbles of broken safety glass, but the mess sat on clean, dry, gray plush upholstery. Whatever had happened to that car had happened that day—or possibly the day before. No earlier.

He called out "Annie?" in the deep silence. His voice echoed. Shifting his flashlight to his left hand, he undid his parka and thrust his right hand inside it. When it emerged he was holding his Beretta. He walked over to the front door, called out "Annie?" again, and listened. Nothing. He reached out with the third and fourth fingers of his right hand to nudge the handle around but, as soon as he touched it, the door swung inward. He jumped out of the square of dimming light that outlined him and at the same time shone his flashlight into the room. There was chaos everywhere he looked. Chairs had been tipped over; broken glass was scattered on the floor. But there was no sign of any human being. A door in the wall opposite him was swinging open; he walked delicately over the cluttered floor and out the door, shutting it carefully behind him.

The ground just outside had been chewed up with footprints. It was easier to see out there, even in the disappearing light, bright enough to notice the body of a man lying on his face near the corner of the cabin. Lucas walked over to him and felt gently for a pulse. The body was cold, very cold. Dead long enough to cool down, but not stiff, he noted automatically. He turned him over. He had been shot twice in the chest and left there in the snow and mud to die. He was dressed in work pants and a dark red-checked heavy wool shirt over a gray sweater; he probably lived and worked somewhere around there. Lucas turned him over the way he had found him. Where in hell was Annie? He retraced his footsteps back to the door in the rear of the cabin and looked around. There was a mess of footprints heading across the meadow in the direction of the woods. He shone his flashlight on them: large feet wearing work boots, he would say, larger even than his; then mixed up in them, at least for a while, smaller hiking boots or work boots—it was hard to tell. But off to one side, there was another set, much smaller than the others, but too large to be animal tracks. He shone his light directly into them. Clearly printed in the soft, almost-melting snow, was the outline of human feet, bare, running across the field.

The bare feet belonged either to a female or a half-grown boy. A sudden vision of Annie, injured and barefoot, running across this field, superimposed itself on the snow, and he tore down the hill after the footprints. The three sets of prints moved along in strict unison until he reached the woods. There the drifts, protected from the sun, still lay deep except directly under the widely spaced, heavy-branched pines. Their thick lower branches, growing close to ground level, roofed over the forest floor beneath them, leaving it free of snow. Lucas was able to follow the two sets of large prints as they blundered down to the stream, but Annie's—if they were hers—disappeared without a trace. He stopped at the point where she had apparently entered the treed area and tried to figure out what she would have done. He shone his light slowly to the right and then to the left, and then in an arc down to the stream. After a second or two, he walked down to the bank to examine it more closely. At this point the water eddied through some large rocks and then formed a relatively quiet—and probably deep—pool.

The heavy footprints churned up the snow along the bank, a foot or two in from the water, creating a well-defined path. He followed them with his flashlight, searching for a reappearance of the bare feet. To the right, the snow on the ground between the line of prints and the stream was thick and undisturbed, the stream bed was wide and rocky, and the water turbulent. Unless she could fly, she had not gone that way. To the left, the trees were thicker and more impenetrable, tracks impossible to see. And down there, the stream narrowed sharply. He walked along the bank to the left, watching for her footprints, fighting his way past overhanging trees, in constant danger of slipping into the icy water. He wondered if that was what had happened to Annie. As the stream narrowed, it deepened as well. How long would she survive in water that temperature with no one to pull her out? The mind, he knew, would give up long before the body did and allow her the deadly kindness of unconsciousness. That was assuming, of course, that she had made it this far. He crouched down, holding his light at ground level and playing the beam up the slope. He could make out patches of snow, boulders, and fallen tree branches in among the pines, but nothing that looked like the body of a girl. She had reached the woods and vanished. He stood up, discouraged, and without looking, put his right foot on a slippery rock; it plunged into the stream up to the ankle before he could yank it out. The icy water seeping in over the top of his boot burned flesh and bone. For a moment, he could do nothing but shake his foot, gasping and cursing softly; at last, he shone his light down on the treacherous hunk of granite. There, beside the track left by his sliding hiking boot, were more telltale and slippery smears of dirt and pine needles. Someone else had slipped on this rock.

He looked across the stream. Here it was at its narrowest, between four and five feet across; a large pine growing on the other side bent its branches over the width of the water. He could swear that there was a faint disturbance of snow and pine needles visible over there. With a deep breath, he grabbed the branch and leaped, hoping that the footing on the other side was good enough not to send him sliding back into the water.

He landed neatly, on both feet, to his intense gratification, and paused to reconnoiter. Here the bank rose much more steeply and was clear of snow—and footprints—as far up the rough, tree-covered slope as his flashlight allowed him to see.

He was getting cold, discouraged, and furious at himself; blundering around in the dark like this, he was obliterating all useful traces of whatever had gone on here. The temperature was dropping rapidly, now that night had fallen, and something wet and cold landed on his cheek. He looked up. The sky, clear an hour ago, was banked with fast-moving clouds. Snow. "Oh, my God," he said aloud. "Now what do I do?" He shone his light up and down and, desperate with worry, called out, "Annie, for chrissake, if you're out there, say something. It's Robin. I won't hurt you and I'm getting bloody cold standing here." He listened to his speech echoing through the trees and felt as great a fool as he must have sounded.

She had just finished dumping the last of the fresh vegetables into the soup pot. She had frowned and chewed nervously on her bottom lip as she considered the problem. Should she risk driving into town tomorrow to get more—and some fruit—or make do with the canned food stacked up on her makeshift shelves? There was plenty to keep her going for a couple of weeks, but the dreary prospect of living for days and days on precooked pap depressed her. It was time she bought a paper, anyway, and found out what was going on. Now that that was decided, she went back to her comfortable spot, pulled off her shoes, and curled up again with her book.

She spent most of her afternoons reading by the west-facing window that overlooked the sloping meadow behind the cabin, staving off the moment when she would have to light the lamps. That was when she felt the loneliest. She had even doggedly cleaned all the windows in the place shortly after she had arrived—windows that hadn't been cleaned in years—to capture every possible ray of light. In fact, she had been cleaning ever since she got here: sweeping, polishing, scrubbing. Maybe she would buy some paint tomorrow as well. And now the western sun shone on the window seat, warming her back as she perched on the old cushions and lazily drowsed her way through an ancient paperback. Today one could believe in the reality of spring. It was almost four o'clock.

She heard a car in the distance, climbing up the township road. Some fool trying for a shortcut, not realizing that once he got down on the other side of the hill he was going to discover that the road had washed out. Again. It washed out every spring, and every spring the township council pretended to find the matter amazing, and every spring they said that something must be done about the road, and nothing was. Not that she minded; it kept down traffic. She went back to her book.

When she heard it again, the noise of the car engine was much closer. Too close. Hell! She had no desire for stray visitors. Only Joe MacDougal knew she was here, and he didn't go in for bothering people—just drifted by every afternoon on his way back home from wherever, his hunting rifle over his arm in spite of the season. He would nod at her, giving her a chance to speak if she had anything to say, mutter something vaguely like good-night and leave. Who else could possibly turn up here? She closed her book and sat up. The car was definitely on her road. She heard it rattle over the logs on the bridge and pull up in front of the cabin. Feeling alone and vulnerable out here, she walked over to the stove, noiseless in her stocking feet, and picked up the poker. She waited for whoever it was to knock.

Instead of hammering on the door, however, he—they— had been doing nothing as far as she could tell. Maybe they're lost, she told herself, and they're just sitting in their car poring over maps. She took a step over to the small window that looked out on the road and hesitated. She had a horror of being caught staring curiously out the window, like some inquisitive old lady. Perhaps if she were quiet enough, they would go away again. She strained to hear what they were up to; there was no sound but the muttering of the brook and the sporadic complaints of a couple of birds. That must have been why the explosive smash caught her by surprise; she jumped and ran for the door in panic. Before she could reach and turn the old-fashioned key that sat in the lock, however, the heavy front door swung open, barely missing her.

Her protests died down before they were made. Coming into the room were two men, one thin and wiry, the other big and powerful-looking. Beyond that, she could not have described them. Both their faces were shrouded by dark blue knitted ski masks that covered all but their eyes.

"Grab her," said the smaller one. He had a cracked, hoarse voice, unpleasantly high-pitched and dictatorial-sounding. She felt as if someone had kicked her in the stomach. She had heard that voice before, in Carl Neilson's apartment; it had frightened her then, too.

The big one had taken hold of her as though she were a naughty child, one hand around each arm, and the poker rattled impotent to the floor. He had sat her down in one of the two hard chairs that were beside the table, and held her with one hand around her throat while he walked around her and grabbed her arms from behind. "I got her," he said calmly. She recognized that voice, too. There was nowhere, nowhere in the world, where one could go and be safe.

"We had trouble finding you, Jennifer, sweetheart—or whatever your fucking name is," said the big man. He gave her body a wrenching shake to emphasize his words. "You caused us a lot of grief."

"Yes," said the other. "You made us nervous, running away like that. What did Neilson tell you about us? Or were you just there, watching?" She said nothing. The small one leaned forward and slapped her sharply across the face. "I asked you a question, you little bitch. What did Neilson tell you?"

"I still can't figure out where in hell she was hiding," said the big one. He dug his fingers into her arms harder.

"She was hiding, that's all—it doesn't matter," said the other one impatiently. "What matters is what she saw and what she told that fucking cop. What did you tell him, sweetheart? You might as well tell us, you know," he added softly. "Because if we don't get it from you, we'll get it from him anyway."

She said nothing.

"And how much Neilson told her. That matters. And what she told the cop. And that lawyer. We know she talked to that lawyer. That was stupid." The big one's fingers dug in harder. "What did Neilson tell you, and who did you tell it to, eh?"

She knew that silence offered her protection; once she had spoken they would kill her as easily as they had killed Carl. She shook her head.

Another slap. "And what is that supposed to mean?" The smaller one glanced around when he finished speaking, leaned down, and picked up the poker from the floor.

"For chrissake," said the voice from behind her. "Don't

hit her with that. You'll kill her. You may not care what she's been saying, but it matters to me."

"Oh, I'm not going to hit her with it," he said and walked over to the stove. He removed the lid and set the poker inside. He walked slowly back and crouched down in front of her. Fear compounded with fury made the blood pound in her ears, and as soon as he seemed to be within range, she moved her right foot back and kicked. He grabbed the foot just before it landed and held it. At the same time his friend jerked her back with such ferocity that she thought her arms had been torn from their sockets. The smaller one began pulling off her socks, both pairs, one by one. "Kick me again," he said, "and I'll break your fucking toes. One by one."

He walked over to the stove and removed the poker with his gloved hand. "Get her other foot, eh?" he said as he walked back, and before she could react, she was being held by one large arm around her body and the other grasping her left ankle. The little one picked up her right foot in one hand. "Okay, what did you tell that cop?" She shook her head again. "That's not an answer," he said and touched the end of the poker to the ball of her foot. She gasped.

"That was just to show you that it's still hot," he said. "What did you tell the cop?"

"Nothing," she said.

He lifted her foot up to his chest level and slapped the poker across the sole, holding it there. She could hear and smell and feel the searing pain, and she screamed.

"Hey, Annie!" A rough voice from outside intruded itself sharply and unexpectedly into the scene. "What in hell is going on in there? Are you all right?"

"Hold her," said the big man, running to the front door. The smaller one stood there for a moment, indecisive, staring at the hot poker in his hand. While he was thinking, she jumped out of the chair, knocking it over, grabbed the table, and tipped it with a smash of breaking crockery in his direction. That slowed him another second or two while she ran for the back door. She had it open before he realized that it existed. By the time he had reached it, she was half-way across the field.

She heard a shot, two shots, thick and muted-sounding, as she left the cabin. She ran even faster through the mud and melting snow. Then a crack of a rifle, and she felt a whistle rippling against the outside of her thigh. She kept running, trying to ignore the searing pain in her foot. As soon as she reached the woods, she fell into a crouch. Here under the trees she felt secure. This had been her playing ground for years, and she knew every contour of the ground, every stone and branch. She threw herself under a large pine growing in a hollow, wriggled under its branches to the far side, and kept crawling silently under the thicker and thicker undergrowth until she reached the stream at its narrowest point. She had done this hundreds of times during her childhood, eluding imaginary pursuers. Without pausing to look behind her, she reached up and grabbed the largest branch hanging over the water, flung herself across and landed on the granite boulder on the other side. Winter frosts had destabilized it in some way, however, and it rocked crazily under her foot. She plunged forward, barely saving herself from a time-consuming and noisy fall with one bone-wrenching thud to her hand. She heard a click like a twig snapping and the boulder dropped with an enormous splash into the brook. Without thinking, she dove into her little cave behind the evergreens.

The voices started up again, very loud in the sheltering woods.

"What's happened?"

"I think I got her all right. That's blood down there, isn't it? Anyway, she fell in the water."

"Can't tell in this light. It might be mud. Doesn't matter, though—she won't last long in there," said the hoarse voice.

She wriggled back to where the rock faces on either side

of her widened and turned herself carefully around; then she curled herself up in the old pine needles and branches on the floor.

She had discovered this little hiding place when she was nine. It had been a pie-shaped crevice some primeval cataclysm had cut in the granite of the Laurentian Shield, but one that a passing ice age had provided with most of a roof, by wedging a couple of chunks of granite into its opening to the sky. Every summer she had dragged small logs over to the open spaces to complete the roof, so that by the time she was twelve, she had created a snug little cave. The continual dropping of leaves and pine needles onto her handiwork had camouflaged it completely; with its shield of evergreens in front of the entrance, it had become invisible.

Now that she felt relatively safe, she had a moment to assess her injuries. She touched her leg where the bullet had whistled by her and felt stickiness coat her fingers. Blood. She tried to ignore the cold and the fear and the pain, tried to push away the thought that, injured and bleeding, she could die in here. Her bolt-hole might well turn into a trap. She pulled her feet up as close to her body as they would come, and reached down to warm them with her cold hands. A stab of pain in her wrist reminded her that she had hurt it, too, as she had fallen on the bank, and tears of anger began to slip down her cheeks.

The sounds made by her pursuers came from farther and farther, until all sound ebbed away, and she drifted timelessly in the soothing darkness. The terror of pursuit was replaced by a kaleidoscopic succession of bright and hectic dreams, dreams of endless icebergs and snowbanks and brooks filled with clear, bright ice water.

Then, lifetimes later, her dreams were interrupted by muttering and cursing on the other side of the stream; that sound was replaced by a lot of heavy-footed crashing and thumping about very close by. "Annie," said another familiar voice, "for chrissake, if you're out there, say something.

It's Robin. I won't hurt you, and I'm getting bloody cold standing here."

She waited for a moment, trying to think what would be the clever thing to do. Awake and trembling with cold and misery, she called, "I'm here, in here," and stretched a hand out through the feathery concealing branches of the trees.

CHAPTER 9

He was close enough to her to touch the icy hand that appeared through the branches. He pushed them aside and shone the powerful beam of his flashlight into a narrow opening, some two feet wide and about four feet high. She was lying there on her side, apparently wedged between two rock faces. Automatically, he reached in to try to get her out.

"Wait," she said weakly, as his hand closed around her wrist. "Let go. Let me do it."

"How in hell did you get in there?" he asked.

"It's not that tight," she said, "especially back here." She was breathing rapidly, ejecting her words in little spates of sound.

He focused the beam on her face. It was streaked with dirt and blood; in the white light, her skin was gray and her eyes hollow and sunken. She blinked under the scrutiny. "How badly are you hurt?" he asked. She shook her head helplessly. "We have to get you out of there," he said, his voice efficient and matter-of-fact. "Can you help?" He said it as if it didn't matter much one way or the other whether she could or couldn't, although he was daunted by the prospect of trying to drag a helpless but sentient being out of there.

There was a long and frightening silence. Just as he was about to reach in for her, however, she spoke, coolly and rationally. "I've sprained my left wrist, I think—it seems to be swollen. Not a great idea to pull me out by that hand."

She paused again for breath. "I've hurt my leg, and I've lost some blood. Walking might be—" She stopped. "And I haven't any shoes or socks."

"Or coat or hat or gloves," he added, gently. "You have to stop going out without a coat. Okay, can you raise your shoulders a little? Then I can pull you out." She nodded and tried to heave herself up, levering herself with her left elbow. She lurched sideways and sank down again; she took a deep breath and repeated the movement. This time she managed to stay up; he stuffed the flashlight in his pocket, reached in and grasped her by the armpits. He pulled steadily until she was out except for her legs. "Now," he said, "reach up and grab me behind the neck." She rolled slightly toward him and placed her right arm on his shoulder. Her grip was alarmingly feeble. He shifted his hold until he was carrying her like a tired child off to bed. "Just one more question," he said. Her head rolled against his chest, and he was afraid she was going to faint. "How do we get to the cabin without wading through that damned river?"

"Up there," she said, with no indication of direction, "to the road. Not far," she added, and lost consciousness.

At least he knew what direction the road ought to be in, and he began to stumble along, following the stream bed upward. It might not have been far, but the ground underfoot was uneven and studded with large rocks that sprang up invisible under his feet. After banging her legs against a tree, he draped her over his shoulder, took out his flashlight again, and started to scramble up the small hill to the road. She seemed to drift in and out of consciousness; unaware, he hoped, of how roughly he was handling her. Back on the road, he shifted her back into his arms; her eyes fluttered open, and she began to shiver violently. Snow was drifting softly onto her face, and she buried it in the waterproof cloth of his parka. If he didn't get her inside soon, he reckoned, she wouldn't make it after all. He wondered how long she had been lying out there in the cold, and lengthened his stride until he reached the graveled parking area. Cursing his own carefulness that had insisted on closing the door when he first came in, he shifted her weight onto his upraised knee and turned the knob.

The lingering warmth from the fire in the stove had heated up the cabin again. He vaguely remembered a battered-looking couch to the left of the door, turned, and cracked his shins against it, and then set her down gingerly on her back. Once he had use of his arms again, the flashlight found him two oil lamps, neatly trimmed and polished clean, up on a shelf beside a wall-mounted match holder. As soon as they were lit, the cabin seemed to blaze with light, and he saw that the stickiness on his hands was blood. He hastily wiped them on his handkerchief and turned his attention to the girl again. She was shivering with cold, or fear, or shock, her eyes anxiously following his movements. The blood had originated from the stiffening mess on her jeans, obviously. He looked around for something sharp, picked up a paring knife from the counter by the wood stove, and carefully enlarged the ragged tear in her jeans and then in the dark-colored long underwear beneath. "What happened to your leg?" he asked.

"I must have been shot," she said. "As I ran away. It was strange. I didn't feel anything. I heard it. I heard it go by. The shot."

As far as he could tell, the bullet had torn away some skin and flesh on the side of her thigh but had not penetrated any farther. He ripped the cloth of her jeans back more, found a couple of clean-looking dish towels hanging from a bar, and wrapped them around the wound.

"Where are the blankets?" he asked impatiently. "Blankets, Annie. You need blankets. You're cold."

"Up there," she said. Her voice seemed dry and faint.

For the first time, he noticed a ladder fastened to a rafter beside the back wall. In two steps he was at the top, and shining his light into a room whose existence he had not suspected. It was a tiny bedroom tucked in under the eaves. It contained a narrow wooden built-in bed with two large drawers under it and very little else, except for a few boxes. An empty duffel bag lay crumpled on the floor right in front of him. He snatched a couple of blankets from the bed, opened the drawers and tumbled as much of their contents into the duffel bag as he could, and hurried back down the ladder to check on her again. Her eyes were closed, but the lids fluttered sporadically. He straightened out the two blankets to make a double thickness and placed them gently on top of her.

Somewhere in the pile of things he had rescued from the drawers he had seen neatly folded socks, he was sure, and he rooted around in the duffel bag until he found them. He moved one of the lamps so that he could see what he was doing and uncovered her bare and agonizingly cold feet. He slipped a sock onto one foot and then picked up the other. And gagged. That oozing filthy mess was beyond him. He put the second sock on top of the first and wrapped the blanket around her legs again.

She stirred, and he turned to look at her. "I'm thirsty," she said. "Very thirsty."

He looked around frantically for water, hoping he didn't have to return to the goddamn stream—which was probably polluted anyway. But on the floor, next to the back door, there was a plastic jug of spring water. He filled a cup and held it to her lips. She drank a mouthful and let her head drop back. "We have to leave," she said. "They know I'm here. They think I'm dead, but they aren't sure, and so they'll be back."

"You're right," he said. "Don't worry." He searched the cabin once more with his flashlight. The beam picked out a pair of hiking boots and a large leather purse with a shoulder strap. Those looked useful. He grabbed them, along with the duffel bag and jug of water, and slung them into the trunk of his car. He opened the rear door, ran back in, blew out the lamps, picked up Annie, tucking the blankets around her as firmly as he could, and laid her carefully down on the backseat of the car.

He thought of nothing but getting away from the cabin until he neared the intersection between the township road and the highway. At that point, far enough back from the main road to keep them from being noticed by casual traffic, he pulled over to consider what to do next. "Annie," he said. "Annie! Are you awake?"

She moaned slightly, and muttered.

He flicked on the overhead light and turned to look at her. "Who knew about this place?" he asked. "Which of your friends?"

She swallowed and licked her lips. "No one," she said at last.

"There has to have been someone," he said incredulously. "Didn't Neilson know?"

"No one," she repeated. "Espe—especially not Neilson." Talking seemed to cost her more and more effort. "How did you—" Her voice trailed off.

"Hennessy," said Lucas. "Your lawyer."

"He knew. No one else. No one." She paused, and when she answered again, her voice was stronger. "I haven't been up here for five years. Joe looked after it after Daddy died. He wouldn't have told anyone."

Joe. That would be the body in the snow, thought Lucas grimly. He wondered if she knew that he was dead. "Was Joe local?" he asked, and winced when he realized he was already using the past tense.

She didn't notice. "Yes," she said, drawing in a ragged breath.

Which meant that to get any information from Joe, you

had to know who he was and where to find him. Which meant that you already knew where you were going. And only Hennessy knew that. Except that Hennessy had told him—but he hadn't passed it on to anyone. Had he? He had told Patterson he was going to check out her cottage. But hadn't mentioned where it was, he was sure of that. And otherwise the location had only been spelled out in his report. The report that he had dutifully filed before lunch. And someone who had access to his report had gone up that afternoon. Or had told someone else about it—who had gone up that afternoon. Which would mean that someone who had access to Baldwin's files was passing information on—probably to the same friends who had found Carl Neilson no longer useful and had disposed of him. "Shit!" he said, and pounded his fist against the steering wheel. The girl behind him stirred and muttered.

He started the car up again. Now that he had put it all into words, the only surprise was that he hadn't thought of it before. It was the logical, if unpalatable, solution. Now where to? First of all, Annie needed help. And if he took her to a hospital with a gunshot wound, the incident would be reported, and the report would land on Baldwin's desk. He had a first-aid kit in the trunk. He wasn't sure how risky trying to look after her himself was going to be, but he certainly knew how risky it would be to let other people get their hands on her. All he needed now was a quiet motel where no one would pay any attention to them.

"I'm not being grim," said Sanders, pushing the candle to one side to get a better look at Harriet's face. "And I haven't been glaring at you. In fact, I'm not in a bad mood at all. Just thinking."

"Thinking!" said Harriet. "I hate to imagine what you're thinking about. Strangling someone, I suppose. I can see it in your eyes—they're narrow and glittering with blood lust." She pointed an accusing finger across the table and then converted the gesture into a grab for the wine bottle that sat between them.

"Shut up, will you, Harriet?" He caught her wrist with one hand and extracted the wine bottle from her with the other. "Something to drink, madam?" he added, and poured some into her glass and then into his. "And I wasn't considering strangling someone—only trying to figure out why Matt Baldwin's case was dumped in my lap this afternoon. It's not like Matt to relinquish his hold on anything."

"Maybe the man is sick," said Harriet. "It must happen."

Sanders shook his head. "I was specifically told that illness was not the reason. Nor incompetence, no matter how justifiable."

"Meow," said Harriet. "I'm shocked, John. It's not like you to be catty about someone. Besides me, of course. And you only do that to my face, as far as I know."

"Absolutely," said Sanders. "Pure gallantry once your back is turned, that's me. But wait until you meet Baldy. He brings cattiness out in the gentlest people. My recurrent nightmare is that Baldy will be promoted over me someday and I'll have to work for him. When I think of that, I break out in a cold sweat and start making lists of alternate careers."

"What's wrong with him?" asked Harriet.

Sanders held up his left hand and began counting points off on his fingers. "He's stupid, a self-satisfied ass, that's one. He's a pompous twit or a cringing, ass-licking jerk, depending on who he's talking to, that's two. He knows nothing and expects the people working with him to cover for his mistakes *and* let him take the credit when things work out. That's three. And he has a foul and irrational temper that makes me look like a cross between a saint and the sunshine fairy."

"Which is four," said Harriet. "I get your drift. You don't like the man. What case is it, anyway?"

"Murder that happened while we were away. A guy who owns a lot of property around the city—"

"Carl Neilson," said Harriet quietly. "Lydia Neilson's husband."

"My God," said Sanders. "Do you know her? Baldwin claims he doesn't want the case because he knows Lydia Neilson. He probably met her once."

Harriet got up and walked across the room over to the CD player. She shuffled through a pile of discs in silence until she finally arrived at one and slipped it into the player. The delicate sounds of baroque music played on a classical guitar stirred around the edges of the room. "Yes," she said. "I know her—or to be more accurate, I used to know her. I haven't seen her for about four years. She's probably changed."

"Was she married to Neilson then?" asked Sanders.

Harriet nodded. She walked back to the table and sat down. She picked up her glass, as if to drink, and then put it down again, too hard, and spilled a few drops of wine on the mat. "I didn't know her before she married Carl Neilson."

"What's wrong with her?" asked Sanders. He imprisoned her hand before she could start fiddling with something else.

"Wrong with her? Oh, nothing. She's very nice. Bright and interesting. Knows a lot about music and art. She did— or was doing—art history in university when she married him. That's how I got to know her. Through, uh—" Harriet stopped dead.

"Your artist friend without the name," said Sanders. "You don't have to avoid any mention of him just because of me. I don't expect to meet a woman of thirty who has never laid eyes on a man before."

Harriet smiled uncertainly. "I realize that. But I have trouble—"

"Talking about him. Given. But we weren't. We were talking about Lydia Neilson, who knows a lot about art and music and is very nice and about whom you also have trouble talking."

She shook her head. "Only because of what happened. Which was strange and embarrassing. And because of your job. I like Lydia, and—"

"And five years ago she told you she wanted to murder her husband. To gun him down in his own hotel, preferably on an afternoon in March, which is her favorite month, with such-and-such kind of pistol, and so on. Is that it? Even if she did, she probably wouldn't have waited five years to do it. As evidence it's pretty lousy."

Harriet had started to giggle alarmingly. "For God's sake, stop. Before I choke on my wine. No, she never told me she wanted to kill him, honest, Officer. But she did tell me she wanted to leave him. She was having an affair with someone—I don't know who—and she was planning on taking the child and running off into the sunset. And then, suddenly, I don't exist. She doesn't call me for those girlish chats. When I call her, she says she can't—doesn't want to—talk to me. She must have decided that leaving him would be too disruptive and was trying to convince herself that the whole episode never happened. And since she had told me she loved this guy, whoever he was, I just reminded her of her folly."

"Or maybe she figured it would be too expensive. Leaving Neilson. He was very rich, I gather."

"It's hard to say. Money didn't seem that important to her. It must have at one time, or she wouldn't have married him, but not when I knew her. It sounds corny, but I guess she'd figured out there were more important things in life." She broke off and looked over at him intently. "She was afraid of Neilson, you know. I suppose the bastard was violent. But Lydia's a very quiet, gentle sort of creature. I doubt if she'd kill anyone. I mean, if he threatened her child, she might pick up an heirloom shotgun and let him have it. Both barrels. She was a fierce mother. But then she would have called the police and explained what she had done and why. You see, she would have felt perfectly justified."

Sanders appeared unconcerned with Lydia Neilson's maternal urges. "Did you get to know Neilson?" he asked.

She shook her head. "Never. Met him once or twice, that's all. I knew some architects who worked for him. General public opinion seems to be that the man was a son of a bitch. With a genius for cheating people out of what he owed them. Whoever killed him did the world a favor."

"Could be, but we're not allowed to work on that premise. Actually, the thing that interests me is not your friend—or erstwhile friend—Lydia and whether she is likely to have done him in. I had really been sitting here looking at that wine and wondering about the champagne in Neilson's hotel room."

"Champagne?" Harriet looked puzzled. "With his money, he could bloody well afford champagne. What's strange about it?"

"There was a girl in the room when or just before he was killed. Someone he probably had up to the room fairly often, if I have pieced together what they found at the scene accurately."

"So he bought his little piece of fluff a bottle of champagne. It's a sad but old story, John. You must have heard of men doing that sort of thing. Even if you never do."

"Did you want champagne? And does that make you my little piece of fluff?" He ducked the blow. "But that wasn't it. He used to order up a bottle of house red for the little piece of fluff—"

"Cheap as well as thieving and vicious." Harriet shook her head sadly.

"And besides, Harriet. When do you open bottles of champagne if you are meeting someone for an afternoon of passion? Or sadomasochistic fun and games, if you're right about him. Before? Or after?"

"I would have thought before, wouldn't you? In most

cases. A glass or two before, to bring the atmosphere up to party level, and then a glass of flat champagne afterward— in the case of Carl Neilson, to wash away the taste. *Aargh.* I could never see how Lydia could have married him. He was so slimy looking."

"Exactly. And the bottle of cheap red rotgut had been opened. The bed bore unmistakable signs of having been used for an afternoon of—passion, S-M games, whatever. Which means—"

"The girl was gone, and he was waiting for some-one else."

Sanders nodded. "Our only problem is we don't know who."

"That's easy," said Harriet. Sanders looked up quickly. "He was closing a deal of some sort. That's the other reason for ordering champagne. I mean, besides weddings and christenings and birthdays and such. Which don't somehow seem to apply. To validate some sort of business deal or project that just finished or, conversely, is off to a glorious start."

"What kind?"

"I don't know. That's your job. Except he probably wasn't launching a ship."

Lucas took another minor road, this one heading northwest. He wanted to put at least a hundred miles between them and that cabin, and headed toward an area just populated enough, he hoped, to have motels open in the off-season. For three hours he drove into the black and starless night, until his exhausted brain began to see menacing visions rise up in his headlights; hydro-poles swayed and danced to the hypnotic music of the road as he approached them. A par-ticularly talented one stepped neatly in front of the car. He swerved back into his lane; his heavy eyes snapped open, and his heart pounded from the shock. He was no longer fit to drive, but if he stopped to grab some sleep, she would never last through the cold spring night once the heater was turned off. He pushed grimly on.

Over the next hill what he was looking for loomed up on his right—a place that looked cheap, seedy, anonymous, and open for business. A place where the management wouldn't inquire too closely about its guests. He parked the car away from the office, walked noisily in, and smashed his hand down on the bell on the counter. Nothing. He smashed it down again, and again, and again. A voice muttered in the background, and the door behind the reception area opened wide enough to allow a head to peer around it. "Yeah?" it said, and looked suspiciously at him. The head disappeared, the door opened wider, and the entire man appeared, rumpled and dirty-looking. A thin line of dried spittle had caked on the side of his face, trailing down to his unshaven chin.

"Hey, buddy," Lucas asked with a leer, "you gotta room? A double? And not too close to anybody else, if you know what I mean."

"Listen, Jack, there are twenty-eight empty rooms out there." His voice was as unpleasant as his face. "Take your goddamn pick. How far away do you want to be?"

"Aw, come on," said Lucas. "Don't get sore. We just got married, that's all, and my girl—I mean, my wife—she's kind of shy, like."

"I'll put you at the end," he said sourly, reaching for a key. "The wife's not gonna like it," he added. "It means farther to walk when she makes up the rooms, and she'll be pretty damned sore about it, but if that's what you want . . ." He paused artistically. "It'll be fifty bucks."

The sign outside promised double rooms for forty, but Lucas pulled out some bills and dropped a fifty on the counter.

"Thanks," he snarled, grabbing the cash with a scowl. "Sign here."

*   *   *

He carried Annie in, half-awake and muttering incoherent protests, set her down carefully on the bed and went back for the first-aid kit. He fetched some clean towels from the bathroom and then stopped to look down at her, uncertain how to begin. She lay with her eyes shut, clutching her swollen wrist. That he could deal with, he thought. Sprained wrists are like sprained ankles. He wrapped an elastic bandage around it and activated a cold pack, which he fastened on clumsily with another towel.

Next he tried to cut the bloodstained jeans off her body with the tiny scissors from the kit. It didn't work. He cursed quietly and set about taking them off instead. "You'll be more comfortable without those jeans," he said firmly. She paid no attention. He struggled with the stiff button, won, and began easing them, together with her torn and bloodied long underwear, over her hips. She was thin—her hipbones protruded sharply on either side of her concave stomach— and was wearing plain white cotton panties instead of the black lace he was somehow expecting. He quickly covered the mess on her thigh with a thick gauze pad. All the time he was working on her, she remained white-faced, expressionless, immobile. Except for her hand. Her nails bit into the flesh of the palm of her right hand as he went doggedly on.

The burn took more courage than he possessed. He picked bits of dirt, pine needles, and broken leaves from its edges and then looked to see what was in his kit. There was a tiny container of antibiotic ointment. He looked at the tube and then at that wound. He couldn't spread anything on that burned and dirty mess, and so he ripped open another gauze pad and squirted most of the gooey substance on it. As he placed the pad gingerly on the wound and wrapped more gauze around her foot, he could feel the shock that went through her body.

He searched the kit for the codeine pills he knew were there. "Take these," he said. "And I'm sorry I'm not very good at this sort of thing." She swallowed them, and let her head fall back on the pillows again. He raised her up, yanked back the blankets, and eased her into bed.

She fell into an uneasy slumber almost at once.

The double bed that she was occupying dominated the room. He looked around for some place to stretch out; his aching body screamed for a few hours' sleep. There was only thin cold carpet laid over the concrete floor. In desperation, he tried lying cautiously beside her, keeping well away from her side of the bed, but she tossed her head restlessly and cried out in her sleep as his weight pulled the blanket down against her injuries. He got up again, dizzy with exhaustion, found an extra blanket, and settled himself into a plastic armchair, with his feet propped up on a corner of the bed.

CHAPTER 10

At 7:00 A.M., Rob Lucas stirred himself out of an uneasy sleep. He struggled awkwardly out of the chair and went to inspect his patient. She was breathing slowly and deeply, lying on her side, her hair spread on the pillow in a mass of tangled curls. If it hadn't been for the cumbersome bandage on the wrist that was flung up on the pillow beside her face, he would not have believed that any of this had happened. That and his own exhaustion. He had an irrational impulse to wake her up, to throw her out of bed, and make her admit that she felt perfectly healthy. Common sense intervened. He found his razor and toothbrush and headed for the shower.

Hot water and a sense of being clean again restored him to something closer to equanimity; he pulled the armchair over to the window and sat down to mull over his position. Problem one: in four or five hours, they were going to expect him back with his witness. And two: the woman lying on the bed right behind him should probably be in the hospital. Preferably in the city. But three: to look at it all in an organized way, her life would be in danger if he brought her back. End of discussion. They'd stay out here. He shook his head, baffled. You're crazy, Robert, he said to himself. You don't know what you're doing. Because if you don't turn up this afternoon, there's going to be a disciplinary hearing, and there goes your job. Which, on the whole, you like. At least some of the time. But if he turned around, he knew he would see the frail, battered body of little Jennifer Wilson lying on that cold concrete floor. "Screw the job," he muttered, and rubbed his tired eyes.

He would temporize, he decided at last. This morning he would call in with some plausible excuse for not returning to the city and for not having found Annie. Something that would keep them happy for a day or so and put off the moment of decision for him.

He considered her again. She appeared to be sleeping soundly enough for him to go out for food and coffee. As he headed for the truck stop across the highway, he reflected that he was probably the worst person in the world to take charge of an injured person. Healthy himself, he had no patience with the ill. He couldn't even imagine how she must be feeling. But he was better than someone who was trying to kill her. He could at least keep her quiet, fed, and full of painkillers.

The restaurant was bright with morning sunshine; its beams lit up the torn leatherette benches and the worn tiled floor with cruel precision. It smelled of coffee, burned bacon, and disinfectant. Only one booth seemed to be occupied—by a couple of men in overalls talking quietly over egg-stained plates—and the room echoed with his footsteps as he crossed it. Eating breakfast in there was not to be thought of. The smell caught unpleasantly in his throat; and he was too restless to sit around and wait. "Give us a coffee, eh," he said to the sleepy-eyed waitress behind the counter. "And coffee, orange juice, and toast for two, to go."

Never had such a simple meal taken so long to prepare. He turned his back to the counter, cradling his mug of coffee in his hands and staring across the highway at the room where he had left the sleeping girl. Finally there was a slap as a bag hit the counter behind him. "That'll be five dollars and fifty cents," said the waitress flatly. He dropped a five and a one on the counter, grabbed the bag, and walked across the room. As he crossed through the broad entrance passage, the bright red of a soft-drink machine stopped him. He dumped all his change in it and added three cans to the bag.

Annie woke up at the sound of the closing door. In one swift motion, he picked her up and carried her into the bathroom, leaving a hot damp washcloth and towel within reach on the edge of the tub, in case she wanted to wash. He couldn't tell from her expression if she was embarrassed, or resentful, or simply too miserable to care at this invasion of her privacy. She didn't protest; in fact, she didn't speak. After he settled her back in bed, she surprised him by consuming her share of the tinny orange juice, the coffee, and most of his toast as well as her own. He opened one of the cans of soft drinks, and left it on the bedside table.

"How do you feel?" he asked finally. He had been avoiding the question, afraid of what her answer might be.

"Not bad," she said. "Thirsty. But I'm not cold anymore."

"Does it hurt?" he asked.

She grimaced. "My foot is—" She seemed to look for words and be unable to find them. "Yes. It does. And my wrist is throbbing. But otherwise I'm okay. Just tired."

He got her a fresh glass of water and shook two more painkillers out of the tube in his first-aid kit. She took them silently, rolled over on her side, and appeared to slip easily back into slumber.

Now he had to put some sort of plan into action before Baldy got alarmed. He couldn't risk doing it from here. She was asleep again, and he looked down at her, frowning with indecision. Leaving her alone seemed heartless, but she'd be a lot more uncomfortable if he dragged her around the countryside with him. Finally he took out his book and wrote her a note, in block capitals, clear and noticeable, explaining tersely that he had to go out, that he would be back, and that she was to stay where she was. "If things get bad," he added after some thought, "don't be a fool. Call the motel office. Lift the phone and dial zero. They will get a doctor. Take care. Robin." Last of all, he dropped into the motel office, where he paid for another day, told the manager's bedraggled wife to stay out of the room, and traded in their used towels for clean ones.

Lucas gave one more worried look at Annie as he dropped off the towels before climbing into the car. He stared at a road map, trying to think. If he was going to be anonymous, the first problem, clearly, was stashing this car. He started the engine and headed back in the direction they had come from.

Eighty miles and an hour and thirty minutes closer to Annie's cabin, he was standing by the side of the highway outside a moderately large town, hitching a ride. A red pickup approached, slowed, and stopped a little way ahead of him. He limped artistically up to it and climbed in. "Thanks," he said. "You going into Deerton?"

"Umf," muttered the driver. "Hurt yourself?" he added after a while, pointing vaguely in the direction of Lucas's lower limbs.

"Skidded into the ditch up that road back there," said Lucas, almost as laconically. "Twisted my ankle."

"There's a hospital," said the driver. "In Deerton."

"For a twisted ankle? Naw. It's okay. Is there a car rental place in town?" The driver grunted, and the two subsided into silence.

In fifteen minutes he was in possession of a new midsize four-door rental car, sober blue in color. In five more, he was standing near the entrance to the New Maple Leaf Grill, on the phone to the city, getting put through to Homicide.

"Inspector Baldwin isn't answering," said an irritating voice.

"Then for chrissake get me Sergeant Patterson," snapped Lucas. "This isn't a goddamn social call."

Patterson answered at once. "Jesus, Rob, where in hell have you been?" he asked irritably. "We were—"

"Been? I'm up in the bloody north woods, that's where I am. Right now. I left this morning."

"The hell you did," said Patterson. "We've had the troops out since ten o'clock last night looking for you. Baldwin decided he wanted to talk to you. Then he couldn't find you, and the shit really hit the fan. Where were you?"

"It's none of your goddamn business, Patterson," he snapped. "I was off duty. Where I was is my business—personal business, as it happens—and the department can keep its nose out of my affairs. I am not the goddamn chief—I'm a lousy sergeant, and the department can run without me. Everything I was doing is in my reports or on my desk. Go look." He paused to take a breath. "And where in hell is Baldwin?"

"Okay, okay, don't get sore. He's walking in the door right now," said Patterson. "Just a minute."

"Don't say it," said Lucas, as soon as he heard his boss's familiar voice. "Patterson just told me. Look, I'm up here in Deerton. I skidded out on a patch of ice this morning, and my goddamn car is in the bloody ditch."

"Oh," said Baldwin. He sounded confused. "Are you all right?"

"No, I'm not all right, damn it. I broke my fucking ankle and I wrecked my shoulder and cracked my collarbone. I can't even use crutches. I am stuck in this goddamn hospital bed, and they tell me I'll be here for weeks. I just called to tell you that, as of now, I'm on sick leave for at least two weeks, maybe three. And I never got anywhere near that girl or her bloody cottage, so you can send someone else or ask the goddamn locals to look for her. They don't seem to do anything else around here. You'll find how to get to it on my desk. Look—I gotta go. The fucking doctors are coming back. I'll call if I ever find out when I'm getting out of here." And he hung up, fast, before Baldwin had a chance to think of anything to say. The owner of the New Maple Leaf Grill looked up incuriously, his damp cloth in his hand, pausing in his attack on the counter in front of him. He considered the large, healthy man who had been describing his pathetic injuries and shook his head in disappointment. He had heard a lot of strange stories told into that phone, and this one was a pallid effort compared to some.

Lucas got back into the rental car and headed out to a shopping center on the highway. The weather had changed suddenly in the past few hours; yesterday's brilliant spring sunshine had given way to flat gray clouds; a chill wind was blowing sheets of old newspapers and greasy hamburger containers around the parking lot. He shivered and zipped up his jacket. The automatic gesture made him consider the question of clothing for Annie. He looked around him. In addition to the supermarket he was standing in front of, there was a hardware store, a drugstore, a women's clothing store, and a bank. He suddenly thought about all those stupid bastards he had tracked down because of the paper trail of credit card slips they had left behind them and headed for the bank.

Thirty minutes later, he opened the car door and pitched in a bag containing a couple of lightweight track suits, size large, and three flannelette nightgowns, just in case. Flannelette didn't fit his image of the girl, but then he had no idea what she habitually slept in. Realistically, he supposed that she was more likely to prefer the white cotton she was wearing to black lace. The groceries sitting back there were just as randomly chosen: fruit, various kinds of biscuits and crackers, lots of odd cans and bottles of things to drink, some yogurt, and cheese. Whenever he went searching for food in the refrigerators of the women he knew, that was what he found, and he had to assume that all women in their twenties lived on this sort of thing. He himself could exist on take-out food from the restaurant across the road from the motel. That was something that six years on the police force had done for him; it had made him appreciate availability over quality in the food he ate.

As he drove back to the motel, he was conscious of a sense of nervous dread, the feeling he used to have as a child coming back from camp or visits away from home. When the taxi turned the corner onto his street, he would close his eyes in terror, sure that his comfortable house and his beautiful, impatient mother and his terrier, Bart, would be gone, replaced by a blackened, burned-out ruin, and everyone would be dead. And one time when he returned, it had happened. Only Mummy was gone, not dead, and the house was for sale, not burned to the ground. But this time, at least, there seemed to be no devastation. The motel sulked quietly under the gray sky. The management seemed to have finished whatever it did for the day to earn its keep, and the place was deserted. He pulled up with automatic caution in front of another unit, walked back, inserted the key without a noise and pushed the door open gently. Annie was lying much as he left her, breathing quietly, asleep.

She opened her eyes at the sound when he closed the door. "How are you?" he asked, a shade too heartily.

"Where were you?" she answered. Her voice sounded cracked and dry, but her eyes were accusing. "I was frightened. Someone knocked on the door, and you had disappeared. I didn't know what to do."

He carried the water glass into the bathroom to dump it out. "I was shopping," he said conversationally. He brought the glass back and refilled it from the jug. "Drink it," he said. "All of it." He put his hand behind her shoulders and lifted her up a little. "I got you a track suit," he said. "Extra large. Not that you are, of course," he added. "But I thought it would be easier for us to get you into it. If it were too big, I mean."

She almost smiled.

"And while you're in the bathroom," he said, "I'll try to straighten out the bed. It's a pity I was never in the army.

I think I'd probably be a little handier at all of this." And he picked her up again.

An hour later Annie was asleep, drugged against the pain, looking pale but reasonably healthy. He paced back and forth, trying to pretend she wasn't there. If they had to stay in this stifling room much longer, he would come to hate her. He brought his map in from the car and spread it out on the battered little table. His finger drew a circle around the motel. He didn't want to spend his time carting her around the countryside, but he had to find a place where he could sleep, too. He considered the possibilities. None of them looked that promising. He shrugged. One more night wouldn't kill him; he'd make his mind up tomorrow.

The afternoon was wearing away to a gray and miserable conclusion when Inspector Baldwin slammed down his telephone and jumped to his feet. He walked twice to the door of his office and then back to his desk again, in an agony of indecision. Finally he threw himself out into the corridor, roaring for Eric Patterson.

"He's not here," said Kelleher. "He'll be back later this afternoon. He had a whole list of people he said you wanted him to see. Now that Lucas is out of the picture." Kelleher looked at his watch. "Actually, he should be back soon. I'll tell him you wanted to see him."

"Don't bother. What did Lucas say to Patterson when he called in? Where in hell was he calling from?"

"The hospital at Deerton, sir. Or that's what I understood."

"Bullshit. They've bloody well never heard of him at the hospital in Deerton," said Baldwin. "He isn't there. I'll suspend him, that's what. I'm taking this up with—"

Kelleher looked up from the pile of material in front of him. "Not necessarily," he said, calmly interrupting Baldwin. "Just because they haven't heard about him at the switchboard doesn't mean he isn't there. It takes a bit of time for information to filter through. Do you want me to try and find out? We could call the locals and get them to check it out."

"Don't bother. I'll look after it myself," said Baldwin.

Lucas had spent the rest of the afternoon trying not to be in the motel room. He had wandered into the snowy woods behind the complex, finding occasional isolated paths. Each one of them seemed to end in a filthy garbage dump or pile of rotting car metal and broken down refrigerators, and his irritation had intensified. On the other hand, Annie seemed to be recovering rapidly, he thought, with a certain amount of pride. She was even gratifyingly hungry. And that presented the problem of what in hell he was going to do with her when she was better. Not keep her here. His nerves couldn't take it. And as he walked into the restaurant for dinner, he realized his digestion wouldn't take much more of this particular location, either. Tomorrow he was going to have to decide. That night he took one of her pillows, settled himself more carefully into the horrible armchair, and fell into a sleep of total exhaustion.

CHAPTER 11

Rob looked down at Annie Hunter in the cool light of early morning and felt a sense of satisfaction. She didn't look half bad today. Well enough to be moved to a classier motel, even. One with two beds in each room and a bit of space. Her breathing was a little fast, maybe, and her color a little gray, but surely that was the effect of expectations. Today, he was expecting her to be better; yesterday, he had expected her to be a lot worse.

She was still stirring restlessly in her sleep when he returned from the restaurant with breakfast. The sound of the door woke her, and she cried out nervously.

"Hey," he said. "It's just me. Come on, let's get you into the bathroom." She felt warm to his touch as he picked her up.

She looked a little better once she had washed, he thought. But after taking a few sips of orange juice and a bite of toast, she put the glass and the paper package down on the table beside her. "I'll finish it later," she said. "I'm not very hungry right now." His expostulations were interrupted by a knock on the door, and once again he chased away the manager's wife with her laundry cart, handing her some used towels and collecting clean linen in exchange.

Ed Dubinsky was leaning against the open door of elevator three, holding it immobile, waiting for John Sanders to fin-

ish reading the directory and figure out where they were
going. He yawned.

"Fourth and fifth," said Sanders.

"Which?"

Sanders shrugged. "Take your pick." Dubinsky pushed
both buttons.

It was a glittering, new, high-speed elevator, designed to
reach the twenty-seventh floor at rocket speed, and it
seemed to resent the briefness of its trip. It lurched to a
reluctant halt on the fourth floor. Dubinsky held the door
open again. "How does this grab you?" he said.

Sanders looked out. The door opened onto a wide hall
with an understated black glossy reception desk manned by
a pale, glossy receptionist. "It'll do," he said. Dubinsky let
go the door and slid rapidly out after his partner. Their feet
sank into the carpet; their sleeves brushed against the pots
of plants that filled up that awful blank space between elevators. "NorthSea/Baltic Enterprises are doing all right, I'd
say," Sanders remarked sourly.

"Or they owe a helluva lot of money to someone," added
Dubinsky.

The glossy receptionist was not pleased to receive another
visit from the police. She would see if anyone could speak
to them.

Out of their shortlist of possible interviewees, it seemed
that the person with the most free time on his hands at the
moment was the bookkeeper. They were willing to see him
first, Sanders admitted, if that made the receptionist's life any
easier, and they were ushered into a glass-and-fiberboard ham-
ster cage badly disguised as a room. The bookkeeper was
sitting at a desk, bare except for a new-looking IBM PS2—
its screen blank for the moment at least—reading a battered
paperback thriller that had sold three million copies several
years ago. He was dark-eyed, thin-faced, and hungry-looking,
and when he dropped his book down on the desk and stood
up, the two police officers towered over him. He sat down

again hastily, pointing at the two chairs on the other side of the desk as he went.

"You are Randolph West, assistant financial officer of NorthSea/Baltic Enterprises?" Sanders remained on his feet, and Dubinsky, with a sigh, followed suit.

"Jesus, is that what they call me?" The thin face broke into a foxy smile, like a dachshund grinning. "I suppose it is. Randy West. I do the books. That's all—I'm not an accountant. I just try to keep everything straight until the professionals come in. And they do. Frequently." He paused to catch the atmosphere of the meeting. "And if we're going to talk, why don't you sit down? Otherwise I'll get a crick in my neck." His voice squeaked, as if he had a case of laryngitis he was trying to ignore; his accent reminded Sanders forcefully of the kids who stole and bullied and fought their way out of his old neighborhood. Like him. Sanders pushed back one of the chairs and sat down.

"Doing the books here doesn't seem to involve a whole lot of work," said Sanders in a noncommittal voice. "Is that all you do?"

Randy looked over at him in astonishment. "Where in hell have you guys been lately?" he asked. "On Mars?"

Sanders shook his head. "On leave."

"Ah. That explains it. See this desk?" Neither one responded. "Empty. See those computers out there, with no one sitting in front of them? Locked."

Sanders looked out the glass wall to his right. "Things do look quiet out there," he observed. "Mostly."

"Oh, you mean that guy. He's not one of ours. He's from the solicitor general's office. An accountant. And a computer whiz. He's going through our computer files. A week ago—the day after the boss died—these guys came in and sealed up everything. Walked out with all my books, all the financial records they could carry, and left shit-face, the ball-less wonder out there, to plow through the rest."

Sanders turned to his partner. "Did we know about this?" he snapped.

Dubinsky paused for a moment. "Yeah, well, we knew that the company was being investigated as a result of—"

"The fire," said Randy gloomily. "The fucking fire."

"That's right, a fire," said Dubinsky. "In a town house built by a construction company owned by NorthSea/Baltic. In which a woman and, I think, a couple of kids were killed." Randy nodded in reluctant agreement. "The timing can't have had anything to do with Neilson's death, though. They'd been in front of a judge for days arguing over the court order."

"That's right," said Randy again. "And now there are all kinds of things that have to be done because Mr. Neilson died, and no one can do them. But they don't think of that, do they? I mean, it doesn't matter to them what happens to a whole company that employs hundreds of people just because some lazy bastard in some subsidiary that Mr. Neilson bought didn't check over the specs for wiring carefully enough."

"Is that what happened?" asked Sanders. His face was expressionless.

"Sure. What else?"

"What happened where?" said a barely cordial voice from behind Sanders.

Sanders turned slowly to look at the man who had just entered the office. He was neat and compact, dressed in banker's gray and oozing prosperity. Sanders had run into him before; in court on rare occasions—his practice did not ordinarily extend to criminal law—but more frequently at headquarters, where he dropped in on his pal Matt Baldwin from time to time. His voice grated harshly on Sanders's ears, as it always did, and raised his hackles. "We were curious about the peace and calm around here, Mr. Fielding. I'd forgotten about the investigation."

"Had you, indeed." Marty Fielding's incredulity quivered

in his voice. "But given the absence of documentation, I doubt that you'll be able to get much help from this department." Randy shrugged his shoulders and opened his paperback again.

Carl Neilson's secretary had been reduced to a state of sulky ineffectualness by her employer's death. She was sitting at a word processor, staring at a voluminous pile of opened mail beside her, and buffing her nails. A small black-and-gold sign on her desk informed the world that her name was Miss S. Cavanaugh.

"I trust we're not interrupting you," said Sanders.

Her ear was deaf to sarcasm. "Oh, no," she said. "That's impossible. Because I really don't know what I should be doing. There's all this mail that Mr. Fielding told me to answer." She flung a venomous look in his direction. "But I don't know what I'm supposed to say."

"For chrissake, woman," said Fielding, "you were his goddamn private secretary—or administrative assistant or whatever else in hell he called you. You answered all his mail, didn't you?"

"Not quite all."

"Well, leave those letters for Mrs. Neilson—no, better leave them for me, and answer the rest."

"When you two have settled all that," said Sanders, flashing his identification in her face, "we would like to go over Mr. Neilson's office. Is it locked?" She nodded sulkily. "Including his desk. Is it locked?" The secretary reached into her top drawer, pulled out a set of keys on a chain and flung them down on the desk in front of the two police officers. "Is this the appointment diary you kept for him?" She shoved it in their direction and picked up the first letter on the pile.

Carl Neilson didn't seem to leave the clutter of his existence lying about in his office. Sanders looked around the large, tidy room and shook his head. "Have we already walked off with everything in here?"

Dubinsky shook his head. "Patterson sent a couple of constables down to do an inventory. Said there was nothing particularly notable in here for anyone to walk off with."

"Well, there wouldn't be, would there? Not after every goddamn thing of interest was seized by court order before we arrived."

"Yeah, well, he pointed that out."

Sanders pulled open the desk drawers one after another. They were almost empty. The deep bottom drawer was bereft of files. The middle drawer contained a small assortment of different sizes of notepaper. In the top drawer he found drawing instruments, rulers, pencils, drafting pens, and colored felt-tipped pens. The wide, flat drawer in the middle of the desk contained a large pad of squared drafting paper, a diary, a passport, and a folder wrapped around two plane tickets for Tampa, Florida.

Sanders picked up the tickets and the passport and carried them to the door. "Hey, you," he snapped. "Miss Cavanaugh. What are these for?"

"They're plane tickets," she said crossly. "What do you think they're for? I picked them up for Mr. Neilson the day before he died."

Sanders ignored the turn of the worm. "No one mentioned that Mr. Neilson was planning on taking a trip."

"Well, really," said Miss Cavanaugh in tones of exasperation. "Why would we? He traveled all the time. Especially down to Florida. Some months he was hardly ever here. Anyway, this wasn't a business trip or anything like that. He was taking his son for the March break."

"And he needed a passport? To travel to the States? Since when?"

"Mr. Neilson had an accent," said the secretary, picking

up the next piece of mail on her desk. As if that answered the question.

"What?"

"He had an accent. And so the customs and immigration people were always stopping him. It's easier to carry a passport than to spend all your time explaining who you are."

"And when was Mr. Neilson planning on leaving for Florida with his son and his passport?" asked Sanders.

Miss Cavanaugh shrugged her silk-clad shoulders. "Around six, I think. The day he, uh, died. It's on the ticket."

"Was he planning to go home first? Get his stuff?"

She looked at him with scorn. "Certainly not. Mr. Neilson never carried luggage." Clearly, in Miss Cavanaugh's world, only peasants like Sanders carried luggage. "He kept everything he needed in his condo in Florida. He used to take a briefcase with him, that's all. And I'd put everything in it that needed attention."

"And that's what you did on March the seventh. The day he died."

The secretary paused a moment. "Yeah. Sure. That's what I did."

Sanders stared hard at her, considering that pause. Her face remained sulkily impassive. "Could you open the safe, Miss Cavanaugh?"

"It's open," she said. "The auditors opened it. There's nothing in it."

"Dubinsky!" yelled Sanders over his shoulder. "Look in the safe." There was a momentary pause, filled with the soft rustle of feet over broadloom.

"It's empty," said his partner.

"What did he usually keep in there?"

"Not much. Cash sometimes, if he was closing a deal, or negotiable securities if we had them lying around. Or important papers. He never used it to store valuable stuff. That all went to the bank."

"He wouldn't have kept his will in there?"

"That would be in Mr. Fielding's office," she replied stiffly.

"Damn," said Sanders. "Has Fielding left?" She nodded. "You got his address there?"

Instead of pulling her Rolodex over and looking up his address, she gave him another astonished look. There was apparently no limit to the ignorance of the police. "It's on the sixth floor," she said. "Suite six-oh-five."

Fielding was containing his joy at the sight of Sanders pretty effectively. "Yes?" he said, drawling out the word insultingly.

"Simple matter, Mr. Fielding. I would like to know the provisions of Mr. Neilson's will. In outline, for the moment."

Fielding looked bored. "I doubt if it'll give you much to go on. Basically he split his estate between his wife and his son. The wife holds the son's share in trust until he reaches twenty-one. If she dies at the same time, or close to the same time as her husband, her sister becomes the child's guardian, with a compensatory sum for her troubles."

"Like?"

"Five hundred thousand, I think. Not much when you consider the size of the estate. She would manage things for him with the assistance of two other trustees until he reached twenty-one. It's a very safe, conservative will. I don't encourage my clients to have wills that are guaranteed to be contested."

"Did Mr. Neilson have any enemies?"

"I've been through all this, you know. You can look it up. Rivals, yes. Enemies, no. Good day, Inspector."

"Now where?" said Dubinsky. "It's almost lunchtime."

"For chrissake, Ed, it's nowhere near lunchtime. You trying to give me a heart attack? We've got a lot to do this morning."

"Just trying to keep you moving. Where to?"

"Thornhill. I want to meet the grieving widow."

Lydia Neilson had been sitting in her comfortable, cluttered study, dressed in tweed slacks and a cashmere sweater, in front of a pleasant fire, when the two men came in. She fussed gently, ordering coffee, removing magazines from chair seats, and in general settling them in as though they were refugees who needed reassurance and comforting.

"Yes, I knew about Carl's will." She stared into the fire as she spoke. "We discussed it at some length. Rather heatedly, I must admit. He wanted to leave everything to Mark, but Marty Fielding convinced him not to. My husband was a rather authoritarian sort of male, you know. Thought that Mark would look after his mother—poor child." She glanced over at Sanders. "Actually the real battle was over Alice. My sister. Carl wanted his mother—who hates children and hasn't been very well—to be Mark's guardian. And if she couldn't manage the responsibilities, then Marty Fielding. Can you imagine? Do you know him? He'd park him in a boarding school for the winter and a camp for the summer and never let him out." Tears sprang up in her eyes, and Sanders remembered what Harriet had said about Lydia's maternal instincts. "I won that one. Alice's only disqualification was that she's rather hard up. I said if he left her some money, she wouldn't be. Eventually he saw it my way. I mean, he wanted what was best for Mark. He really was fond of him."

"I gather he was going to take him to Florida for the March break."

Lydia Neilson was now sitting erect and looking at Sanders with an expression of horror on her face. "To Florida!

You're crazy. He wasn't taking Mark to Florida. Not out of the country. Not without me."

"There were two tickets—"

"That doesn't mean anything. He went down there all the time. He owned a development firm down in Tampa. A subsidiary of NorthSea. He was probably taking someone from the office—or that, uh, some friend—with him. He never said anything about taking Mark."

Sanders eased away from the topic. "What private papers did your husband keep at home?" he asked.

"Private papers?" Lydia Neilson's eyes slipped away from Sanders's face again, and she returned to her contemplation of the fire. "Not much, really. He had a safe here. I had to get the manufacturer to come in and open it in case there was something important in it."

"Was there?"

She looked up, startled.

"Anything important in it?"

"Oh, things like life insurance policies. You're welcome to look at it. I don't know what you consider to be important. It's in his study."

Carl Neilson's study resembled his office. The light and expensive furniture in it was almost lost in the sweeping space. There were few books, fewer comfortable chairs, and a general air of chill joylessness in the surroundings. Lydia Neilson walked across the room and opened a door into a closet. "It's in here," she said, standing aside.

The door to the safe was swinging open. Dubinsky reached in, pulled out a tiny pile of documents and handed them to Sanders: house insurance, an insurance policy taken out on the life of Mrs. Neilson, a warranty on a recently installed furnace, and underneath it, a key to a safe-deposit box. Sanders took it and held it up in front of Lydia Neilson.

"I don't know," she said. "I thought it was the key for our safe-deposit box in our local bank, but I found that in his desk drawer. I looked in that one. I don't know what used to be in it, but when I checked, it had been cleared out. I have no idea which box that would be."

"Take it, Ed, will you? We'll have to try to track it down." She shook her head helplessly. "Did your husband have any enemies?" Sanders added casually, handing her back the insurance policies.

Lydia Neilson looked at him for a long time and then sighed. She walked over to her husband's desk, set down the policies, opened the top drawer, pulled out two small, cheap envelopes, and handed them to Sanders. They were addressed to Carl Neilson at the Thornhill house, and each contained a single sheet of lined yellow paper with a few lines of writing on it. The script was unformed and messy-looking, and the words were chilling: "Your lawyer can protect you in court, Neilson," the first one said, "but he won't help you once you step outside." The second was messier and more chilling: "A wife for a wife, Neilson. I'm sorry you only have one child. That doesn't seem fair, does it? You owe me two children. How well will your house burn?" They were unsigned.

"How long have you known about these?" asked Sanders abruptly.

"I knew that the man whose house had burned down— you know about that, I suppose—had threatened Carl. He told me to be extra careful about Mark. But I always am. I didn't know specifically about these particular letters until yesterday, when the man came to open the safe. They were in there. They're sad, aren't they?" Her eyes filled up with tears, and she turned her face away. "I'm sorry, but every time I think about them, they make me cry. That poor man."

"You never mentioned to anyone that your husband had received threats? That poor man might be the person who killed him," said Sanders.

"I guess he might," she replied. "I didn't say anything because I really didn't think the threats were anything more than the cries of a very unhappy man. You can't blame him for hating Carl. And I didn't want to sic the police on him. He's suffered enough already."

"Jesus," said Sanders. "There's turning the other cheek if I ever saw it." He slipped the letters in his pocket.

She paid no attention. "Two children," she said, shaking her head. "They were just eight months old and three, you know. It was horrible."

"And his wife," said Sanders.

"And his wife."

"We need to track that man down," said Sanders as they drove away.

"Can't be too hard," said Dubinsky. "His picture was plastered all over the papers, television, you name it. Shouldn't take more than a couple of hours. Do you think he shot Neilson?"

"How do I know?" said Sanders. "He probably hated him enough. But would he know enough about him to track him down to the hotel?"

"Sure," said Dubinsky. "There were lots of articles in the paper about other buildings that Neilson owned or built. Just to make the people who lived in them feel secure. You know, 'Developer of fatal firetrap subdivision renovates famous downtown hotel.' That sort of thing. Neilson was probably about to be in big financial trouble. Would you want to move into one of his buildings?"

That day there was not even a pretense of anything for Rob Lucas to do. He walked around the woods again, checking back on Annie every thirty minutes or so, trying to convince himself that all she needed was more rest and she'd be fine. By six, he was dejected, tired, and cold. He picked up a grilled cheese sandwich to go and came back for the evening. Annie's eyes were bright and her cheeks pink. "Hi," he said. "I have a disgusting grilled cheese sandwich here for you."

She shook her head silently.

"In that case," he said with false heartiness, "you can try some of the other delicacies." He opened the back window and took in the yogurt and a can of ginger ale, set them down beside her with a spoon and some melba toast. "There," he said triumphantly. "Dinner. Eat some of it."

"I can't," she said. "I just can't."

He looked sharply at her. All that bright color didn't look very healthy anymore. "Well, then," he said, "have something to drink."

She took a minute swallow of the ginger ale and dropped her head back on the pillow. Lucas reached over and placed a hand on her forehead. It was burning; he felt her neck, her hands, her forearms. He walked over to the window and stared out into the gray parking lot. At last, he turned back to her, his decision made. "We're getting out of here."

Tears sprang up in Annie's eyes. "Why?" she said at last. "I can't do it," she added. "I can't move around anymore. I don't care if they kill me, Robin. I don't care anymore. Just let me stay here and rest."

"To hell with that!" he exploded. "I haven't dragged you all over hell's half acre to have you fold up and die on me. Damn you, you're going to pull yourself together! And shut up." He stalked into the bathroom and began to throw things into his bag. He picked up the sack of groceries, grabbed the unopened tins and bottles, and tumbled them back in. In minutes he had the trunk filled with their possessions. He came back in, wrapped Annie in the blankets he had brought from the cabin, picked up the pillow he had brought along with them, and settled her into the backseat again. "Watch your foot," he snarled, still unreasonably angry. "Don't let it hit the side of the car." And he pulled out.

Less than a minute down the road, he was stopped by a

panicky and uncontrolled voice from the backseat. "The codeine. It's still beside the bed. I can't—I'll never manage without it."

He swung around in a U-turn and headed furiously back to the motel. He had also forgotten to leave the room key. He patted his pocket to check that it was there and touched a plastic vial, just where he had put it. "I have them," he said, "in my pocket." His exploring fingers hit the room key in the same pocket. They were almost back at the motel. Might as well leave the key where someone could find it.

He slowed down and put on his turn indicator. As his hands began to swing the steering wheel toward the parking lot, he saw the crowd: two cruisers with flashing red lights and two unmarked cars, obviously containing more law, all converging on the space in front of their old room. He flicked off the indicator, put his foot back on the accelerator, and drove quietly past the scene at something very close to the speed limit.

"Where are we going?" asked Annie. Her voice slurred drunkenly.

He pulled over to the shoulder and turned to look carefully at her. "How do you feel?" he asked. "And for chrissake, don't tell me fine—you look like hell."

"Worse," she whispered. "I'm sorry, but . . ." Her voice drifted off.

He started the car again. "Let's go," he said to himself.

"Where?"

"To visit an old friend of mine who ought to be able to help you," said Lucas with an assurance he certainly didn't feel. "Get some sleep. It's a fair distance from here."

"Oh," she said, and sank back into her half-conscious feverish haze.

The fastest way to Mike Chalmers's house would be to go down to the expressway, drive east forty or fifty miles and head back north again, but Lucas was reluctant to take such a well-traveled road. He braked, turned left, and headed north. If he remembered this neck of the woods accurately, there was a lousy little secondary road that would take him there more or less directly, passing through thirty miles of dreary scrub forest and rock on its way. At least along there—in the isolated silence of early spring—if some other vehicle tried to hang on to his tail, he'd notice. He pushed the car five cautious miles into the darkness without meeting anything but one startled deer who hustled out of his way. Just beyond the deer crossing a small road snaked off to the right into nowhere. It had no name, no number, no road signs along it at all. The only indication that it might go somewhere of any significance lay in the indisputable fact that at least once in its long life it had been paved. With a silent prayer, he swung onto it, picking up speed, screeching and bouncing around the unbanked curves and over the steep hills, muttering apologies to Annie every time the car gave a sickening lurch sideways. He was beginning to feel doubts about his fantastic brain wave. He wasn't at all sure—now that he had had time to think about it—that Mike would or could help him, but the alternative wasn't good. In fact, there wasn't an alternative. He reckoned that any hospital that looked at her would insist on keeping her at least overnight for observation. And by that time, judging by the speed with which things had been happening, half the world would know where she was.

He crested a slight rise in the absolute darkness and down in front of him a pool of light signaled that he had finally reached a town. He slowed down for the intersection where this little road angled in to meet the main street, searching for a road sign that would announce where he was. There wasn't one. He had arrived here—wherever they were—by the unmarked back door. He stopped and looked carefully around him. The shabby gas station and slick grocery store that faced each other at the corner looked vaguely familiar.

He cruised slowly down the street; it was garishly lit and empty. Here and there a cardboard coffee cup or a brightly colored paper bag from the local take-away blew in front of him in the cold wind. Drugstores, hamburger joints, paint stores. It could be any town in North America north of Florida and south of the Bering Strait. Until at last his eye picked it out. A faded sign on the aged hardware store boasted the name of the town—Cedar Hill. He passed the commercial block and started searching for street signs.

He turned the corner down the peaceful little road where Mike Chalmers had his veterinary hospital, eased gently up the street, and pulled into the driveway with a surge of relief. Warm light glowed through the curtains in the Chalmerses' living room. They were home and still up. He jumped out of the car and in seconds was pounding on the front door.

A shadow passed across the milky glass panel, an outside light flipped on, and Mike Chalmers's stocky frame filled the doorway. He peered into the darkness and then stepped back, startled. "Rob? Well I'll be damned. It's—"

Lucas cut short the traditional noises of surprise. "Look, Mike—sorry to barge in like this, but I brought you an emergency. I need your help." He gestured in the direction of the car. "She's in there."

"Accident? Badly hurt?" He nodded. "A car?"

"No," he said. "Shot and—"

"Jesus," he said in disgust. "Bastards. How big is she?"

Lucas blinked in surprise. "Not that big. Maybe a hundred and ten pounds—I don't know exactly."

"That's big enough," he said, raising one golden eyebrow. "Okay, carry her in by the door on the other side of the garage—I'll open it. I think we'd better take her straight into the operating room. No point in moving her back and forth, not a dog that size. I'll meet you there."

Before he could correct Chalmers's misapprehension, his

friend had disappeared. He shrugged and went back to get Annie out of the backseat.

She was lying on her side with her knees tucked up in the cramped space. He opened the door on the driver's side. The pillow he had jammed in the corner for her fell half out, and her head turned with a slight spasmodic jerk. He reached in, got his arm under her torso and pulled her gently out. She stirred and muttered as he lifted her up. "Where are we?" she asked.

"Getting you some help," he said. I hope, he added silently.

Not even draped with a blanket that covered her completely did Annie look like a large dog, he decided. But what the hell. It was too late now. He carried her in the open door to the hospital, turning her carefully to avoid hitting her feet on the frame and heading down the short corridor between the waiting room and the hospital. Two dogs barked sleepily in another room, a swinging door opened, and Mike Chalmers was standing there, drying his hands on a piece of paper towel. He stared at the bundle in Lucas's arms. Lucas went past him through the swinging doors and laid her down on a steel table in the middle of the room. She moaned slightly, and he uncovered her head.

"Jesus Christ, Rob," said Chalmers in a despairing voice. "What in hell do you think you're doing?"

"Mike, wait. Before you say anything, let me explain. Please." He grabbed him urgently by the arm. "Come out here."

"For chrissake, Rob, use your head. You can't leave her alone on that table in the state she's in!" he snapped. "Keep a hand on her." He took a step nearer. "Okay, now what is this?"

Lucas glanced uneasily down at her. Her condition had worsened considerably in the past hour or two. He had no idea whether she was conscious enough to hear or to understand what she heard; but he hated talking about her as if she were a piece of soft sculpture someone had tossed on the table. Most of what he had to say—the death of Jennifer Wilson, the way every move he made, every piece of information he collected, seemed to be known to the people who were pursuing her—would terrify her. But Mike was giving him no choice, and he whispered the whole tale into his ear.

"Couldn't you do something to help her? She lost blood from a wound in her leg. And maybe it's infected. She seems to be a lot worse now than she was yesterday. And I've already carted her forty miles cross-country to get to you."

"Jesus," said Chalmers, and ran his hand over his short red hair in perplexity. "This is one hell of a mess. You do realize what'll happen to me if I get caught, don't you? I mean, that will be the end. The authorities take this sort of thing very seriously." As he was speaking, he walked over to the table, pulled the blanket down to her waist, and looked at her. He reached up and turned on the powerful overhead light. "Let's get this goddamn chunk of filthy wool off her—didn't anyone ever tell you about septic wounds?— so I can see what we're up against," he said. "I'll raise her up and you get rid of it." Lucas carried the blankets over to the corner, caught Chalmers's eye, and took them out to the corridor before dropping them on the floor. "Now, what's wrong, as far as you know?"

"She was shot in the leg and burned her foot—it looks godawful, let me tell you. I almost puked when I saw it. And maybe she sprained her wrist."

Chalmers walked over to the sink at the wall and began to wash his hands again. "You realize that she's probably already picked up God knows what in the way of infections—not counting on what she'll get from us." He lifted her right arm and explored it with gentle fingers, ending up feeling for a pulse and checking it. Then he picked up the swollen arm and felt down to the wrist. "This has to be Xrayed," he said, almost to himself, "but it can wait until later. Which foot?" Lucas pointed silently. Chalmers picked it up and looked at the stained bandage.

"It's bad," said Lucas. "Really nasty. She walked on it after it was burned."

"Ran, actually," a hoarse voice croaked faintly.

"Good heavens," said Chalmers. "I'm not used to comments from the patients. How did you burn it?"

"With a hot poker," she said, and fell silent.

Chalmers raised an eyebrow at his friend, who nodded. "That will need to be cleaned up some," he said. "And now for the gunshot wound. Which is where?" he asked.

Lucas pointed at her left thigh.

"How badly is she hurt?" asked Lucas, when the leg was exposed.

"Just a minute," grunted Chalmers, working swiftly and systematically to ease off the bandage and swab away the accumulated dried blood and dirt on her leg.

"This is probably the least of her worries, I would say," he replied at last, as he finished cleaning up the edges of the wound. "It's shallow, and it looks clean. It'll probably leave a messy scar, but there's not much I can do about that now. It looks as if the bullet just tore the skin and did relatively superficial damage to the muscle tissue. That foot and the wrist are more worrisome, I think. And her general condition. When did this all happen?"

"I'm not sure," said Lucas. "What's today—Friday? Wednesday. In the afternoon. It was after seven when I started searching for her."

"It was between four and five," said the small voice again.

"It doesn't matter. Are you allergic to anything?" he asked. "Novocaine, stuff like that? Penicillin or penicillin-related drugs?" She shook her head. "Good. You know, Rob, I might just get hooked on having patients who can answer questions. It's very handy." He turned to a shelf of vials on the wall and looked them over, selected one, opened a drawer and took out a neatly packaged hypodermic needle.

"How do you know how much to give her?" asked Lucas nervously.

"Well, she looks to be somewhere in between a German shepherd and a Saint Bernard, wouldn't you say?" asked Chalmers with a wink.

An hour and a half later Lucas carried Annie into the waiting room and put her carefully down on the couch. Her thigh and foot were neatly bandaged, and her arm was in plaster from just below the elbow to the hand, leaving only her fingers exposed. Chalmers had banished him from the operating area some time before, and had been working quietly away in there on his own. Lucas pulled up a chair and sat down looking at her with worry carved across his face. She looked cold. He got up again and spread his coat over her bare legs. She made an attempt to open her eyes, failed, and lapsed into sleep.

Chalmers appeared a few minutes later and beckoned him over to the chairs on the other side of the room. "Sorry to throw you out, old man, but I didn't want you distracting me by passing out," he whispered. "Or breathing into her open wounds. The conditions in there weren't exactly ideal." He frowned. "She's in fair shape, I would say. The wrist is broken. A classic Colles' fracture—the radius and the ulna." He pointed to the bones on his own wrist as he talked. "Comes from falling forward onto it with great force. It'll take several weeks for it to heal, and, Rob, she should have it looked at again by a competent orthopedic man. I only know about this kind of fracture because Christy did the same thing skating. I cleaned up that hole in her leg—it should be okay. Just keep an eye on it."

"How do I keep an eye on it?" he asked, panic-stricken.

"I'll tell you in a minute. The worst injury is that foot.

It's a nasty second-degree burn, badly blistered; not too extensive in area, but she did a hell of a lot of damage to it running around on it afterward." He shook his head. "With some luck and care, the body will be able to deal with it. But it's infected. I'll give you a pile of fresh dressings—look after it, eh? And if it doesn't start healing, you're going to have to take her to a hospital, no matter what the situation is." He lowered his voice even more. "There's no point in trying to save her life one way by letting her die in misery from septic wounds."

"Is that likely?"

"I don't know. I've given her a healthy dose of penicillin. I'll give you some more for her to take for the next ten days. Otherwise, just make her stay off it until it's clearly healing—and I mean that absolutely. That foot is not to touch the floor. And pray, that's all."

"Thanks, Mike," he said and stood up. "God, what a feeble thing to say, but I mean it. She really is in danger— I meant that, too. And whoever is after her—"

"Doesn't she know who it is?"

Lucas shook his head. "This guy who was killed may have had mob connections. That means she's probably never seen the person sent out to get rid of her. Anyway, someone connected with it has a direct line into our communications. So don't mention that we were here, eh? Even if the local cops turn up to ask nice innocent-sounding questions."

"That's the least of your worries, old pal." He ran his fingers through his hair again. "If this gets out, I'll be charged with practicing medicine without a license. Believe me, Rob, you're just an old school friend. I haven't laid eyes on you for three years—not since we bumped into each other at the horse show. Before that I hadn't seen you since we worked together at the track. In fact, I was wondering what you were up to these days. Okay?" He got wearily to his feet. "Stay with her. I'll be right back."

Chalmers appeared in a few minutes carrying two pill containers. "Hi," he said to Annie, who was opening her eyes again. "How do you feel?"

"Not bad," she said, forming the words with difficulty. "Thirsty."

"Good girl. You need to drink lots. Get her some water, you idiot," he said to Lucas, nodding in the direction of the water cooler in the corner. As he talked, he opened up the vials and removed the paper labels that were curled up inside them. "There," he said. "The capsules are antibiotics—three a day, every eight hours without fail. The white pills are painkillers, one every four hours if necessary. Do you think you can remember that?" He handed the two containers to Lucas, who was crumpling up the tiny paper cup that Chalmers supplied with his cooler. "I don't like to send you out with pill containers with my name and handwriting all over them—but I'll give you some plain labels to write the instructions on if you like."

"Don't worry. Capsules three a day, pills every four hours for pain. What kind of animal were these for?" he asked suspiciously.

Chalmers laughed. "Some quack prescribed the capsules for Christy when she had the flu, just in case she had strep throat. She didn't, and so she didn't take them. She doesn't like pills. And the painkillers were mine—I got kicked by a horse. Jesus, did that hurt. I took one and found out I couldn't stay awake, so I stuffed them in the medicine cabinet. They're safe enough, just a bit strong."

"Okay, young lady," he said, walking over to her and picking up her good hand. "You have to take good care of yourself, do you understand?"

"You don't have to call her young lady, you know," said Lucas, irritated at his patronizing tone. "She has a name."

Chalmers held up his hand. "I don't want to know it," he said. "It's better for both of us if I don't. You're down on my records as Tara's Bridget of DerrynaFlan—a nice big

Irish wolfhound—and that'll account for the supplies I used. We'll leave it at that. Anyway, don't touch that foot to the floor until it heals, drink lots of liquids no matter how you feel, get lots of rest. Take those painkillers so you can sleep—and be a good girl, Bridget. Most of all, don't chew that cast off, even if it gets itchy." He got a very small and remote smile from her at last.

"You think she'll be okay?" asked Lucas as they walked away from her again. "And no bullshit."

"I don't know," he said. He sounded tired and discouraged. "Maybe. I hope so. In the short run, she's made it so far, in spite of shock and all that. She seems to be sturdy. She yours?" he added casually.

"God, no," said Lucas, startled. "She was private property of the murder victim, as far as I can tell—bought and paid for. My interest in her is purely professional. She's a witness."

Chalmers looked thoughtfully over at her, stretched out asleep on the fake leather of his waiting room couch and then at his watch. "You two better get out of here and find a place to spend the night. I'd ask you to stay, but—"

"Not a chance," said Lucas. "Someone might happen to remember that you're a friend of mine."

Chalmers nodded. "Just a minute. She should be okay on her own for now. Come here with me."

Lucas followed him through to the house. "Where's Christy?"

"She's visiting one of her sisters for a couple of days. The kids are off school this week, and they're driving her crazy. This way they can play with their vile cousins. And speaking of my wife's relations," he said, leading his friend into a large bedroom with an unmade double bed in the middle of it, "you were lucky to find me in. I was up at another sister-in-law's cottage today, checking it over for them. I just got back. They left for Mexico a couple of days ago. For a month. Lucky bastards, eh?" He rummaged in a drawer and came up with a pair of yellow track pants. "That cottage is a hell of a worry in the winter. My brother-in-law has it done up like some kind of royal ski resort, and these sons of bitches with snowmobiles are all over the place, looking for places to break into. Of course, he just built it, and he put in enough security to hold back an invasion." He tossed the pants on the bed and turned back to the drawer. "Anyway, they stocked it up this winter with enough food to last a year, I swear. Most of it will just get thrown out, too. But do you know where the stupid oaf keeps the key? On a nail under this hideous sign that says The Buchanans, with little gnomes or something carved in the corners. Anyone could get in." He pulled out another drawer and tossed things around inside. "The area's pretty deserted. Now that there isn't much snow, nobody goes prowling around there. It's on the Wanitake Lake Road, right at the very end. You get a choice of driving into a tree or down my brother-in-law's little private road." He discovered a top that matched the sweatpants. "I was tempted to stay there for a while, actually. It's unbelievably isolated, like I said, and completely winterized." He handed Lucas the two pieces of clothing. "Put those on her. They're soft and comfortable, and they're clean. Remember what I said. Everything I said. Lots of luck."

On that slightly ambiguous note, they went to collect Annie and put her back into the car.

"Where are we going?" she asked again, very faintly this time.

"To a nice cottage on a very remote lake," Lucas answered. "Where nobody knows where we are. It's going to take us a while to get there, and the road in probably isn't very good, so try to sleep."

CHAPTER 12

Occasionally in later years a stray sound or scent would trigger some unexpected train of thought that hurtled Rob Lucas back to those weeks in early spring. And in the half-life of memory, the days all had a bright, feverish clarity, as though he, too, had seen them filtered through pain and delirium, and the sun never ceased to pour its brilliance down on the pine woods and bare birches and ice-rimmed lake. From the time he had carried Annie Hunter into the cottage until the day he left, the deserted landscape had changed from winter to the promise of summer, yet for him the entire episode took place on one long, silent sun-filled day.

It was very dark at the end of the Wanitake Lake Road. He left the car outside a suburban-looking garage, took his flashlight, and went to find the key. There was the name, carved with flourishes on a pale varnished board fastened to a post. His fingers ran lightly across the bottom of the smooth surface, found a hole, reached in and pulled out the key to a high-security lock. He shone his light over the back of the cottage. There were acres of dark rounded siding— the fake log-cabin look that he didn't much care for—but no door. He followed what he assumed to be a path beside the cabin—down a slope, through patches of snow and leaves and pine needles and over small treacherous stones. The corner of the building sat on bare rock, smooth granite that appeared to sweep cleanly down to the lake. He scrambled up it and found himself standing on a broad deck. The air was still and cold; it smelled of winter still, of pine and snow. The almost total silence was broken only by the soft night murmur of lapping water. At least part of the lake must have thawed. He ran his light over an expanse of metallic security shutters that covered most of the walls from roof to deck, but there was no way through them by key from the outside. He turned the corner. More decking, more shutters. At the end, he dropped off the decking by swinging under a rail and landed a considerable distance below in the middle of a patch of prickly juniper bushes. Swearing, he scrambled up a steep and pathless slope until he reached the point where the building contours coincided with the land again, and of course, there it was. A path ahead of him, a concrete pad, neat and free of obstruction, a broad concrete step, and a door.

A rush of stale, cold, inhospitable air hit him as he turned the key in the lock and thrust the door open. So much for winterized cottages, he thought grimly, reached for and found a switch beside the door. It flooded the room with discreetly indirect light and revealed a kitchen. A clean and useful-looking kitchen. Fastened to the refrigerator with a magnet was a large piece of paper headed "Mike." He stepped over to look at it. "The thermostat is on the wall across from the counter," it started out. He looked to his right. There was a broad counter jutting out from the outside wall that divided off the kitchen from the rest of the building. On the wall across from it was the familiar round shape of a standard thermostat. He turned it up to above seventy—Annie needed warmth—and returned to the instructions.

"The hot water heater switch is beside the laundry room door, marked." There was an arrow pointing to the left. He followed it to a door, found the switch and turned it on. "There is a fire laid; use it by all means. It's the least we can offer you! More wood in back. Lots of beer, wine, etc., in the laundry room. I hope you and Christy manage

to get up for a weekend or two. Leave the kids behind!
You'll have more fun.

"The food in the freezer is left over from skiing. It has
to be used before summer, so anything you don't eat, we'll
be throwing out when we get back. You can take your
garbage home with you or leave it at the dump. Map in
drawer by refrigerator. Rest of keys are in the laundry
room. Be sure to lock shutters before you go, please. (And
could you give Muffin her shots before we get back?
Thanks.) Love, Susie."

He walked through the rest of the structure, finding and
flicking on light switches. He was in a great barn of a room,
divided between dining and living areas by a giant freestand-
ing stone fireplace whose rough-tiled hearth spread far into
both rooms. The walls were covered with vast expanses of
drapery, corresponding to the steel shutters outside. In the
living room, two couches faced each other at right angles
to the fireplace, one a single bed, dressed up with a brightly
colored rug and fancy cushions, the other having the square,
lumpish quality of something that would convert into a double bed. Warmth began to ooze up from every corner. He
turned on a couple of lamps that crouched on small tables,
pulled out the sofa bed, turned off the intrusive overhead
light, and went to fetch Annie.

Susie Buchanan, who was obviously a woman of infinite
kindness and sterling character, had left both beds in the
living room made up. He set Annie carefully down on the
sofa bed. Her eyes fluttered open and then shut again. After
a rapid search, he found a pile of pillows, neatly encased in
clean linen, inside a large painted box that defined one end
of the single bed; inside the matching box at the other end,
he discovered two eiderdowns. His search for a bathroom
took him into a master bedroom, countrified but sumptuous, behind the living room. Its adjoining bathroom was—

except for the cedar-lined walls and ceiling—not countrified at all. Merely sumptuous. He considered putting Annie into the splendour of the master suite and rejected the idea. In the living room he could sleep on the single bed at her feet, and she would be near him; he wouldn't be tempted to spend all night getting up to make sure she was alive. He settled her for the night, trying not to notice her vague and unfocused eyes, and collapsed, exhausted, into the smaller bed.

He was dragged from heavy sleep by a husky voice; in an instant he was crouched on the floor, taut and alert. The sound stopped. He held his breath, listening for some indication of where it had come from, reaching one hand out, slow and silent, to find his weapon. He heard the voice again, close enough to make him jump. He sighed and sat up. It was Annie. He pulled himself up off the floor and glanced at the clock—4:10. He turned on a light.

Annie's face was flushed, and her eyes glittered in the lamplight. He put his hand on her forehead. It was hot, frighteningly hot. Her lips were bright with irritation, cracked and painful-looking, like a dried up, muddy river-bed, baking under the sun. Liquid was his first panic-stricken thought. He tried to remember back to illnesses in his childhood. Surely there had been a time when his mother had sat by his bed when he was feverish. What in hell had she done? Nothing. It had been Mariana, of course, who had sat by his bed. His nanny, small and pretty, who rocked him and spoiled him. He remembered that cracked little soprano voice singing to him in Spanish to take his mind off the pain and misery of an earache. And glasses of orange juice mixed with soda water and ice, very cold and diluted. And more ice that bobbed musically about in a bowl with water, in which she dipped a cloth and cooled his forehead. He pulled on his discarded clothing and raced into the kitchen. There was frozen orange juice in the refrigerator and ice. He threw the juice container into the microwave oven and began searching for soda water.

"Who are you?" she said, staring at him when he returned with a glass of watered-down orange juice and a bowl of ice water. "Leave me alone." She made a feeble pushing gesture with her hands. "I don't want you around tonight." She turned her head away. "I'm cold," she added. And he noticed that she had begun to shiver.

"It's me. Robin." She stared up at the ceiling. "Can you hear me, Annie? I've been here all the time."

"Not Annie," she said. "Don't call me that. Not Annie." She rocked her head back and forth.

He tried to straighten out her bedclothes and get the eiderdown over her. She shivered and then pushed the coverings away. "If you're not Annie, then who are you?" he asked, curious in spite of his alarm.

She stared at him, unseeing. He dropped a face cloth into the ice water, wrung it out and placed it on her forehead. She sighed. He lifted her head and put the glass to her lips. Some of it seemed to go into her mouth. He sponged her burning cheeks with the cold cloth.

"I am no one," she said suddenly. He wrung out the cloth again in the ice water and pressed it to her forehead. Still staring, she clutched him awkwardly on the wrist with her good arm. "I come from nowhere." She shook his arm for emphasis. "I come from nowhere. I am no one." Her voice drifted off. He propped her up again and poured a little more liquid into her mouth. She seemed to find swallowing difficult. "I am no one," she muttered. "I come from nowhere." Suddenly her eyes flew wide open again and she clutched his arm once more. "I have no soul."

"What?" he said, startled in spite of himself. This went beyond anything he could imagine—having a weird philosophical discussion with a delirious hooker at four in the morning. Her hand relaxed its grip, and he forced some more juice into her mouth. She coughed and swallowed and subsided into silence again. He looked around him for a radio; if he was going to be sitting there all night, he wanted something less spooky to listen to than her demented ramblings. Like music—any kind of music. He put her hand, which had somehow found itself caught in his, down beside her and went to see.

Of course there was a radio. Tucked into a corner of the dining room was an expensive stereo system. As he turned on the receiver, it all suddenly made sense to him, and he laughed. Music. That was it. He had forgotten she was a singer, too. And in her feverish state she was running through *Lulu*. Because it was Lulu who had no soul. Not Annie. He fiddled with the dial until he got a country and western station and a girl singer breathily telling him her woes. That was reassuringly normal. Annie was mixing herself up with Lulu. He walked back over to the bed and looked down at her. She was quiet for the moment, sleeping again, he hoped. He pulled a chair over to the bed, dipped the cloth into the ice water, and went back to sponging her face and shoulders.

When he woke up, he was still seated on the chair but twisted around and half lying on the bed beside Annie. The room was still plunged in profound darkness, except for a trickle of light escaping from the bathroom. Annie was stirring restlessly; that meant she was asleep. He knew her well enough now to realize that, awake, she lay as still as a mouse that suspects there is an owl nearby. Only in sleep did her body reveal its misery. He got up awkwardly, stretched, and slipped into the bathroom to throw some water on his face and check the time.

Light was pouring into the room through the windows set high up against the ceiling. He looked at his watch. 7:45. He turned on the shower, stepped into the elaborate oval tub, and tried to restore himself to normal with a rush of cold water. By the time the water coming through the pipes was hot, he was wide-awake and starving. He remembered Annie, jumped guiltily out of the shower, and set out to do what he could with her.

He pulled the curtains back to wake her up. The room was still plunged in deepest gloom, and he remembered the shutters. Every expanse of glass wide enough to admit a body was covered with steel shutters. He turned on a light and began looking. The French doors were locked at floor level; in the laundry room, as promised, he found a board of keys, removed the one marked Windows, and set to work in the dining room. The key fitted, the glass slid back, and his hand touched cold steel. He searched around the frame looking for a device to raise them, found a switch, and turned it on. There was an unhappy whine of machinery; nothing happened. He looked again. Another lock fastened the shutters into the floor. And, sure enough, back in the laundry room, there was another key marked Shutters. In five minutes the huge room was flooded with light. He stepped outside to investigate his surroundings in daylight.

The sun was blinding after the darkness of the room. It poured down on the granite, bleaching it to a pinkish off-white; it glittered off the chunks of ice that slid across the water of the lake. Then he shivered in the chill air, remembered Annie, stepped back inside, and pulled the window shut. Her eyes were open, looking fixedly at him.

"Would your friend Lydia murder her husband if she suspected he was going to run off and take the boy?" asked Sanders. The couple at the next table turned their heads, startled, caught his cold glare, and, embarrassed, returned to their steaks.

"Wait a minute," said Harriet. "First of all, let's stop calling her my friend. I haven't spoken to her for four years.

And what happens if I said yes, she would? Or no, she wouldn't? That's a hell of a question to dump on someone between salad and dessert." She frowned. "Was he?"

"I don't know." Sanders shook his head. "He told his secretary he needed two tickets for Florida because he was taking his son with him. But he could have been lying. For all we know, he was taking a girlfriend. He didn't mention the trip to his wife." He looked across the table. "I did, of course. And if I'm not wrong, I gave her quite a shock."

"If you gave her a shock, then she hadn't known what he was going to do. And that means that she didn't—" Harriet nibbled her lower lip. "Unless the shock was that you knew about it, of course."

"You're getting cynical, Harriet," said Sanders. "Hanging around me too much."

"Don't flatter yourself, John. My cynicism comes from having survived the world for this long." She stared thoughtfully across the cherry-red tablecloth, seeing nothing. The waiter's hand crossed her sight line, and she looked down. "Why in hell did I order apple pie?"

"Because it's that sort of place—and I told you to. This is probably the first instance since our relationship began that you have done something because I told you to. Don't knock it. The pie is good."

"Mmm," she said vaguely, and ate a mouthful. "Did Lydia kill him?"

"It wouldn't surprise me. But then, nothing much surprises me these days. Except for your extremely mellow state of mind," he added, reaching over and touching her cheek lightly with his fingertips.

"Pay no attention to it." Harriet caught his hand, dropped a light kiss on it, and returned it to his side of the table. "I'm still suffering from post-holiday euphoria."

"But other people hated the man as well. Did you hear about the fire in Markham? It was the night after we left for the coast. A woman and two kids were killed. Well,

Neilson owned that development. His company built the house. Of substandard materials. The husband survived because he worked night shift. Anyway, he threatened to kill Neilson and to burn down his house—wife, child, and all."

"Did he? I mean, kill Neilson. Obviously he hasn't burned down Neilson's house, or we would have heard."

"I don't know." Sanders shook his head. "Lydia Neilson gave him to us, saying she feels terribly sorry for him. Handing over his threatening letters with sweet reluctance. You know—Gee, Officer, I hate to do this to the poor guy, such an unhappy man, but here they are, waiting for you, encased in plastic to preserve fingerprints, if any."

"She didn't," said Harriet. "Not Lydia."

"Well, not quite. But she dredged him up in one hell of a hurry once we started talking about her kid."

"I told you she was hysterical on the subject of that child. Otherwise she's quite a rational woman." Harriet toyed with the crust of her pie for a moment. "Motherhood does strange things to people—I see it all the time in my friends."

"Anyway, to get back to your question," interrupted Sanders, alarmed at the direction the conversation was taking. "As soon as we find the man, we'll ask him. He didn't try to conceal his identity. The letters were handwritten; he referred to himself quite clearly. He didn't sign them, but he didn't start with 'Dear Carl,' either. If he killed Neilson, he'll probably tell us."

"Where is he?"

"How the hell should I know?"

Harriet put down her fork and looked gravely at him.

"Okay," said Sanders irritably, "he's probably with relatives somewhere. We'll find him soon enough."

"What's going on with you, John?" Harriet pushed aside her plate and settled her elbows on the table, leaning toward him. "You're uncommonly prickly tonight. The case getting on your nerves?"

"I don't know." He stood up abruptly. "Come on, let's get out of here. I feel like walking."

Sanders put his arm around Harriet and steered her through the Saturday-night crowds on Danforth Avenue. Lovers, late-night shoppers, families wheeling bundled-up, sleepy babies all swirled around them as they walked in the direction of Harriet's apartment. "The case can damn well look after itself at this point. I'm more worried about— Do you remember Rob Lucas?"

"Rob Lucas. Rings a faint bell, but I can't place him."

"You've met him. He was part of my group for a while. Big blond guy with a broken nose."

"The gorgeous one! With that English public-school-boy face. I remember him. Didn't remember his name."

Sanders looked down at her in disbelief. "Public-school-boy? The Harriet Jeffries system for classifying physical types is beyond someone as dull-witted as I am. Well, gorgeous or not, he's disappeared."

"What do you mean, disappeared?"

"Just that. Disappeared. He had a line on a witness he'd misplaced and went tearing off to interview her out in the middle of nowhere, someplace between Haliburton and Bancroft, and the next we hear, he's been in a car accident on the way up there and they've taken him to a Deerton hospital, which should be miles out of his way. We got this from him—he called in. But when Matt calls Deerton to ask how Lucas is, they've never heard of him. When they check the cabin where the witness was living, they find a corpse. Murdered, rifle bullet. No witness, no Lucas. But the cabin looks as if a war was held in it, and the witness's car has been smashed to pieces. And now Baldwin's instituted a province-wide search. The owner of a motel somewhere east of Bancroft reported that a highly suspicious character bearing a striking resemblance to Lucas was staying at his place, but when they got there, he'd gone again."

"That's it? Has something happened to him?" she added hesitantly.

"Well, he rented a car in Deerton, which is I don't know how many miles west of the cabin, and took a pile of money out of his bank account. That sounds as if he planned out what he was doing. We should be able to find that car, but it's disappeared, too. They found a sweater belonging to him in the cabin, by the way. He was there."

"Why would he want to disappear?"

Sanders shook his head. "Or take his missing witness with him. Because the man who rented the motel room had a girl in the room. She had black hair and slept all the time."

"You mean that she was drugged?"

"It's hard to believe." Sanders sounded as if he was finding it only too easy. "Lucas is an odd guy in some ways, but not like that. I can't imagine him kidnapping a witness—which is what it looks like. And I can't figure why, once he found her, he didn't bring her down here."

"Maybe he decided he didn't want to," said Harriet as they turned the corner onto her street. "Maybe he's one of those weird guys who likes to collect his women safely under lock and key. Maybe he has a whole lot of strange girls stashed away somewhere."

"Jesus, Harriet, if that's the best you can do, then shut up. I can think up things like that without your help. Anyway, I can't imagine anything worse than having a room full of vicious broads like you, all locked up, ready to murder me once my back was turned. Rob is too bright for something like that."

"Why, thank you, Officer," said Harriet sweetly. "I appreciate the compliment. Are you coming up?" she asked, reaching into her pocket for her key. "I must show you this collection of helpless males I keep in the basement. A nuisance to look after, but sweet. Do come in, Officer."

Reaching around her with both arms, Sanders took the key, opened the door, picked her up, and carried her awkwardly into the hall. "Never mind," he said huskily, as he kicked the door shut. "I can still win arguments by brute, stupid force." He set her down gently, turned her around, bent down, and kissed her with a desperation that startled her.

CHAPTER 13

John Sanders had wasted the better part of Monday morning reading through material compiled before he had taken over the investigation: maddeningly incomplete reports; vague statements from witnesses that should have been checked before now and found wanting. The writer of the threatening letters to Carl Neilson, whom he had expected to trace instantly, was still missing. Dubinsky was off pursuing his favorite daily occupation—harassing the auditors from the solicitor general's office, reminding them yet again that homicide was at least as important as fraud.

"Nothing." His partner's voice interrupted a highly complex sketch he was adding to a sheet of paper with a three-line interview statement on it. Dubinsky dropped his coat over a chair. "But I think I've convinced them that if they don't start looking into some of his other business enterprises, I'm going to start breaking shinbones. They're obsessed with that goddamn development that caught fire. The boss man got himself 'a promising line of inquiry,' he said. Anyway, one of the other guys is going to start in on the two restaurants this afternoon. I suggested La Celestina."

"Why?"

"I dunno. I have a few not-so-good memories about that place. I wouldn't mind seeing it up to its elbows in shit."

Sanders yawned and pushed aside the paper he was scribbling on. "Speaking of the restaurant, I want to talk to the pimp."

"Was that any particular pimp you wanted?" asked Dubinsky. "Because there are a hell of lot them around."

"The one who was tried for the murder of the hooker in the restaurant. Neilson's restaurant. The one who got off. Maybe he knows something, off the record. Say, about Neilson, that he didn't bother mentioning to us or to the judge."

"The La Celestina pimp. Sounds kind of neat, doesn't it? I'll see what can be done." Dubinsky reached for his phone and punched in some numbers. There was a long pause, punctuated by low-voiced murmurs. "No shit," he said at last, his voice flat. "That's a real bitch. Who got him?" After a further pause he muttered what could possibly be construed as thanks and hung up. "The pimp's dead. Someone took his head off with a mortar or a guided missile or something. Hardly enough left of him to identify. In Peel—that's why we never got it. They wrote it off finally to turf battles." He sighed. "They were so damned glad to get rid of him, they didn't exactly bust their asses to find out who did it."

"What the hell—you can't win them all. If we can't get the pimp, let's go take a look at the restaurant," said Sanders.

No one had intended the restaurant La Celestina, as the sign outside called it, to be seen in the harsh light of Monday morning. The vacuum cleaners were still being run over the stained red carpeting; the deep red curtains were pulled back to allow the sun to fight its way in through the dirty windows. A waitress was moving slowly from table to table, covering each with a white and then a bright red tablecloth that clashed violently with the rug and the curtains. It was eleven. By noon, no doubt, it would be too dimly lit to notice such infelicities. Cooking smells drifted in from the double doors leading to the kitchen.

"We're not open yet," said the waitress, in a voice that was neither hostile nor friendly. She yawned. "You should be able to get something in thirty minutes or so. Except that Monday morning the chef is always late with the specials. But we can do you a sandwich or something."

Sanders raised a hand to stop the sleepy flow. "This place have a manager?" he asked.

She nodded in the direction of a smaller door in the back, marked Exit and Washrooms. "Through there. At the end."

The manager's door proclaimed him to be a Mr. Horvath; the tall, thin, balding, and hollow-eyed man inside greeted them without surprise. He glanced at Sanders's identification and pointed at two empty chairs in the crowded room. "I wondered when you guys would turn up," he said. His voice was as hollow and gloomy as his eyes.

"Why is that, Mr. Horvath?" asked Dubinsky genially.

"Why? Because someone shot Mr. Neilson, that's why," snapped the manager. "On top of everything else. I've been expecting to be up to my ears in police for the last week."

"Sorry to disappoint you," said Sanders. "We had other fish to fry. They said you were the manager—"

"I am the manager," said Horvath sourly.

"How much did you see of Mr. Neilson on a day-to-day basis? How much control did he exert?"

"Not much and a lot," said Horvath. "Meaning, he wasn't hanging around every day tasting the soup or anything like that. Jesus, I've worked for owners who thought they knew something about food." He shook his head. "It's godawful. Chefs get mad and quit. No, Mr. Neilson used the place for entertaining. I guess his wife didn't like parties much, and we're a big operation. We can handle a party of two hundred or more without any trouble if we close the dining room. We can put sixty upstairs *and* run the dining room with a few days' notice."

"So otherwise he left you to manage things on your own."

"Well, sort of. I do what you'd expect. Inventory, ordering, beverage control, food cost. But then everything is done over again, in a way. The bookkeeper—"

"Is that West?"

"Yeah. You know him? Randy. He comes in every night, tallies the cash, picks up the printouts I work from, and checks it all. I guess. Banks it and reports to Mr. Neilson. Stupid."

"Unless he didn't trust you."

"So let him fire me. Or audit me. Who knows why he did it? Owners are weird. I asked him once. He said he believed in double-checking everything."

"When did you see him last?"

Horvath scratched his earlobe. "Dunno. Two weeks before he died? He had a lot on his mind. The investigation and everything. Too busy for us. Anyway," he said, standing up, "you want to know anything else, come back after lunch. I got work to do."

"Interesting," said Sanders, as they walked back into the dining room. The curtains were drawn; the soft lights were on. "The place looks almost worth eating in."

Dubinsky yawned. "Not my kind of food. Besides, where are the girls? You could at least have asked about trafficking, rake-offs—all the good stuff."

"Softly, Ed. This is just a start."

"Can I get you guys anything?" said the sleepy waitress. By now the tables were supplied with napkins and cutlery, and more staff lounged around chatting.

"Just a little information," said Sanders.

"Jesus, I shoulda known," she said. "One look at you, and I shoulda known. Am I out of it today. We've been expecting you guys. So?"

"Tell me about how things work around here," said Sanders. "Money—that sort of thing."

"That little prick Randy does the money," said the waitress. "Except on his days off, when I do it—or Mr. Horvath.

And he skims tips, Randy does. I know. The day I catch him at it, I skim his balls off."

"You don't care for Mr. West?"

"I like that. Yeah, I don't care for Mr. West. He can't keep his greasy hands off the girls—or the boys, I wouldn't be surprised. And mean as hell if you do anything about it. One girl bashed him across the ear with a tray, and he went straight to Mr. Neilson and had her fired."

"Were they friends? West and Neilson?"

"I wouldn't describe them as friends. Being as Randy's a miserable little ass-licking son of a bitch when Mr. Neilson's around. Or was around. Maybe he got on better with the other owner."

"Which other owner is that?" asked Sanders cautiously.

"I don't know his name. I only know there's another owner because I heard him once when I was in the washroom. They were holed up in Horvath's office, and he was mad—saying something about as an owner, he had a right to know what was going on." She shrugged. "Places like this, it's hard to find out who owns what."

"Tell your friends at the solicitor general's office that we need some more information about this place," Sanders growled to his partner as they walked back outside. "Before all the witnesses die of old age."

For three more nights the fever had raged. Each morning Rob Lucas looked at Annie, appalled at the responsibility he had cavalierly taken on himself, and decided it was time to throw in the towel and take her to a hospital. But each night as he sat up with her in the dim light of one small lamp, he was haunted by visions of Jennifer Wilson's dead body, by memories of the chaos and destruction at the cabin, and he changed his mind. Looking after her consumed every hour of the day. He coped badly with changing her dressings, and worse with trying to keep her warm, clean, and dry. He had discovered extra bed linen and a washer-dryer in the laundry room, and conscientiously changed her sweat-soaked sheets each morning. Every night he lowered the shutters, in case somehow someone tracked them to Lake Wanitake. In that time she did not speak an intelligible word, didn't appear to know he was there. He sat by her anyway, afraid that if he turned his back, death might catch her alone in that big room. When she seemed to be awake, she stared out at the water or up at the wood-paneled ceiling. Otherwise she slept, fitfully and restlessly, moaning in her sleep, or worse still, lost again in a delirious trance, she raved at him with an intensity of fear and despair that appalled him. She screamed to some invisible hordes of devils to leave her alone, she grasped his arm and demanded his name, and from time to time she returned to *Lulu*: "I do not know; I am no one; I believe in nothing." His constant preoccupation was a never-ending fight to keep her from dehydrating; for hours he held her in his arms and forced liquids down her throat. Some she swallowed, some spilled, some she coughed up again. He carefully mopped her face and began to despair.

On the fourth morning he woke up with a start, his heart pounding, and lifted his head in alarm. He was stretched out on Annie's bed; she was on her side next to him, her arm in its awkward plaster casing flung high against the stuffed back of the couch. She was breathing deeply and regularly, the slow, even breathing of those who sleep soundly. The small lamp remained burning in the corner, but beyond the steel casing on the windows he could hear a bird singing. It was morning. The last thing he remembered was forcing a painkiller and an antibiotic capsule down Annie's throat at midnight and making her drink something. He slipped off the bed and walked into the bathroom. The sun was pouring through the windows. He looked at his watch. It was seven minutes past nine.

They had slept for nine hours. Nine hours without interruption. He looked at his four-day growth of beard in the mirror and grinned. To hell with shaving, to hell with spit and polish, to hell with greasy hamburgers and cold, scummy coffee. He wasn't a cop—he was a man who had just tilted with the windmills and won. He stripped and showered for the first time in days, got himself some clean clothes, and moved quietly back into the living room to have a look at his rescued maiden.

She was sleeping quietly, looking pale and thin and very sick, but the taint of fever and madness that had been a physical presence hovering over her was gone. She was a person again.

He opened the two sets of French doors in the dining room, unlocked the shutters, closed the doors again, and flipped on the raise switch. Green, woodsy light filled the cottage, and he went into the kitchen to make himself some coffee—some real coffee. And some breakfast instead of the crackers and cans of soup he had been living on. He was famished. He moved his down jacket from the freezer lid, lifted it, and discovered a treasure hoard. There were coffee beans, packages of bacon, loaves of bread of all kinds and descriptions, plastic bags filled with Danishes. Susie was a woman who knew how to live. And to shop.

Between microwave and oven, stove top and toaster, he had Danishes warming, bacon thawed and now frying, bread toasting, and freshly ground coffee dripping through its filter. He was searching through the refrigerator, looking for interesting jam, when he heard his name. Startled, he snapped upright, so rapidly that he hit his head.

"Robin—are you there?" This time the voice sounded worried.

"Sure," he said, rubbing his head. He reached over and turned down the heat under the bacon before heading around the fireplace and over to the bed. "Of course I'm here. How are you feeling?"

"Can you help me into the bathroom?" she asked. Her

voice sounded husky and unused. "I'm not sure I can make it on my own."

"I am," he said, reaching down and picking her up for what seemed like the hundredth time at least. And each time she had felt lighter and lighter. "Sure you couldn't make it, that is. Don't even try. Not yet." He got her into the bathroom and turned to go. "I'll get you a clean nightgown. I didn't like to wake you up earlier," he said, and left, suddenly embarrassed. He hovered nervously outside the door, listening for a thump as she crashed to the floor, wondering if she hated being dependent on someone like him, a stranger, hostile, someone with no connection to her at all except the accidental one of his job.

After a decent interval he knocked, walked in firmly, and reached down to take off her rumpled nightgown. She looked up at him, startled. "No point in getting prudish," he said. "I've been changing your clothes and trying to give you sponge baths for three days now. Sorry, but Mike said it was important to keep you clean and dry. You sweated a lot sometimes."

"Three days?" she said weakly.

He nodded, grabbed a clean washcloth, and rinsed it in hot water. "You want to wash your face?" he said, holding it out to her. "And maybe eventually I can even organize brushing your teeth. And your hair." She buried her face in the hot, damp cloth, handed it back, and began to try to pull off her nightgown. In one rapid gesture, he had it over her head and the clean one dropped in its place; then he picked her up again, and carried her back to bed. "I'm cooking breakfast," he said unnecessarily. The room was filled with the odor of bacon. "Would you like something?"

"I'd love some coffee," she said. "It smells—I don't know—nice and ordinary."

"One coffee coming up. How about orange juice? And some toast?"

*   *   *

She put down her coffee mug and leaned heavily back on the pillows Lucas had arranged behind her. "I'm tired," she said. "But I guess I'm okay."

"Good," he said, setting his plate down on the coffee table and picking up a glass of water. "Drink this. You got very dehydrated." He laughed nervously. "I thought you meant to dry up on me."

"I knew I was dying," she said quietly. "And I didn't give a damn. I felt so awful . . . and so tired. And you kept shoving things down my throat. Instead of just leaving me . . ."

He waited for her to finish what she was saying, but she turned her head and looked at the blank windows, silent again. He got up and began the slow routine of unlocking all the shutters and raising them. The strong spring sun flooded the room, and Annie dropped her head back as far as it would go. In a minute she was asleep again.

Inspector John Sanders walked into the room, took off his gray, pin-striped suit jacket and draped it with elaborate care over the back of his chair. His face was white; his features frozen, thin-lipped, immobile. He sat down with the same care that he had expended over his suit jacket and grabbed for a file. He opened it and inspected the first page it contained. Five minutes later he was still staring at the first page.

"You want a coffee?" said Sergeant Ed Dubinsky, who up to this point had been pretending to ignore him.

"No," said Sanders.

"So what in hell happened up there?" asked Dubinsky. "Before you have a heart attack and can't tell me."

"It's going over to internal affairs." Sanders glanced up for a moment and then returned to his file.

"Turn the page," said Dubinsky. "Then tell me what's going to internal affairs."

Sanders closed the folder sheepishly and looked over at his partner. "Lucas. Dragging us all upstairs was Baldwin's idea. Everybody else was happy to wait until we found the stupid idiot and asked him what in hell he thought he was doing. But Baldwin thinks Lucas was on the take, got himself mixed up with Neilson's murderers, and is getting out while the getting is good. He claims he's been suspicious of Lucas from the very beginning, that Lucas kept turning up where he wasn't expected—looking into aspects of the investigation he wasn't supposed to be worrying about."

"Could be," said Dubinsky with his usual skepticism.

"I dunno," said Sanders, running his hands through his hair. "He never struck me as the type. Which doesn't mean a thing. Those pretty, clean-cut types can get away with murder." Sanders winced. Harriet's cry of "gorgeous" was still ringing in his ear. "Baldwin says he was chasing that witness so he could get rid of her."

"Or somebody was," said Dubinsky. "Anyway, what difference does it make? They can't do much until they find him."

"They're stepping up the search. I hadn't realized until today how much Matt hated him."

"So what else is new?" said Dubinsky, yawning. "But I wouldn't worry about Lucas. He's not as stupid as you think. He'll be all right. Anyway, you want to hear what I got from the auditors?" Sanders leaned back in his chair and closed his eyes. "Their reason for concentrating on Neilson's land development deals is that they were sent in there on account of the fire and those people being killed. That good enough for you? Anyway, it's slow because everything he did was very complicated. Got it? It took them forty-five minutes to explain those two things to me. But what they're pretty sure of—it'll take weeks before they pin down the proof, understand—is that Neilson was expecting the roof to fall in on him and was moving every asset he had out of the country, out of reach of Canadian courts."

"You mean, he was going to leave the country for good?"

"They wouldn't say, of course. But that's what it looks like. And with two plane tickets—"

"Take the kid with him." Sanders sat up and opened his eyes again.

"Bingo!" Dubinsky leaned back in turn. "And something else. While you were farting around up there, raising your blood pressure for no good reason, Collins and McNeill tracked down that safe-deposit box key. I told the manager we'd be there at two. That gives us time for lunch."

The manager of the large downtown bank where Carl Neilson had his safe-deposit box did not like police on the premises. He was waiting at the door; he pushed them through the public areas as if they were plague carriers, hustled them into a private room and into the box almost before they could identify themselves.

Instead of cash reserves, negotiable bonds, whatever it was that Sanders had expected to see, only two items occupied the space. A standard business envelope and, under it, an eight-and-a-half-by-eleven brown manila one. Both were unmarked and unsealed. Sanders picked up the smaller envelope and looked inside. It contained one strip of developed black-and-white negatives, 35mm. From the larger envelope he pulled out six black-and-white prints, eight by ten in size, set them on the table, and picked up the top one. And drew his breath in through his teeth in a muted whistle. "Pay dirt, Ed," he muttered softly. "You better get the car. We're off."

The house in Thornhill slumbered in the strong spring sunshine, clean, innocent, and rich-looking. They surprised

Lydia Neilson on her way out to the stable, turned her around and back into the house. She led them into the study, smiling politely and automatically, but as she turned to gesture them into chairs, Dubinsky pulled the manila envelope out of a large plastic bag. Mrs. Neilson paled and sat down abruptly.

"Mrs. Neilson," said Sanders briskly, "while going through a safe-deposit box rented by your husband—"

"Where did he keep them?" she asked. Her voice was hoarse.

"At his downtown bank."

"Yonge and Bloor?"

"No, right downtown."

"I didn't know he had another bank," she said. Her shoulders sagged, and her face settled into a mask of absolute misery.

Dubinsky took out the top photograph and handed it to Sanders. "We found this and other photographs of you—"

He held out the picture, but she shook her head vehemently and wrapped her arms protectively around her body.

"I've seen them," she said. "I don't ever want to see them again. They're disgusting—absolutely disgusting."

"Is that you in the photograph?" asked Sanders. "You might want to consider for a moment before—"

"Oh, yes, it's me. But I didn't—" She stumbled, searching for words. "It was a setup. I never went in for Carl's sick games. And I would never, never, never have done anything like that with a child present. That was pure Carl, that touch. He knew how I felt about child pornography."

"What do you mean—a setup?" asked Dubinsky.

Lydia Neilson's fingers were digging into her upper arms as she clutched herself more and more tightly. She stared down at the carpet. "A setup. The kind of thing Carl was good at. That's why people hated him." She looked up a moment, surprised. "Or admired him, too, I suppose. Anyway, I was ready to leave him. He was disgusting—but that doesn't matter here. I fell in love with someone—a normal human being—and Carl opened a letter from him and discovered I was going to leave. He didn't give a damn about me, not really, but he was furious that I meant to take Mark with me. Mark was his son, you see. His property. He never told me about all of this until later, by the way. Anyway, it was my birthday, and he threw a big party for me, a costume party at La Celestina—that's one of his businesses. I'd never been there before. It was hot and smoky and filled with people I didn't know. I remember being very thirsty and feeling very strange, and someone taking me somewhere to lie down. I don't remember anything else until I woke up in the hotel with my lover in bed with me and someone taking our picture. Both of us felt like hell. Carl came in right after that with a couple of guys and that pile of pictures. I threw up when I saw them."

Sanders looked at the top picture. Lydia Neilson was lying on a double bed, naked, with one man on top of her, and a second man reaching out for her while being fondled by a boy who looked no more than ten. Her eyes were shut and her face was slack. Unconscious? Possibly, he thought. "Is one of these men your boyfriend?" he asked abruptly.

She shook her head. "The idea was that Carl would go into court and say that not only did I have a lover but I went to parties where I—" She stopped in momentary confusion. "Parties like that. He said if I ever tried to leave, or had anything to do with my friend or any of his friends again, he would divorce me and produce these pictures in evidence—including the one they had just taken—and I would never see Mark again. He said the two men in the pictures would swear that I—that this wasn't the first time. My friend got dressed and left, and I've never seen or heard from him since." Tears began running down her face. "You can't believe how happy I was when that policeman told me Carl was dead. I felt guilty, because he was a human being and afraid of dying and deserved to live his life, but

I was happy. No one was going to be able to take Mark away from me now. That was all I could think of." Lydia Neilson unwrapped her arms and fished in her pocket for a handkerchief. "Someone like me killed him, Inspector, some desperate person, and I feel so sorry for him, because you'll catch him, whoever he is, and all he was doing was trying to save himself from being destroyed by my husband."

"You mean, you don't care who killed him?" asked Sanders quietly.

"Not particularly. And don't look at me like that. I didn't kill him. I couldn't put Mark at risk—what would he do with his mother in prison? No, I couldn't do that. Besides, I've never killed anything in my life. But someone did, and Carl deserved it."

"The problem with Mrs. Neilson," said Dubinsky, yawning and taking the top off his coffee, "as I said yesterday, is that although she has motive written all over her, motive she admits to, we can't place her anywhere near the scene. It's a long way from her house to the hotel. The housekeeper didn't see the car go out, and none of the neighbors saw her driving to or from the house."

"No one saw her out riding, either," said Sanders.

"Okay, no one saw her out riding. But there is someone who was right there while that bastard Neilson was still bleeding all over the carpet, and that's Rob Lucas's mystery witness who has disappeared, with or without Lucas. Has it ever occurred to you that she might have taken her little twenty-two and popped a couple of tiny bullets through his brain as well?"

"Yeah, it's occurred to me. From time to time. Stupid thoughts like that are always occurring to me at four in the morning. But you know what really occurred to me while I was listening to Mrs. Neilson? That her husband was a vindictive, blackmailing son of a bitch by nature. Maybe we should concentrate on his business partners for a day or so—if we can find out who they are. He probably did the same sort of thing to them. Anything new from the auditors?"

"Come off it," said Dubinsky with pain in his voice. "I just got in."

"Christ! They've probably been working since dawn. Call them." Sanders turned back to his desk and began his morning paper shuffle once again.

It was after lunch before Dubinsky turned up again, looking sleek and well fed. "Okay," he said. "Here's what we've got. The guy who's been looking at Neilson's restaurant and hotel business says that for the last two or three weeks before he died there was a serious hemorrhage."

"What does he mean, hemorrhage?"

"Well, there's a hell of a lot of money coming in to the restaurant, for instance. Much too much. I asked him if it could be drugs and girls, and he said he hadn't the slightest idea. Neilson had it covered in his books, sort of. Then the money disappears. Not just the extra cash, but all the money. And now the books for the restaurant wouldn't stand up to a five-minute scrutiny, he said. So I asked this guy who Neilson was trying to fool, and he said it wasn't the auditors. And it wasn't the tax people. Maybe some very gullible business partners for a very short period of time. Because pretty soon even they would figure it all out. In a week or so, at the rate he was going, there wasn't going to be enough cash in that business to pay the cook."

"What about the guys sniffing around the premises? Anything new?"

Dubinsky shook his head. "They're still looking. The place is getting too respectable. But they're still digging."

"So as far as Neilson's death goes, we're back where we started."

"I don't know about that. Try this on. Randy West's been inside. He served five years of a fifteen-year sentence for embezzlement. Got out five—six years ago and has worked for NorthSea/Baltic ever since. I found that so interesting, I made an appointment with Mr. West at the restaurant for a little talk. You're welcome to come along if you want: five-thirty."

They were met at the door by Horvath in a dinner jacket. Its neat and severe lines made him look gloomier than ever. Before he managed even the briefest of good-evenings, Sanders had him backed over to the relative privacy of the coat-check counter. "Do you remember a birthday party that Mr. Neilson gave for his wife here? One of those two-hundred-people, close-the-dining-room kind. Costume."

Horvath wiped the surprise caused by their sudden entrance off his face and restored his features to their habitual melancholic impassivity. "For Mrs. Neilson? You're sure?" Sanders nodded. "It must have been before my time. I've never met Mrs. Neilson. I heard she didn't like going out much. I didn't know she'd ever been here."

"Do you get a rake-off on the girls?" asked Sanders casually.

Horvath stiffened. "Look," he said, leaning one long thin finger on Sanders's chest, "I don't run places like that. Understand? You can bring your family here. Your mother. Dinner. Dancing if you want. No girls. No funny stuff. The bar is run clean; the staff is clean. I watch these things." His face was growing pink with agitation. Sanders gently put aside the hand that stabbed at him. "Okay," Horvath said, as if conceding some great point, "when Mr. Neilson bought the place it had a lousy reputation. And there was a lot going on for a couple, three years. That was one reason he hired me. We got a new bartender; I put Addie there," and he paused to nod at the sleepy-eyed waitress, "in charge of the dining room. We redecorated, updated the kitchen, everything. This is a clean place." The unaccustomed color began to recede from his face. "You saw for yourself. The money, inventory, everything—it's all checked three times. Me, Randy, Mr. Neilson. We all did it."

"But you don't actually count the money in the till."

He shook his head. "That's Randy's job. Except on his days off, Addie does it. That's usually Sunday and Monday, when business is light. Not much money comes through here, though. Mostly credit cards." He pulled together his cloak of professionalism. "What can we do for you this evening? It will be getting busy pretty soon, so—"

"Just a cup of coffee and some quiet corner where we can talk to Mr. West. He's expecting us."

Randy West sat in Horvath's crowded office surrounded by piles of paper, rapidly entering data into the computer on the desk. He looked up wearily as they all crowded in: Horvath, Sanders, Dubinsky, and Addie with two cups of coffee. She set them down on the desk, gave West a poisonous glare, and swept out, dragging Horvath in her wake.

"So what's your scam here?" asked Dubinsky genially. "Besides screwing the waitresses out of their tip money. Maybe we should warn you that the books from this place smell like last week's stew—you might want to start working on a good line for the boys from the solicitor general's office."

Randy West pulled himself upright, quivering with virtue. "What do you mean, scam," he said. "Listen, I got no scam, okay? What do you think I am, some kind of genius? I just enter figures, check the math, count the bills. That's all. Mr. Neilson set up the system for this place with the chef and Horvath. I just do the numbers."

"You know what I think you are, Randy? I think you're someone who embezzled half a mil out of a parts manufacturer over three years and never got caught until the owner died. That's smart, Randy. You're good. I have trouble imagining you running a clean operation with all that talent."

"Okay, so I did. So I got caught. I did five years for that, and I'm out."

"Did Mr. Neilson know about your talents, Randy? And how you used them?"

"Sure he did." West was looking pale. He kept flipping a pencil in his fingers, pushing it down on a stack of computer printout, and flipping it again. It made a soft, irritating sound. "You can't keep something like that from someone. Mr. Neilson was willing to give me a chance. Jesus! I don't know what I'm going to do now. No one else is going to hire me to do this kind of work. I was really grateful—but I put in a hell of a lot of hours for him. Working nights and all."

"What did Neilson have on you?" asked Sanders quietly.

"What do you mean?"

"He must have had something on you, just to make sure you stayed in line. To keep your fingers out of the cash. He liked having things on people, didn't he, Randy? He was that sort of guy."

West smiled, a big open smile, and swallowed hard. "You guys are great kidders, eh? Real sense of humor. You don't need to have something on a bookkeeper who's been in for embezzling. Think about it. I needed this job. Real bad. And I dunno where you get this stuff about Mr. Neilson. I never heard any of it."

"You remember Mrs. Neilson's birthday party, Randy? Maybe you helped Mr. Neilson organize it. It was here. Lots of people, lots of booze, everything. Costume party, wasn't it?"

The big open smile returned to his face. "A birthday party for *Mrs.* Neilson?" He looked puzzled, very puzzled, and shook his head. "Gee, I don't remember anything about that. Mr. Neilson had parties here sometimes, but Mrs. Neilson never came. I don't even know what she looks like. She's one of these real quiet ladies, I guess. Homey type."

"Where does the cash go after you've finished counting it?" snapped Sanders.

"To the bank," said West, opening his eyes in candid innocence. "Oh, you mean after that. Well, strictly speaking, Mr. Neilson didn't own the place. It's owned by a corporation. NorthSea owns fifty percent of the corporation. Anyway, I deposit the receipts in a special NorthSea account, the bills get paid out of that, and the auditors make sure the corporation gets what it's supposed to get."

"Who owns the other fifty percent?"

The smile came out again. "Who knows? Could have been Mr. Neilson under another company name. He had pretty smart accountants—very good at setting up things to minimize taxes and stuff like that. All legal, of course. But very complicated."

"Then who is the guy who came here to talk to you, who seems to think he owns part of the place?" By now, Sanders's voice was very soft.

"Are you kidding? There's no one like that. Who told you that? You find him for me. I'd like a good laugh right now. Look, I got to get this done before the evening rush starts. If you don't mind."

"We'll be back, Mr. West," said Dubinsky, rising to his full height and leaning over the little bookkeeper. "You could just try to remember the name of your friend who thinks he owns the place. Because next time we come, we could be feeling a little less patient than we are now." His voice was gently caressing.

Randy West started entering figures with furious haste onto the numeric keypad.

Annie had slept most of Tuesday and Wednesday, waking to eat, a little more each time, and obediently drinking whatever liquids Rob thrust at her. Her conversation was limited to monosyllables; either she was too weak to talk or she had no taste for it. Once he had helped guard a witness who spoke only Arabic, sitting, the two of them, in a hotel room, one shift on, one off, for four days. That had been bad. This was worse. Then he had been able to watch television, dreary as it could be sometimes, to pass the time. And he had felt that the man would have talked to him if he could have. Now he could only pace around the echoing room. When she was sleeping, he ventured outside in the sun, shaking himself like a bear come out of hibernation, stretching and stamping his feet and taking great gulps of outdoor air. He was impatient for her to get better, to tell him exactly what had happened, but he felt a strong reluctance to pry.

On Thursday he was awakened by a thumping sound, looked up, and saw her hopping across the room, leaning heavily on pieces of furniture and the wall as she maneuvered her way into the bathroom by herself. When she emerged again, he was leaning against the wall outside the door.

"Tired?"

"Not that tired. I can manage," she said irritably.

"Why not let me help you back," he said, picking her up again and carrying her to her bed. She felt more solid, less likely to crack if he grabbed her too hard. And heavier. "How about some real breakfast this time?" he said, as he dropped her down.

She nodded silently and turned to look out the window.

After breakfast he went out into the woods and began to look for a suitable piece of timber. He found a pine branch, relatively straight, ripped green off its tree by some violent winter storm. He had already picked up a hunting knife and a whetstone from the garage; he settled himself in the sun on the deck and began to turn the branch into a usable cane. Stripped of its bark and sanded a little, it gleamed palely in the sun. He purloined a heavy-duty rubber tip from a leg of the barbecue and slipped it on. He sacrificed one of his cotton T-shirts to make a padded handgrip on the top, fastened on by four neatly placed tiny nails. He returned the tools to the garage, walked back into the cottage, and solemnly placed the cane at the foot of her bed.

She stared at it. "It's for you," he said at last. "A cane. Crutches would have been better, I suppose, but they're harder to make."

"Thank you," she said at last. "That's nice of you." Her voice was dull and unenthusiastic.

He was nettled. He wasn't expecting long speeches of gratitude, but he had spent a hell of a long time making that thing. He reverted to silence. Two could play that game. He fetched the medical bag that Mike had put together for him and began the daily routine of changing her dressings. The gunshot wound was not beautiful—the scar was red, thick, and jagged—but it had almost healed; the skin around it looked clean and healthy. There was no point in replacing the dressing, he decided.

The foot had always been a different story. Scarlet, inflamed, oozing, infected, for days it had looked unstoppable, intent on eating away her flesh. Only massive willpower had kept him from gagging whenever he uncovered it. But that day, as he carefully peeled the old bandage off, small areas of thin reddish new skin were visible around the edges of the wound. In his excitement he forgot his punctured self-esteem.

"It's getting better," he said, as he cautiously placed a new pad where the old one had been and then bandaged over it. "A lot better. All of a sudden."

She nodded. "Thank you for the cane," she said. "It will help."

On Friday she sat up most of the morning. She had insisted on negotiating the potentially hazardous path to the bathroom entirely by herself, leaning on her pine cane, and the sense of independence it gave her seemed to have cheered her up. She still only spoke when he goaded her into it, and he was beginning to realize how very dependent on human conversation he was.

In a celebratory mood, he opened a bottle of beer, some smoked oysters and other oddities he found in the Buchanans' well-stocked cupboards, and set out a small hors d'oeuvre plate on the bed before lunch. Annie was drinking fruit juice mixed with soda water—something she seemed to have acquired a taste for in her delirium—and looking soberly out at the lake. In the eight or nine days since they had arrived, the ice had almost disappeared, even from the shaded coves. The only trace of winter was the occasional patch of snow trapped under thick growth in the woods.

"You know," he said. "People keep telling me you're a singer. Why don't you sing?"

"What do you mean?" she asked.

"Even my mother used to sing sometimes—under her breath, and not very well, but she sang. When she was happy, I suppose, or concentrating on something."

"The only thing I concentrate on when I'm singing," said Annie coldly, "is singing."

"I suppose I deserved that. So sing something. Concentrate."

"What would you like?" she asked. As if he had suggested that she make him some lunch. "Opera? Pop? Folk moderne? Folk genuine? Folk artsy? English madrigal style? Lieder? Italian or French art song? Take your pick. If there's one thing I got, it's repertoire. I am not equally good at all of it, but you pays your money and you takes your chances."

He shook his head. "Sing something you like—something you feel like singing," he said, and walked over to the window, in case she was put off by having him three feet away.

"Then I shall sing 'Down by the Salley Gardens,' " she

said. "Nothing fancy. It's Yeats, you know, and very pretty."

She straightened up a bit, settled her shoulders, and sang, "Down." Her voice quavered, lost, and began searching for the note she started with, turned husky, and died away. He stared at the lake, burning with embarrassment, unable to face her. For chrissake, she was absolutely awful. He should have known better.

"Sorry," she said calmly. "It's been a while. Wrong key. Drastically wrong key." This time "Down" was pitched higher—much higher. It grew and then faded softly, gathered strength, and the figure of the first line soared upward. He turned back in astonishment. Her voice, clear and rich, and yet totally unornamented, filled the room. He held his breath, terrified now that it could not last, that the hoarseness and quavery pitch would return. Almost without wanting to, he came closer and then crouched by the coffee table to bring himself down to her level. Here he realized that she didn't see him at all. She was singing to a huge audience somewhere out across the lake, and he looked down at the floor, making himself a part of that audience. She toyed lightly with every playful, heartbreaking word of the little song until, with a wry grimace, she came to "But I was young and foolish, and now . . ." She paused. "—am full—" Her voice hoarsened, cracked and stopped again.

He looked up, surprised. The tears that were supposed to end the song were pouring down her face. She shielded herself from his gaze with her right hand and clumsy, plastered, left wrist, sobbing now, helpless to control her grief. He got up and walked over to the bed, sat down beside her, and put an arm around her shoulders.

"Don't touch me," she gasped, and then began to cry even harder.

He got up again and headed for the bedroom, reached into his overnight bag, and extracted a large, clean linen handkerchief, elegant, expensive, monogrammed—another little offering from his stepmother. "Here," he said, once he was sitting down beside her again. "This works better than plaster of paris." He opened up the handkerchief and thrust it into her good hand. Now she buried her face in it, still sobbing.

He waited for a minute, two minutes. "I don't know if it will help," he said. "But you have a magnificent voice. I was overwhelmed." It didn't seem to help. She continued to cry, each sob turning into a huge gasping intake of breath.

He couldn't stand watching her so unhappy and comfortless, with no one to turn to but him—and he was clearly the last person she wanted to depend on. "Annie," he said helplessly, "Annie, darling, please—" and, astonished at himself even as he did it, he wrapped his arms around her and pulled her against his chest. She stiffened and then let herself fall against him, burying her face in the harsh wool of his sweater. He wanted desperately to lift that unhappy face, to kiss the tears from her eyes and cheeks, to murmur mad things in her ears, and now it was his turn to hold himself still and in check. It was one thing to comfort a weeping woman who was sick and in distress—anyone could do that; it was quite another to transport a wounded, helpless creature forcibly to a remote spot in the woods and then to rain kisses on her. There were nasty terms for that— many of them in the criminal code—and in his innocence or stupidity he had never thought this out. "Christ," he murmured into her tangle of black hair, "this is one hell of a complication."

When had he fallen for her? Listening to her sing? Way before that, he realized. Before he nursed her through those dark nights or carried her away from her cabin or spent all those hours searching for her. It must have been when he thought she was dead and then saw the body of the real Jennifer Wilson—and suddenly he could see her gray eyes mocking him, could see her holding up the sleeve of his sweater and telling him he was beautiful. Don't kid yourself, Lucas, he said to himself. Ever since the day you met her, you've been pursuing her like some demented fool.

The convulsive sobs began to ease, and he had to fight not to hold her tighter. He ran his right hand lightly over her hair, smoothing it back, allowing himself the luxury of resting his cheek against it for an instant. She began to straighten herself up, and he released her hastily. He turned away to hide his burning cheeks and said the first thing that came into his head. "Listening to you sing, it suddenly came to me why all those rich bastards, the bloated robber barons of this world, go batty over singers. Imagine having all that—"

Annie blew her nose fiercely and turned to face him. Her nose was red, her eyes swollen, her face blotchy. Unlike his stepmother, who could cry at will—and did—and look both pathetic and elegant as she did it, she did not cry well. She hiccuped. "Was that supposed to be funny? Or just in appalling bad taste?" she snapped. It was almost the longest unprompted sentence he had heard from her since they had arrived at the cottage. "I'll have you know that I never ever sang for—" She couldn't bring out the name. Her eyes began to look watery again.

"You're not going to believe me," said Lucas, furious at his thoughtlessness, "but I was thinking of Callas captivating the shipping king. I had forgotten all about Neilson. I find it very easy to forget him."

"I find it pretty hard," she said bitterly.

"I wouldn't have thought he was that memorable," said Lucas. "After all, if the relationship was purely business, he can't have been much of a personal loss." There was a nasty edge to his voice, and he had no trouble identifying it. Jealousy.

"My God, what do you think of me?" she said. "No, I know what you think of me. You've sure as hell told enough people. You think I'm a cheap, nasty little whore. You'd prefer me if I called myself a hooker and went out and picked up anybody on the street, wouldn't you? That would appeal to your goddamn perverted masculine vision of women, wouldn't it? Then I could have been the prostitute with the heart of gold. As it is, you think I'm a cheap whore with pretensions—the kind that calls herself an artiste or a model or something. Only in my case it's a singer, isn't it? You were surprised that I can sing, weren't you? I saw it—you were bloody astonished. You couldn't have been more surprised if that chipmunk out there had started singing Puccini. Admit it—you were surprised." The thought of his reaction brought a grin to her face in the midst of the blotchy cheeks and scarlet nose.

He blushed, hating himself. "Okay, I admit it—I was surprised. I didn't ask you to sing to trap you, though, if that's what you think. I was just trying to make conversation. Honest." He stopped for a moment. "And I'm sorry it made you unhappy. Believe me, I'd never have asked you to do it if I had thought it would make you unhappy."

She looked at him oddly for a moment and then shook her head. "It wasn't your fault. I shouldn't have sung that song. It runs too close to the bone. And besides, it reminds me of my mother. And the old days, before things got so . . . complicated." She fell back on the pillows. "I'm tired," she said. "I'd like to be left alone, if you don't mind. Can't you ever leave me bloody well alone?"

He grabbed his jacket and went out by the kitchen door, followed a small path through the woods down to the smooth granite that edged the lake. He sat down and stared into the water. At last he picked up a small rock and threw it, hard, into the smooth surface. A gull came gliding around the point, looking rather hopeful. "I'm going crazy," he said to it. "Locked up here with a nutty woman. Whom I am falling madly in love with against my will, and she hates me. No wonder I'm going crazy." The gull was either uninterested or on her side. It gave him a distinctly cold look and reversed its direction. "To hell with you, too," said Lucas vehemently and threw another rock into the water, this one right off its port wing. It squawked, shook its feathers, and flew off to the east.

Rob Lucas sat on the smooth, cold granite and stared into the icy lake. His mind darted about in a multitude of directions: love, desire, suspicions of complicity in murder, haunting melodies. He was doomed to have that song in his head for days. He stood up with a sigh—he seemed to be doing a lot of sighing lately—and turned to go back to the cottage. He couldn't stay out here forever. He'd die of exposure. And besides, he was hungry.

One step, though, and he halted. Bouncing over the lake, from its far western end, he heard a sound so foreign to this deserted place that it took him a second or two to identify it. But no more than that. It was the sound of a noisy internal combustion engine. A car with a faulty muffler or a motorcycle.

CHAPTER 14

A panic-stricken voice calling Rob's name sent him racing back up the path toward the cottage. The kitchen door was swinging open. He caught it by the edge, using it to propel himself inside.

Annie stood in the kitchen, one hand on the counter, the other clutching her makeshift cane, in nightgown and bare feet, her face gray with terror. "There's a car coming."

"It's okay," he said. "I heard it. Go back to bed. As fast as you can." He closed and bolted the door, pulled the curtains over the horizontal slits up near the ceiling that acted as windows, and turned off the light. "Turn on the lamp beside the bed," he called. "I need it to see what I'm doing." Then with speed born of practice, he lowered and locked the shutters on all the French doors. The engine noise faded away; a delusion, he knew. Those shutters were partially soundproof. He looked around. Light seeped in from the master bedroom. It, too, had broad window slits placed high on the wall; he yanked its lined curtains closed.

He raced into the bathroom. Once again he could hear the sound, closer now. This bathroom had no curtains. Susie must have felt that the window had been placed too high for privacy to be a problem. Lucas had less faith. He grabbed all the towels, face cloths, bath mats and toiletries he could carry and dumped them on the bed. One more glance assured him that the room looked at least temporarily unused. He went out and closed the door. He had never used the other bathroom between the master suite and the kitchen. He shut that door as well. The noise of the engine was now very loud. That should be— "Dammit!" he muttered. The laundry. He ran back into the kitchen, into the laundry room. It had a rather ordinary window, covered with a mesh security grill, through which one could see the driveway and the garage. And be seen. He tumbled all the clean and dirty laundry into the basket and slipped out, shutting the door behind him. The engine noise was deafening now in the silence of spring. He walked back into the living room, dropped the basket of laundry, and sat down on the foot of Annie's bed.

"You'd better turn out the light," he murmured. The engine noise stopped, and Lucas could hear Annie breathing like an exhausted sprinter. She leaned over and turned out the light. The darkness was almost complete. Lucas slid over to the couch he had been sleeping on and reached under the pillow for his pistol. He walked quietly back and set it down beside the lamp. He could feel, rather than hear, Annie crying beside him.

"Move over," he whispered, and sat, one leg stretched out in front of him and the other on the floor, leaning against the sofa back. He put his arm tightly around Annie's shoulders. "Don't worry," he murmured in her ear. "We're pretty tightly locked in here."

"What are they doing?" she whispered back.

"Walking around the place. Looking for a way in."

"Who are they?"

"Small town hoods. Or maybe the police. But it doesn't matter, Annie. They can't get in."

"They might have a key."

"Won't help. The kitchen door is dead-bolted shut."

"It's them," she said. She began to shake. "I know it's them."

"Sh. If it is, they won't get anywhere near you. Sweet-heart, I'm a cop. I'm armed. I'm even trained. I have to be good for something."

A heavy thump interrupted him. "Shit!" said a loud voice. "Locked up tighter 'n a monkey's ass. Shoulda brought Glen's welding stuff—we coulda torched the place open."

"For chrissake, don't be a fucking asshole. You wanna start a goddamn forest fire and have the whole fucking system coming down on us—helicopters and everything? Try the window."

There was another loud thump. "Jesus. You got any more stupid ideas? Who in hell can get in that window? It's too fucking small."

"Jimmy could."

There was a pause. For thought, presumably. "Naw. That's dumb. You bring Jimmy out here and shove him through that window, the whole town knows in five minutes. That kid don't know how to shut up."

"I thought your ma said someone was living here."

"For chrissake, don't you ever listen? She was over cleaning out the MacDonald place and said she saw someone outside. That's all. So we can tell her no one's here. That should be good for twenty-five bucks. That's all we need. I mean, she's supposed to keep an eye on things, isn't she? Now she doesn't have to come out. Anyways, let's get the hell out of here. If Ma finds out . . ." The voices drifted off. The engine started again with an ear-pounding roar and began its long journey away from them.

Rob Lucas realized that he was clutching Annie's shoulder so hard she must be in pain. He loosened his fingers and gently massaged the offended place.

"Have they gone?" she whispered.

"Oh, yes, they've gone. I doubt if they'll come back. And even if they did," he added, "I think we could buy them off with fifty bucks."

"It was just kids." Her voice was tight and strange. "Just

kids. And I was scared, Robin. I wanted a little dark closet to hide in."

He shuddered and rubbed her shoulder again.

"Robin," she went on, "there's just one thing—"

"Mmm?" he murmured vaguely, giving most of his attention to the dying engine sounds.

"What are we doing here?"

"What did you say?"

"I said, what are we doing here? Way out in the middle of nowhere, just the two of us? What are you doing looking after me?"

He turned to try to see her expression in the darkness and failed.

"If I'm a witness, why aren't there other cops around? Don't you get time off? And whose cottage is this?"

"Have you been worrying about this since we got here?" he asked. "You should have said something."

"No. Actually, it never even occurred to me until today. And then I began to wonder why they would send one cop off to look after a sick witness for a week or so without any relief. Why wasn't I in the hospital? I mean, you are a cop, aren't you? Not just one of those guys—"

"—who likes to lock women up in private hidey-holes? Oh, Jesus, no, Annie. I'm not sure if I'm still a cop, either. And the reason we're alone is that no one knows where we are—except for a friend of mine who sort of lent us the cottage. It belongs to his wife's sister."

"Then what in hell is going on?"

"Listen to me, Annie. There's a reason for all of this. Remember when I dropped you off at the motel? Well, I filed a report, saying where you were. Okay? Standard procedure. Next thing I hear, your motel room has been entered forcibly and you are gone. I think I am chasing someone called Jennifer Wilson. I find out where she lives, file my report, and Jennifer Wilson is murdered."

"Oh my God." Annie drew her breath in horror and

began to tremble again. "Jennifer? My roommate, Jennifer?"

Lucas nodded. "I'm afraid so."

"Because I used her name? I didn't mean to involve her. I was so scared that it was the first thing that came into my head." Her voice died away.

He put both arms around her and held her. "It wasn't your fault. If anything, it was the fault of the woman next door. Some man came around asking questions, and she identified a bad description of you as Jennifer. Anyway, I finally found out who you were and the name of your lawyer. He told me you were at the cabin, I filed a report, did a few other things, and then drove up to talk to you. Someone got there before I did. I may be slow, but by this time even I have figured out that I am the connection. Someone is reading my reports and passing on the information to the people who killed Neilson. And they want to get rid of you because you saw them."

She shook her head, still muffled in his sweater. "No, I didn't see them. I was hiding in the apartment. I heard them."

"Heard them? Where in hell from? Not the coat closet. You would have had to move the body to get out. And the body wasn't moved."

She shivered. "No, not the coat closet. I was in the linen cupboard in the bathroom. Behind the bath towels. It was a tight fit."

"Well, I'll be damned," he said, with admiration. "It didn't occur to us anyone could get in there. You are a resourceful woman, Miss Hunter."

"No, a skinny, terrified woman."

"Could you recognize their voices again?"

"Oh, yes. I'll never forget those voices. And I've heard them twice, remember. All that ear training, Sergeant. It comes in handy sometimes."

"Well, to get back to my story, I may be a slow thinker,

but it finally occurred to me—once I got my hands on you—that letting anyone know where you were might be worse for your health than me looking after you. So here we are. My superior officers are probably livid with rage. I phoned in and said that I was in the Deerton hospital with multiple fractures. They must have figured out by now that I'm not there. I expect I've been slung out of the force."

"But why? Why have you done this? Why risk—"

There was silence. "I'm not sure," he said finally and changed the topic. "Do you want me to raise the shutters?"

"Oh, please don't. In case they come back." She reached over him, brushing her hair across his face, and turned on the small lamp beside him. "There. I hate talking about important things to someone I can't see. It's like fighting on the phone. Can't be done satisfactorily." Her voice had changed in a subtle way that he couldn't quite assess.

Lucas's first impulse was to turn the light off again and hide his desperate need under cover of darkness. Blood was pounding through his arteries with uncontrollable violence; his face must be scarlet. Every breath was ragged and undisciplined. Annie sat up beside him, pulling her uninjured foot under the other leg, perched like an inquisitive child. "I think I'd better go," he said hoarsely, "and see if those kids did any damage to the place." He pushed himself up.

Annie caught him by the arm. "Don't go," she said. "They didn't do anything. We would have heard if they had. Stay here and talk to me."

His arm burned under her touch; desire coiled in him like a tightly wound spring. He laced his fingers together and sat straight, his back rigid, concentrating on two thoughts: you kidnapped her, Lucas; she is sick and injured. "Really, I better go out and check the place," he said again. He tried to move, but the hand on his arm seemed to fasten him to the spot. He could no more shake it off than tear off his own arm.

He took a deep breath and tried to concentrate on something else this time. "Do you ever call yourself Anne?" he asked.

"No," she said. "Never."

"Why not?" he said desperately. "It's a very nice name."

"That may be, but my name isn't Anne, so I don't. It'd be stupid to call myself that, wouldn't it? You don't call yourself Jason, do you? Or Frank?" She pulled her hand away from his arm in irritation.

That was better. He could deal with his lust when she was feeling combative. "So—what is your name? Or are you really Annie? No, I'll bet it's Anna. I've known a couple of Annas. But they would have killed anyone who called them Annie."

"No." There was a pause. "No one calls me by my real name. Well, my mother used to. My dad never liked it, though. He was the one who called me Annie."

"So what is it? You have me intrigued. Very intrigued. All sorts of interesting possibilities are running through my brain: Augusta? Hermione? Cleopatra. How about Delilah?" His subconscious mind was beginning to do odd things to him.

"Not that interesting. Although it is an odd name around here, I suppose. It's Irish—quite common, really. Grainne. Rhymes with Sonia, spelled G-r-a-i-n-n-e, but no one can remember how to spell it or pronounce it, so it's a drag sometimes."

"Grainne," he said softly. "It's beautiful. Grainne," he repeated, drawing the syllables out.

"Grainne Mary Dermot Hunter. That's me. My mother was Irish."

"That seems evident," he said. She smiled and placed her hand on his arm again, poised as if to say something. His stomach lurched, and his precariously gained self-control fled. "I really must go out and check," he muttered, and pulled himself free of her. He swung his left leg off the couch and set his foot on the floor beside the other one.

"Robin, what's the matter with you?" she asked, whether in malice or innocence he couldn't tell. "Are you angry?"

"No. I am not angry. Far from it. Or not at you. At myself, maybe." He gripped the arm of the couch until his knuckles whitened. "For chrissake, Annie, just let me get out of here."

Suddenly her eyes filled with tears again. "I'm sorry," she muttered. "I keep forgetting. You're stuck here because of me, and you must be going stir-crazy." She tried to laugh. "It'd be different if I was a gorgeous blonde, wouldn't it? Not just some—" Her voice died away and she turned her head.

"Oh, my God," he said, twisting his torso around to face her. "Annie—Grainne—whoever you are, do you have any idea what you're up to? Do you enjoy teasing the hell out of me? Or are you just being incredibly stupid?" He grabbed her face, forcing her to look at him. "What color is your damned hair, anyway?"

"My hair? It's nothing special. Not this color." She blinked the tears out of her eyes, blushing with embarrassment. "And I don't know what I'm up to. All I know is that sometimes you're absolutely wonderful, as if you like me, and then suddenly you treat me like a piece of dirt. I'm confused, Robin. I'm not very good at figuring men out. I've never had much to do with them, except as friends, you know. I always worked too hard—we all did—for going out and things like that, and anyway, lots of the guys I know are gay and so—"

Lucas's bitter laughter cut her off. "Oh, Annie—" He turned his back to her again. "It's not confusing at all. I am an ordinary heterosexual male who has fallen in love with you, and I can hardly keep my hands off you, and I'm suffering hideous pangs of conscience and a sense of violated ethics." Her face turned scarlet. "Dammit, don't you see? If you could simply call a cab and waltz out of here, it would be different. I'd be plying you with champagne and soft music and chasing you all around the furniture, no doubt. But you can't chase a woman who can't run. You can't. And so—I think I'll go for a walk."

"Wait," she said, breathlessly. "Don't I have a say in this? What if I didn't want to run? Wouldn't that make a difference?"

"You did want to—I could tell. I can always tell."

"Only because you looked at me like—"

"Sh." He turned back to look at her again. "That was temporary insanity on my part. Occasioned, I fear, by jealousy. Jealousy I had no right to." He began to stand up.

Grainne Hunter caught the back of the couch to balance herself and stretched out her left arm in its awkward cast. "Wait," she cried again. There was desperation in her voice. "Robin, look at me. You can't do this. You can't say things like that and then just walk out. It isn't fair." He turned slowly back and found himself staring into her eyes. Suddenly they filled with tears. "It's just an excuse, isn't it? I've got it backward. You don't want me," she said flatly. "I'm too covered in filth. Because of—" Her voice shook with contempt and loathing for herself, and her cheeks burned once more. "Damn it," she said, and let herself fall onto the pillow.

"Oh, Annie," he murmured helplessly and sat down again. "What in hell am I supposed to do?" He lifted her gently by the shoulders and pulled her toward him; she turned her unhappy face in his direction. Without pausing to think, he kissed her eyes, letting the salt of her tears linger for a moment on his tongue, and then brushed her lips tentatively with his own. He felt a tremendous shudder run through her; her lips swelled and softened in response, and her body pressed against him, melting into his. He released himself gently for a moment. "I've never wanted anyone or anything more desperately in my entire life," he said, his voice uncertain. He looked up at some invisible censor hovering above him. "Dammit, I tried. You can't say

I didn't try." Giving up at last, he pushed her nightgown up, running his hands over her with ferocious hunger. She raised her right arm and ducked out of the voluminous garment, sliding it awkwardly over the cast. He lowered her gently back down and regarded her for a moment. It was the first time he had allowed himself to see her as anything but a collection of hurt places and surfaces that needed to be kept clean and dry. In that gentle side light, casting its shadows across the planes of her body, she was awesomely beautiful. He ran an exploratory finger lightly between her breasts and down across her concave belly before standing up abruptly.

She lay back, watching him with solemn eyes as he pulled off his boots and heavy sweater and struggled impatiently with shirt buttons and belt buckle.

As much as he wanted to prolong gentle preliminaries, to prove to her, somehow, that his affection would wait for months if need be, his gallantry was a dismal failure. He tossed his clothes on the floor and slipped down beside her quietly, suddenly afraid of her pallor and fragility and determined again to hold back. It was a foolish notion. At his first tentative touch, she turned to him, energized with a fierceness he could not hope to withstand. She pulled him to her; he abandoned thought, consideration, technique. They clung to each other like drowning swimmers for a few brief minutes until her low-pitched sobbing cry and final spasm carried him along with her, and it was over. Then, guiltily, he tried to ease his weight away, but she fastened her lips on his and wrapped her arms more tightly around him. He fell to the side, carrying her with him, and she slowly released her grip. It occurred to him, looking over at her as he searched with one hand and his feet for the eiderdown to pull over her, that he had probably never made love with less finesse and skill in his life, or with more passion.

She lay curled against his side, her plaster cast lying across his chest like a bandolier, and her head on his shoulder. "I

was right. You really are beautiful," she said. "Especially
with your clothes off. Much too elegant-looking for me, I'm
afraid," she added, with a small noise that he finally identified as a giggle.

"Well," he said, "handsome is as handsome does, as
someone said. And you can't have been that impressed.
Next time, I won't be so anxious."

"Impressed?" She paused for a moment and hid her face
in his shoulder. "This is the only time in my life someone
has made love to me because I wanted him to." Her voice
was almost too soft to hear. "It was . . . it was a . . . a
revelation. I really didn't know what it could be like."

"Are you serious, Grainne?" he said, raising himself up
on his elbow to look at her.

She nodded.

"Well, I wasn't just doing you a favor. I wanted you so
desperately, I couldn't think. And since I pride myself on
my sophistication and technique, that's a very embarrassing confession to make. Next time will be better—we'll have all
the time in the world to think about each other."

"But all I wanted was you," she said. Then, with a sly
sideways look, she added, "And how does it feel to be a
sex object, Sergeant? Loved for your beautiful body and
golden hair?"

He half sat and looked down at her. "You're not bad-
looking yourself," he said, and found his voice beginning
to do odd things on him again. "A little scrawny, maybe,
and a trifle beat-up looking, but otherwise, the most beautiful woman I ever saw in my life."

"Except for my hair."

"Except for your hair. I hate that color. How long is it
going to take you to grow it out?"

"It might look better when I wash it—maybe. You want
to try? Oh, Robin, can we? You'll have to help me, or I'll
get my bandages wet. It'd be easy if we had a flexible
shower head."

"I think there is one," he said. "In the other bathroom."
And so there they were. In the bathroom, with the heat
turned up, and Grainne sitting on the floor on two folded
towels, with Lucas kneeling beside her, distracted and
amused to the breaking point by their nudity and the situation, holding the shower head and staring at her massive
quantity of hair as it spilled into the tub. "Now what?" he
asked.

"Get it wet, you idiot," she said laughing. "Didn't you
ever wash your hair? It's not sex-specific, you know. It's
just hair." She reached out with her right arm and poked
him in the ribs. "To work."

"Okay. Here goes. Don't blame me if I mess it up." He
began to wet the ends very cautiously; then with added
confidence he worked his way up to her scalp.

"That feels marvelous," she murmured. "I feel as if my
hair hasn't been washed in years. Now get the shampoo,"
she added in a brisker, more practical voice. "Don't
skimp—I have a lot of hair."

He set down the shower head, flipped open the cap, and
squeezed a long, sticky pink ribbon of shampoo smelling of
herbs and nut oil onto her wet hair. He considered it a
moment and squeezed another smaller ribbon onto a different place. "You're sure you want me to—"

"Robin, I can't do it with one hand. And it's too late
now. Once you begin, you have to finish it properly."

He started with a tentative circling motion on top of her
head; not much happened. He took a courageous breath
and plunged his fingers into her hair, rhythmically rubbing
her scalp, creating mountains of foam, which he coaxed
farther and farther along her hair until they diminished to
a trickle and dried up.

He squeezed out more shampoo, picked up the curling
strands—almost waist-length and almost straight under the
weight of the water—and let them run through his soapy
hands. Grainne dropped her head back even farther over

the edge of the tub, stretching out her long pale throat; he bent over and kissed her, a warm, lingering, damp kiss, moving his hands up to massage her scalp. "Is that enough?" he asked at last, piling the sudsy mass up on top of her head.

"Enough?"

"Washing. Do you think your hair's clean?"

"My hair," she said, startled. "I'd forgotten about it for a moment. It should be. Now rinse the hell out of it."

"Yes, ma'am," he said. He picked up the shower head and looked at her. "If you got in the tub, with your cast over the side, and your bandaged foot over the back, I could give you a shower. Let me lift you in." Without waiting for a reply, he picked her up, set her carefully in the tub, and began running the warm water all over her.

She lay back, her eyes closed, passive, motionless, and devoid of expression. He began to wonder if she had fallen asleep. "Don't forget my hair," she murmured at last. "Or it'll get dried out and sticky."

He turned the water onto the piled-up mass on top of her head, watching mesmerized as it fell down, curl by curl. He brought the spray close to her scalp, driving the thick suds out. But as the shampoo ran off in streams of water, so did her hair color. Up to a point. A well-defined point, about six inches down each dripping lock. "Jesus," he said. "Annie, all the color is washing out of your hair."

"Oh, that," she said. "That's just the black goop I put on to cover the roots. It washes out."

"Your hair's brown." He said this flatly, almost accusingly.

"I know it's brown. It's my hair, after all." She opened her eyes wide, prepared for battle. "What's wrong with brown hair?"

He ignored the question. "What are you going to do with it?"

"Do with it? What do you mean?"

"Are you going to dye it again?"

"No, I hate it that color. When the roots are long enough, I'll cut off the black ends."

"You mean, like now. The roots are long enough now, Annie. Just a minute."

Fifteen minutes later Grainne Hunter was sitting in the living room, on her bed, wrapped in an eiderdown, and staring at herself in a small hand mirror. What she saw was a pair of gray eyes surrounded by an undisciplined mass of damp, light brown hair. At that moment, Robin came in with a paper bag, containing an enormous pile of wet black hair. "What would you like me to do with it?" he asked.

"Let's start a fire—a really big fire—and burn it," said Grainne. "The end of Carl Neilson." A shadow flickered across her face. "And then eat. I am absolutely starved. Aren't you?"

He knelt by the bed and took her hands, the one half-encased in plaster of paris and the long, slender one, and kissed them each in turn. "You are so beautiful, and funny, and clever, and sexy, I can't stand it. But yes. A huge fire, and a monstrous meal. And champagne, if I can find any. Because, my darling, you are never going to get rid of me. And if you won't marry me, I shall become one of those bachelors in evening clothes who goes to all of your concerts and sends you bushels of flowers, until I gradually fade away into a little pile of devoted dust." He let go her left hand and placed a silencing finger on her lips. "Don't say anything. I don't want to ruin this day with arguments. Besides, I have to start a fire."

CHAPTER 15

The late-afternoon sun poured through the only west-facing window that Lucas had left unshuttered. Yesterday's scare—although in retrospect rather anticlimactic—had been salutary. It had reminded him that the castle drawbridge was worse than useless if you couldn't get it raised before the enemy rode in. Not every vehicle coming down that road was going to give ten minutes warning time of its approach. Nevertheless, he had risked building another fire in the baronial fireplace. And here they luxuriated, Rob propped up against the side of the sofa bed, Grainne stretched out beside him, her head on his lap, watching the flames, drowsy with satisfied desire.

"We can't stay here forever, I'm afraid," said Rob, leaning over to brush her cheek with his lips.

She yawned. "Why not? I mean, at least until your friend's sister-in-law comes back. Does anyone mind? Or is the food running out?"

"It's not a question of anyone minding. It's a question of anyone finding out where we are. These beautiful fires are producing smoke for all the world to see. Our friend's ma could get suspicious and send out the cavalry." He tried to sound lighthearted and amused. "I have to get in touch with Toronto and find out what's going on."

Her reaction was even worse than he had feared. She stiffened in alarm; he could feel her trembling, even though her voice was almost steady. "Does that mean you're planning to take me back to the city?"

"Listen to me, Grainne. It's all right. We won't show our faces until they're all in jail—everyone who's after you. And if that means never, then never. We can go anywhere, you know. London, Paris. We don't have to stay in North America." He leaned over again and playfully ran a finger down her nose. "How does Oxford sound? I was thinking of going to Oxford once. Or Italy or Germany? Surely there must be superb vocal coaches all through Europe."

Grainne pushed herself up on her good elbow and stared at him. A peculiar look crossed her face. "You make it sound so . . . so plausible," she said. "As if one could just throw a few things in a bag and take off for Florence or London or Salzburg."

"What's wrong with that? One can. Do you have a passport? Somewhere in that mess of stuff I brought along?"

"Yes, I have a passport," she said crossly. "Of course. Not here. It's in my safe-deposit box. That's not the problem. Robin, my pet—and you are a pet, you know—what would we live on? You can't count on getting jobs over there, you know. There are all kinds of restrictions." He opened his mouth to respond, and she cut him off ruthlessly. "And don't tell me fellowships. They're chancy and take months to apply for. You've been too isolated working for the police force. Stuck in your little ivory tower with a government job and a regular pay check. You have no idea what it's like being poor—really poor. So poor, you can't pay your rent, you've got no cash to buy groceries, and you have no idea when the next check is coming in. It's soul-destroying. You simply don't understand the financial realities of this world." The tension had begun to seep out of her muscles as she talked. She lay down again and then flopped over on her belly, her chin resting on her good arm. He reached over and started to rub her neck and her shoulders.

"I have some money," he said cautiously to the back of her head. "In the bank, I mean. Apart from my salary."

"And how long would that last?" Her voice was slightly choked and muffled from the effects of the massage. "Oh, Robin, that's sweet of you—and I'd love to throw in my couple of thousand, and we could take a holiday and go to Europe, but in the end we'd have to come back and—"

He straightened up, releasing his hold on her, and scratched his ear. "It should be enough to live on. Or it was the last time I looked."

"Exactly how much money are we talking about?" said Grainne sharply, raising her head and looking suspiciously at him.

"Well, something over a million." He paused and then went on very rapidly. "To be precise, it was a million and a half when I was twenty-one—which was when I got it— and I haven't spent any of it, so the interest keeps being reinvested. And my grandfather left me some as well. It's probably quite a lot now. I don't bother looking at the statements." By this time Rob Lucas's face was scarlet.

"A million and a half dollars!" Grainne looked appalled. "We are talking about dollars, aren't we, not pesos or lire?" He nodded, still red and uncomfortable-looking. "Why not spend any of it? And why are you living like an ordinary mortal when you've got all that cash?"

"Well, first of all, you know, it's not *that* much money. And I didn't spend it because my father set the trust fund up for me, and I was furious at him at the time. It sounds very childish, doesn't it?"

She stared at him without answering.

He went on doggedly. "My mother had just left him, and I assumed that it was his fault. And then a couple of years later he married a thirty-year-old leggy blonde who thinks it's cute and funny to try and seduce me—and that made me even more furious."

Grainne considered this outpouring of information and settled on one portion of it. "Was it your father's fault?"

"I don't suppose so. Not entirely, anyway. I think my mother was bored. She went off and had herself rejuvenated, and now she bops around the Mediterranean with beautiful young men, looking terrific and having a wonderful time. Or so she says when she calls. She's terrified that I'll come to visit her—she's trying to pass herself off as under forty."

"And that would be difficult with you around?"

"Sure. It would have made her ten or twelve when I was born. And in answer to the question you didn't ask, I'm twenty-eight years old and in excellent health. I have a university degree (Trinity College, history); I have no neuroses or peculiarities except the ones you have already noticed. But I do have too much money, if that's a problem. And this is the first time in my life that I've been grateful for it, because it means that we really can go away—far away— until this country is safe for you."

"Whatever made you join the police force?" she asked, her eyes wide in amazement. "Instead of traveling around Europe or whatever it is rich people do."

He turned to stare into the fire in embarrassment. "Bloody-mindedness, I guess. Everyone was so damned sure that I would go to law school or into the diplomatic or something nice and prestigious like that. You know—my son, the ambassador to Tehran," he said bitterly. "Because I wasn't stupid and did well at school. I couldn't think of any career that would shake up my parents more. At least, any career that appealed to me. And it did. It was fascinating." He stopped and looked with some alarm at the expression on her face. "Does it bother you?" he asked. "That I have all that money, I mean."

"Yes, I think it does. Now I'll always wonder if I fell for you because you're rich—"

"Nonsense. You fell for me against sense and better judgment when you thought I was just a dumb sergeant in the police force. And when I said I was going to marry you, you had visions of yourself with a string of babies, struggling along on a policeman's salary—which isn't as bad as you think, by the way—and lamenting your lost singing career. Don't deny it—I saw it all running across your face. Now you find out I'm rich, and you decide that you can't have me because it would be immoral. Come on, Grainne. I'm still the same person. There could be strings of babies if you wanted, only we could afford a nanny. And that would mean you could still study. Money's not all bad. And having spent a lot of time and energy chasing you all over the countryside, I am not anxious to let you go." By now he was breathless.

"But why do you have to get in touch with Toronto? As soon as they hear from you they'll start searching even harder for us. For me."

"Look, Grainne, you don't want to *have* to leave. All right? I've nothing against living in Europe if we want to, in fact, nothing against living in Europe if we have to, but the best solution is to dispose of the people who are after you. Legally." He took a deep breath and grasped her hand. "You must know something, Grainne, something that can get them caught and convicted—otherwise they wouldn't be so anxious to find you. If we can get that information back to the department, to the right people at the department—"

"Who is it?" she asked quietly. "The wrong person in the police department?"

"I don't know," he said, with a certain desperation in his voice. "But there's only one person who saw all my reports, who insisted on knowing everything I knew almost before I knew it—and getting around him is going to be a hell of a problem. But it can be done, if you'll tell me what you know. Grainne, if you didn't see anything, then what did you hear?"

"Only gunfire. And then their voices when they were searching the apartment. They were sure I was there because of that stupid perfume and everything, but they didn't find me."

"What did they talk about?"

"Just that. The fact that I was there, and then they crashed around swearing because they couldn't find me."

"Men?"

She shivered. "I think so. Both of them. Although one was fairly short. Still, he moved like a man, I think. I'm not positive, though."

"I thought you said you didn't see them?"

"Not there. I saw them at the cabin. Their faces were covered with ski masks, but the one with the loud voice was a really big guy—as big as you, maybe bigger. The other was smaller. Thin build, maybe five foot nine."

"Not that small."

She shook her head. "Only in comparison with the first one. And he was strong. They both were."

How strong was strong, compared to Grainne? Not very, he concluded. Irrelevant detail. He was getting nowhere, fast. "And they didn't say anything you can remember?"

"They wanted to know what I had told you."

"Me? Did they mention me by name?" His mind raced through the other people who had known he had interviewed her, trying to come up with one who was five nine and wiry.

"I can't remember. I can't remember if they said your name or just called you the cop who interviewed me." She rolled over and looked up at him with a worried frown. "Sorry."

"That's okay." He smoothed her forehead with a gentle hand. "Did they say anything else?"

She shook her head.

"Well, how about Neilson? Maybe he said something. Was he expecting them to turn up?"

She closed her eyes. When they opened again, they were suspiciously damp, but she was looking at him with steady calm. "Something was going on that afternoon."

He opened his mouth to ask, and she raised a hand.

"Let me just tell you what I can remember before you interrupt me. Now, it was something big. Because there was champagne in the refrigerator. I'd never seen him be that extravagant before. And he was in a wild mood, prancing around like a billy goat, pleased as hell with himself. He brought a huge wad of money out of his pocket right after he poured the wine and peeled off twenty-five hundred dollars in fifty- and hundred-dollar bills. He told me to put it toward my pension, and then he laughed like crazy. I shoved it in my skirt pocket, and he thought that was pretty funny, too." She paused for a moment, staring into the fire before recommencing. "And then he said that he was getting the last installment on his pension that afternoon as well, and he hoped that I would spend mine as happily as he was going to spend his. Which I took to mean that he had a very big deal closing that afternoon. Money affected him like that. He hadn't touched his wine, and already he was higher than a kite. I think that was all, except that when they knocked on the door, he told me to hide in the bathroom. He didn't want them to know there was anyone in the apartment with him. The rest you know." She turned her head away to avoid his eyes.

Lucas thought of the tangled bedclothes and the thick reddened lips of the corpse. What she had told him was far from all; he was profoundly grateful for that.

"Why did he call it a pension?" he asked, hastening to break the thickening silence growing between them.

Grainne's voice had become brittle; she propped her head up on her arm and stared ahead of her into the fire. "I don't know. I didn't think about it at the time, and I've been trying very hard not to think about it since. A pension. I assumed he was referring to the amount."

"Could he have been giving you the golden handshake?"

Her head swiveled in his direction; her eyes widened in surprise for a moment, and then she giggled suddenly. "Firing me? With two months' pay in lieu of notice? What a bizarre thought. I suppose he could have been. Farewell performance, lights out, and it's back to auditions on Monday? When you put it that way, it's quite possible."

"It sounds as though he was expecting someone to turn up with a huge amount of money, and then he was planning to take off. Somewhere pleasant. But not, thank God, with you." He picked up her hands. "Grainne, let me ask this one thing—and then, I swear, I'll never mention it again. Just tell me why you got involved with him. If you know."

"You really want to know?"

He nodded.

"And you'd never mention it again?" Her voice was heavy with scorn. "It wouldn't be your favorite subject every time you're angry or irritated?"

"I'm positive," he said calmly.

"Well," she said, an edge of doubt creeping into her voice, "if you want me to talk about it, I suppose I'd better get it over with." She turned her head away from his gaze and then grabbed a blanket to pull defensively over her. "I certainly know why I did it," she said flatly. "I was broke, I owed two months' rent, and my father had died. As far as I could see, I was facing stark poverty, and there was no one, basically, to ask for help."

"That's not true," said Lucas. "You weren't thinking clearly. There are an awful lot of people trying to help you." He raised his hand to prevent her from commenting. "No, just listen to me for a minute. I have a whole lot of messages for you, and what with one thing and another, I forgot to pass them on. But Mrs. Dubchek wants you back at the Faculty—she swears that there are grants just waiting for you to pick up. Your singing coach is devastated that you've disappeared and wants you to come back and start working again and stop worrying. Mr. Hennessy sounded as if he and his wife wanted to adopt you. I have a helluva lot of competition from other people wanting to look for you."

Tears welled up once more in Grainne's eyes, and she shook her head. "I was scared. I was frightened that I'd end up waiting on tables or working in a store, too tired to practice or go to class, and I'd have thrown away years of work and hopes—everything. Anyway, Mrs. Neilson brought Carl to see a production of *Lulu* that I was in—"

"In which you sang the lead," added Rob. "Brilliantly. I've been researching you."

She blushed. "And there was a party afterward for the patrons—apparently Mrs. Neilson had donated a lot of money to the Faculty, and so they were invited, of course. I don't suppose Carl liked music that much, but he really went batty over the Lulu costume, including that horrible hair color. He asked me out to lunch and made me this incredible offer. It was like something out of a nineteenth-century opera. I didn't know things like that still happened. Anyway, it seemed to be the answer to all my problems. Lots of money—by my standards, if not by yours—and limited demands on my time. What I didn't know," she added bitterly, "was that Carl Neilson's money poisoned everything it paid for. I couldn't sing, not while I was dependent on him. I tried to explain that to him," she added in an uncertain voice, "but he seemed to feel we had some sort of unbreakable contract, and he just kept sending Cassidy— the chauffeur—to get me." She stopped and took a deep breath. "There's one other thing I want to do." She sat up, allowing the blanket to fall to her lap, and gestured impatiently over at a chair where Lucas had thrown her large leather purse. "Could you get me that?"

Lucas walked over, picked up the purse, and handed it to her. She unzipped the wide opening and took out a smaller purse. From it she pulled a roll of bills. "There it is," she said. "I kept it because I was frightened, and I thought I might need it to get away again. But it paid for the motel room where I was almost caught, and for the groceries at the cabin, and look what happened there." She looked intently at him. "Do you swear you won't leave me up here? Because once I'm in the city I can look after myself. Swear?"

He nodded, speechless.

"Then throw it in the fire. It belongs with the hair. It's cursed, that money, and if I gave it away, it would just wreck the person I gave it to. Please."

"With or without the elastic band?" he asked, taking the roll as coolly as if he frequently kindled fires with hundred-dollar bills.

"Without. That was mine." Her face cracked in a half smile. "Besides, it would smell."

He took off the elastic band and tossed the money into the heart of the dying fire. It blazed up merrily for a moment or two and then died away. He reached for another log and covered the place where it had been.

"Good-bye forever, Carl Neilson, you slimy, vicious bastard," said Grainne, staring into the blaze. Sitting there, unselfconsciously naked to the waist, she looked like a bizarrely ripe ten-year-old, performing some childish, solemn rite, and his heart ached in sympathy. She turned to Lucas, her face grave and composed. "And now you'll never know whether I made that beautiful and heartrending gesture because I really am a wonderful woman who doesn't give a damn about money, or whether I was just trying to impress the hell out of you because I found out you were rich."

"Mercenary little bitch," he said, kneeling beside her and catching her in his arms. "Now that you are penniless and at my mercy, I shall take you to my castle in the country and lock you up with my other wives." He smothered her

giggles with his lips. "I think," he said, as he came up for
air, "that I'll close the shutters, raise the drawbridge, lower
the portcullis, and shut out the world. We don't want to be
disturbed, do we?"

"No," she murmured. "We don't."

By ten o'clock Monday morning, Lucas had been up for
four hours, trying to restore the cottage to the state of clean-
liness and order that Susie would expect. At nine he had
awakened Grainne, who showed signs of possessing an
unlimited capacity for sleep, now that she was recovering,
and they had eaten the last of the bacon and frozen waffles
from the Buchanans' freezer. He had given Susie's list one
last check in reverse, torn a page from his notebook, and
written quite simply, "Dear Mr. and Mrs. Buchanan. Someday I will thank you in a better fashion. I hope this will
reimburse you for everything we used. R.L." He had slipped
it with five hundred dollars into an envelope he had found
in a drawer.

While he had been looking around for a place to set the
envelope, Grainne had limped in from the bedroom, cautiously allowing her weight to settle on the heel of her
injured foot. She had stopped in front of him, fully dressed,
a hiking boot on one foot, heavy sock on the other, her cane
clutched in her hand, and tears in her eyes. "I'm ready," she
had said, in tones of one standing under the guillotine.

"What's wrong?"

"I don't want to leave. I've been so happy these last few
days. I never knew I could—" The tears threatened to spill
over. "Why do we have to go back now?"

"Sit down," he had said quickly, afraid that the wave of
sentimentality generated by her words would engulf him
completely. "We have to. And that's why. So we can be
happy. Everywhere. Not just here." He knelt on the floor

to bring himself to her level and placed his hands on her knees. "Grainne, I'll go mad if I have to live with the thought that someone is— No. Let me say it this way. I want you to be able to stand on a stage anywhere without worrying that someone wants to kill you. If I don't succeed, then so be it—I'll hide you as well as anyone was ever hidden. But I have to try. God, that sounds melodramatic," he said bitterly. "But dammit, that's what it is." He stood up again. "I'll get the car started and then come and get you." And he rushed out. Once the car was warm, he came back in, gathered her up in his arms, and carried her out, just as he had carried her in so many ages before.

And now he was looking for the least conspicuous route back to the city. The car and its license plates were bound to be on everyone's wish list; any passing local or provincial patrol car might notice them and have some dim memory that they were of interest. Grainne sat silent beside him, taut and apprehensive, staring out over the brown, muddy landscape of early spring.

They crested a rise; there was a tiny hamlet in front of them with a shabby store and an outside telephone. "I think I had better make some phone calls," said Lucas.

"Who to?" She looked ready to run at any moment.

"I'm looking for another quiet, pleasant, and very safe place to stash you, my love," he said, as he slowed down and pulled over onto the concrete in front of the store. "So I don't have to worry about you." He smiled and dropped a kiss on her forehead before getting out. In two minutes he was back. "There," he said. "Easier than I expected."

"Where are you taking me?" she asked fearfully.

"Into the bosom of my family, so to speak. Than which there is no place safer, I assure you."

"In Toronto?"

"Where else?"

"We'll never get that far. They'll be looking for us."

"Very true. Which is why in an hour or so we will pick up another car which will discreetly transport us into the city. Don't worry."

Ed Dubinsky picked up the telephone and identified himself with a yawn. "Yeah, that's right," he said and paused. "How long have they been there?" he asked. A certain alertness was beginning to creep into his voice. "No," he said after a while, "leave them. We'll pick them up." He dropped the phone down again and turned to John Sanders. "That was Mr. Sigurdson from the hotel," he said. "He wants to know what to do with Carl Neilson's suitcases. They've been sitting there since the day he was murdered."

"Jesus," muttered Sanders. "And no one mentioned them?"

"Apparently not. Didn't think they were interesting enough, I guess. The chauffeur dropped them off with the deskman, and they're still there."

"For chrissake, didn't someone interview the chauffeur?"

"Must have," said Dubinsky. "All the help was interviewed first off. Just a minute—I'll get it."

"Okay," said Dubinsky five minutes later. "The chauffeur was interviewed the day after Neilson was killed—"

"Who by?"

"Pat Kelleher. Here it is: 'I drove Mr. Neilson to the office at ten-thirty, and we got there at eleven-fifteen. At twelve-thirty I drove him to lunch and picked him up again when he called. That was at one forty-five. I drove him to the Karlsbad Hotel. He didn't need me to come get him. I was supposed to pick up the kid from school instead. I often did this when Mrs. Neilson was busy.' And that's all there is. Not very informative, is it? And no mention of any suitcases."

"I want to talk to that chauffeur. And send someone over to the hotel to find out what's in those damned suitcases."

*   *   *

Sanders walked into the interview room and was met by a lazy stare from the tall man lounging by the table. "Joe Cassidy, Neilson's driver," said the constable tersely. "You want me here?"

"Don't bother. Ed's on his way. Okay, Mr. Cassidy. What else happened the day Neilson died that you didn't bother putting in your statement?" He dropped the offending document on the table. "Besides the carful of suitcases."

"Suitcases?" His voice quivered with contemptuous wonder. "What about them? Mrs. Howard packed the suitcases, like she always does—"

"So Mr. Neilson did take luggage with him when he went to Florida?" asked Sanders with a touch of muted triumph. So much for Miss Cavanaugh. "Those were his suitcases?"

"Huh? Yeah. Of course. And the kid's. He was going, too."

"Did Mrs. Neilson know about that?"

He shrugged. "How should I know? She wasn't around when Liz—Mrs. Howard—was doing the packing. But she sure didn't act like he was going away for a week. So maybe she didn't. What the hell, she never knew what was going on. Talk about out of it." His gesture indicated just how far off the planet his boss's wife was, in his estimation. "Anyway, I put them in the car and gave them to Len—he was on the desk—after I dropped Mr. Neilson off. He was going to take a limo to the airport and I was supposed to bring the kid. From school."

"So how come you never took the kid to the airport?" said Dubinsky.

"They called me and told me not to."

"Who called you?" asked Sanders.

"I dunno. Someone from the office called on the car phone."

"And you didn't check?"

"Why the hell should I? Mr. Neilson was always changing

his mind. And the call had to come from the office. No one else knew the car phone number. Mr. Neilson never gave it out to people. So I just went and got Mark at three-thirty and took him home. I never thought about those suitcases, though. I should've gone back and gotten them."

"And why in hell didn't you admit all this to the officer who interviewed you?" asked Sanders, irritated. "It might have helped."

"Why should I? He never asked."

That hour was one of the most nerve-racking of Lucas's life. Twice they passed a patrol car and were unable to tell whether they had been noticed or not. Anxiety pressed at him to speed; fear nagged at him to slow down. Either course would draw attention to them, and he drove at a steady hundred kilometers an hour through the countryside, easing back to fifty without fail for every village. At last he came to the crossroad he was looking for. There she sat, in her new red Jaguar, a scarf over her head, buffing her nails with the air of one who has all the time in the world. He pulled up behind her. "Wait here," he said to Grainne, jumped out, and began to pull their luggage from the backseat.

A tall, mink-coated vision in dark glasses and green boots stepped out of the Jag. She waved cheerfully in their direction and opened the trunk. Rob Lucas slung his bag and Grainne's duffel bag in and slammed it shut, turning back to fetch her. He lifted her, protesting, out of the front seat. "Tricia, I'd like you to meet Grainne Hunter," he said, gravely presenting her. "Grainne, my stepmother. And I don't think we'd better hang around here much longer."

"This is so exciting," said Tricia, as she put the car in gear and skidded off the shoulder at a ferocious pace. "I've never helped fugitives from justice before. What did you do?" she asked, glancing over at Grainne, who was sitting beside her in the front seat.

"She didn't do anything," said Rob, leaning forward between them. "She's just a witness. And if you don't slow down, we'll be stopped for speeding, and that'll be it as far as both of us are concerned." He slouched back down in the rear seat.

"Well, all right. And someday you'll have to explain to me in words of one syllable why it is that a policeman and someone who is just a witness are hiding from the police. Because I really don't see it. But if you say so, sweetheart, it must be true. Robin," she said, turning to Grainne again, "never tells lies. It's one of his most disagreeable characteristics. If you've been spending a lot of time with him lately, I suppose you've discovered that already. He's like what's-his-name, with the ax and the cherry tree. You ask him what he thinks of a dress, and he tells you it makes you look like a scarecrow that died last week sometime. And of course, he's always right. That's what's so awful. Anyway, I'm so glad he called me—I really am, you know," she called back to the rear seat, "because Bertie—that's my husband, Robin's father—well, Bertie's gone off to Switzerland to ski or count his money or something and left me here, and I was getting bored. What do you do?" she asked Grainne suddenly, just as she was making a rapid left turn and then a right in order to swoop onto the expressway.

Grainne shut her eyes as the car darted into a tiny space between a truck and a van, to the accompaniment of loud horn-honking. In the momentary silence, Lucas filled in, "She's a—"

"I'm a graduate student," she said firmly. "At the Faculty of Music. Opera school. I should have finished this spring, but I took a year off. I'll be going back in the fall."

"How exciting," said Tricia. "A singer. I love opera. The

only trouble with it is that Bertie keeps falling asleep—especially during Wagner. It goes on for so long, you know. And if I poke him to wake him up, then he jumps and starts applauding and everyone glares at him. Very embarrassing. Maybe you'd like to come with me instead. What a brilliant idea. Let's do it. I promise I don't hum, and I'm very careful not to applaud in the wrong places, and we have absolutely wonderful seats."

"Tricia," said Lucas. It was a warning growl, a grimness in his voice that Grainne hadn't heard before. "Shut up and stop harassing Grainne. She's been through enough already."

"She's not harassing me," said Grainne. "Offering me a ticket to the opera hardly constitutes harassment."

"That just proves how innocent you are. Survive that, and she'll start asking you to family parties—"

"And knitting? Are you the person who knits?"

"That's me," said Tricia, changing lanes to pass a truck on the left, two cars on the right, and then another truck on the left. "I love knitting, and Bertie hates thick wool sweaters. They make him itch, he says. And they're too hot. So I knit for Robin. I keep hoping my little sister will get married and have some children—then I can shower them with booties and little sweaters with bears on them. And, Robin, speaking of sweaters, there's a sweatshirt back there. Fold it up and put it under Grainne's head. She might as well take a little nap while we're getting there."

"Are you sure?" asked Harriet, looking up at the stuccoed front and blinking neon sign that announced the restaurant La Celestina. "I didn't realize they actually served food here. Isn't it one of those places where you rent a plastic hamburger to leave on your table in case the dive gets raided?"

"You're hopelessly out of it, Harriet. No one does that anymore. I can guarantee that there really is lunch, cooked by a real live chef, and served by real waitresses with sore feet and at least three kids each. Anyway, we have no choice. I told Dubinsky to meet us here."

Addie greeted them with muted warmth. "Morning, Inspector," she said. "You here to eat or ask questions?"

"Eat, mostly," said Sanders. "We're expecting my partner. If you happen to notice him, send him over."

"He's hard to miss. By the way, what in hell did you say to Randy?" she asked, leading them to a quiet table in the corner. "Tips doubled over the weekend. You must've put the fear of God in him."

"I think he's just considering the error of his ways," said Sanders. "We'll have an Amstel. Each, that is. And what's worth eating today?"

Harriet watched until Addie was out of earshot and turned to John. "What was the waitress talking about?"

"Oh, that. Randy was skimming tips. We just sort of prodded him, that's all. Nothing much. He seems to scare easy. It's nice Addie's getting her money."

"He's the bookkeeper."

"Right. And if cash is being skimmed wholesale out of this operation, Randy has to know about it."

"Is cash being skimmed? And why does he have to know about it? Maybe he just keeps everything straight from this end—so much coming in every day, so much going out in food and heat and light and salaries and whatever. He hands the balance over. And then Neilson gets his hands on it and grabs a huge chunk instead of putting it in the bank. Easy. And so poor little Randy is innocent of anything— except cheating Addie and the rest of them out of their tips, of course," she added uneasily.

"Right. Skim tips today, skim entire operations tomorrow. Anyway, he used to be a big-time embezzler. And I want to know why Neilson hired him. Would you hire an embezzler to do your books and handle all the cash from a profitable operation? No, you'd have to be crazy. But he wanted someone with experience. In fraud. One question is, did he want Randy because he could recognize fraud? Or perpetrate it? The other one is, when you hire a crocodile to protect you, how do you keep it from eating you first? Which leads me to wonder if Neilson had something very big on him, to keep him in line." He waved in the direction of Ed Dubinsky, who was threading his way through the tables in their direction. "And that makes me wonder what Randy was doing on the afternoon that Neilson was killed."

"Was Neilson a blackmailer?" asked Harriet. "Along with everything else?"

Sanders nodded.

"Who was he blackmailing?" asked Harriet. "That you know of?"

Sanders opened his mouth and suddenly thought of the pictures of Lydia—Harriet's friend Lydia—in bed with two men and a boy. But Dubinsky and Addie arrived simultaneously, saving him from having to answer. Sanders turned to Addie as she handed his partner a menu. "Was Randy here the afternoon Mr. Neilson was murdered?"

Addie paused for a moment. "Sure. Well, most of the time, as far as I know. He was here at lunchtime, and then he must have gone out for a while. Couldn't tell you when. I only remember because Mr. Horvath was looking for him that afternoon. There was a major screwup on the ordering, and we needed him. I called the office, and they didn't know where he was—maybe doing something for Mr. Neilson. We even thought about closing. Not because of Mr. Neilson's death or anything. No one gave a damn about Mr. Neilson," she added, lowering her voice, "but because we'd run out of stuff, head office was going crazy, and we needed authorization to buy emergency supplies. The chef was ready to quit."

"But you opened."

"Yeah. The chef went into the till, took all the cash, and sent the busboy out to a supermarket. Problem solved. Horvath worries about doing everything according to procedure. You know. Randy got back in time to straighten things out anyway." She paused. "I don't know what was going on at head office earlier, but it can't have been because of Mr. Neilson. They called Randy to let him know what happened just before we opened. Between five and five-thirty."

"So Randy was in and out. How about Mr. Horvath?"

Addie looked shocked. "Mr. Horvath was here all day. He's always here. Except when he was out shopping with the busboy, of course. But no—he was here."

Sanders looked over at the impeccable elegance of the manager and wondered. "Have the corned beef sandwich, Ed," he said gloomily. "It's Monday, the chef's hung over, and the goulash didn't turn out."

"Okay—and a beer," he said to Addie's retreating back. "According to Miss Cavanaugh, no one called the chauffeur and told him not to pick up Mark Neilson. The only people who ever dealt with the chauffeur—who even knew the telephone number—were Cavanaugh, that bitchy receptionist, a person they called the office manager, and maybe Randy West. I got that same story from everyone, by the way. But remember, the chauffeur wasn't sure, but he thought probably it was a woman who called. I asked all of them, including West, and they all said that it was the last thing on their minds when they found out about Neilson's death. Which, by the way, wasn't until just before five. And the chauffeur must've gotten that call before three-thirty, when school gets out, or he would have driven Mark Neilson to the airport when he picked him up. And before three-thirty, we didn't even have the identification of the corpse. So that call—if it existed—came from whoever shot Carl Neilson."

"Where does that leave us?"

"Okay. No one called the chauffeur, no one around this place was thinking of anything but food, and no one at the office knows anything about anything. That leaves us with Mr. Neilson, or Lucas's girl in the apartment. She seems to me to be the likeliest candidate. She was there, her prints are all over the place, her prints are all over the other girl's apartment, and she's disappeared with one of the investigating officers."

"And where is he?"

"Dead," said Dubinsky flatly. "Probably didn't expect any girl to be that dangerous. Nice guy, but he had his limitations, you know. No respect for the power of women."

"Then who called the chauffeur?"

"No one. The chauffeur and the girl are in it together. He probably picked her up lots of times, got to know her. That's where the weapon's gone. He took it away, and as soon as he was safely gone, she called us."

"Motive?"

Dubinsky shrugged his shoulders. "Money. Probably. How do we know there wasn't another suitcase stuffed with it that he hung on to? They keep telling us Neilson's cash is disappearing—well, that's where it went."

Sanders pushed his sandwich away and picked up his beer glass. "Not very plausible."

"Why not?" asked Harriet.

"Why in hell would anyone in her right mind help to commit a murder and then, before the corpse has stopped twitching, call in a report on it? And if the girl and the chauffeur had the money, they would have disappeared together. We would never have laid eyes on either one."

"Not if they wanted to go on living in the city," objected Dubinsky stubbornly. "As soon as they took off, the whole world would be out looking for them."

"Anyway, I just can't see Lucas dead somewhere in a snowbank. Or being part of it, either. And your crazy theory doesn't take into account the report from the motel."

"If that was Lucas," said Dubinsky. "And even if he was traveling around with her for a while, all she had to do was wait until he fell asleep. We haven't had a whisper about

him for a week or two. And they're looking for him all over
the place."

"Three coffees," called Sanders in the direction of the
tired-looking waitress. "You have a point. And we'd better
start taking the chauffeur apart on that phone call."

Grainne woke up as the Jag pulled to a stop in front of a
three-story warehouse on King Street West. "Where are
we?" she asked, looking nervously around.

"When did you two meet?" asked Tricia. "It's home, sort
of. Okay, Robin, love. We're here. Any special instructions?"

"Just don't let anyone know who she is, don't leave her
alone, and don't let anyone, especially the police, into the
apartment." He leaned forward and caught Grainne by the
shoulder. "Take care of yourself. Don't call me, just in case.
I'll be in touch. You're much safer with Tricia than you are
with me right now."

Tricia got out of the car and walked around to the trunk,
opened it with elaborate care, and scuffled noisily about
inside for Lucas's suitcase.

He pressed his cheek against Grainne's. "Stay hidden,"
he said hoarsely. "I'm not sure I'd survive if anything happened to you." He let go abruptly and jumped out of the
car. Grainne turned to watch him stride casually up an alley
beside the warehouse.

"What if they're watching for him?" she asked in panicky
voice as Tricia got back in the car.

"He said it doesn't matter. But he doesn't live here. His
apartment's up on Adelaide Street. He just didn't want them
seeing this car with you in it." Tricia gave her a comforting
pat on the knee, put the car in gear and made a rapid and
heart-stopping U-turn.

Minutes later, Tricia pulled up in front of a soaring building down by the waterfront. She jumped out, tossing the

keys to the doorman. "My cousin's gear is in the trunk," she said. "Could you have it brought up?"

"Certainly, Mrs. Lucas." He didn't twitch a muscle as Tricia opened the door and assisted a woman with one boot on and the other in her hand up the stairs and into the building.

The elevator took them directly to the top floor. Grainne limped into a huge apartment and sat gratefully down on an enormous chesterfield that gave her a view of the lake; Tricia tossed her coat onto a chair and sat down near her. "It's getting late," she said. "We'll have some lunch, and then we'll put you to bed for the time being. You look very tired." She turned and called over her shoulder. "Mrs. Henderson."

An efficient-looking woman in a white uniform appeared in the doorway. "Yes, Mrs. Lucas?"

"Something nice for lunch for my cousin as soon as you can manage it, please. And would you call Mrs. Kovacs and say that I am much too ill to attend the meeting this afternoon? I think we should put Miss Hunter in the small bedroom—it's quiet and cheerful. She'll be staying for a few days." As soon as she left, Tricia turned back, kicked off her shoes, and curled herself up in the corner of the chesterfield. "I'm so glad Robin called me," she said. "It's not easy being a stepmother to someone who's practically your own age, you know. This is the first time he's ever let me do anything for him."

"Except knit him sweaters," said Grainne. "It's a beautiful sweater. He let me borrow it once when I was very cold."

Tricia laughed. "You can't mother someone who's twenty-eight, can you? I've tried treating him like any other male friend, but that doesn't seem to work, either. So I knit."

Just as Grainne was opening her mouth to explain to Mrs. Lucas how her stepson viewed her offers of friendship, a heady smell of rich soup drifted in from the dining room and wisdom prevailed. "That smells wonderful," she said. "I'm absolutely starved."

"No, he can't call me back. I'll call him later." Rob Lucas slammed the telephone receiver down. He looked at his watch. One-thirty. The bored voice at the other end of the line had told him that Inspector Sanders had gone to Freyfields to interview Mrs. Neilson "a little while ago." He tapped his thumb against his upper lip and considered his options. Was it worth driving out to Freyfields on the chance that Sanders would still be there, and could be reasoned with, before this whole thing got even more desperately out of control? It was risky. He had borrowed Kelleher's name to make the call, but his voice on the telephone had probably been recognized. Someone in the department was probably figuring out right now what Lucas was likely to do, and would turn up at the estate to pick him up. But as long as Lucas had an opportunity to talk to the inspector first, it didn't matter so much. He would chance it.

But first, he needed a car. He looked uneasily at his telephone. If they were monitoring his calls . . . He slipped down the stairs, out the back entrance, and into the back door of the restaurant behind the building. "Hi, Lum," he said with his usual casualness. "A sandwich to go—anything that's fast—while I'm telephoning." He walked out of the kitchen and around to the pay phone beside the washrooms.

Tricia had no objections to lending him the Jag. "I've got Bertie's car. I really don't need two. Where shall I drop it off? And don't worry, Mrs. Henderson's here. She won't let anyone near Grainne."

Eight minutes later the Jag screeched to a halt at the corner of King and Bathurst. Tricia leapt out, leaving it running, and before Rob had a chance to say anything, she had one elegant arm in the air, flagging down a cab. " 'Bye, love," she called, as she climbed into the taxi that had miraculously appeared, "see you later."

Lydia Neilson appeared behind him as he stood in front of her door, waiting. "I thought I heard someone," she remarked. "Come on. I'm in the stable." He followed her numbly around the house, convinced that coming here was a mistake; Sanders was nowhere in sight. "Now, what do you want?" she asked, as they walked slowly around the paddock. "I was under the impression that you had murdered Carl and were on the run. If you did, by the way, you have my profoundest gratitude—but I don't suppose you've come to be thanked."

He stopped, leaning against the white fence. "Is that what they're saying about me?" he asked, unsurprised.

"According to Marty Fielding," she said. "Of course, Marty is a mine of gossip and half-truths. It doesn't do to take him seriously. But he does report what people are saying—he doesn't give a damn if it's true or not. You've replaced me as everyone's favorite murderer."

Lucas shook his head. "I didn't kill your husband, Mrs. Neilson, and I don't suppose you did, either, but someone thinks that I—" He was interrupted by the sound of car engines.

Lydia Neilson's head swiveled in the direction of the driveway. "Just a minute," she said, holding up a hand. She ran lightly over to the edge of the house. In a second or two she was back and reached out a hand to grab his. "Come on," she said. "To the stable."

"What?" he asked, scrambling to follow her.

"It's your friends from the police department. Two carloads of them. Perhaps they heard you were here."

"Jesus," he muttered breathlessly. "Where—"

"Into the woods," she said. "You can't get a car onto the bridle paths." She flung open the door, and the spring light flooded in on the restless figure of the enormous gray gelding. "He's ready to go—you caught me just before I took him out. You'll need boots," she said, in horror, looking at his running shoes. As she spoke, she rummaged in the tack room, appearing seconds later carrying a pair of boots and a hat. "Here, quick. They're Carl's, but they should fit well enough. As soon as you get far enough away, just dismount, hitch up the reins and give him a slap. He'll come home. He did it often enough when he threw Carl."

As her voice ran on in an urgent, breathy whisper, she was lengthening the stirrup leathers; he was pulling off his running shoes, stuffing them in his pockets, yanking on Carl Neilson's boots—a little large—and cramming the hat—a little small—on his head. "Ready," he said.

Lydia ran to the door. As soon as she opened it, a voice called out across the paddock. "Anyone home? Mrs. Neilson?"

"You'll have to mount in here. Duck as you go out. Hurry up!"

In an automatic movement he had almost forgotten, Rob grasped the saddle, settled his foot, and vaulted onto the gelding. It snorted with disapproval.

" 'Bye, Achilles," Lydia said brightly. "Show us what you can do." Her slap on the gelding's rump sent him scrambling precipitously out of the stable.

Rob's leg muscles quivered as they adjusted themselves to his mount; it had been five or six years since he had ridden, and for a few moments he felt disoriented and awkward. Then Achilles swerved and headed at a canter toward a grass-covered primitive road that ran between a meadow and woodland behind the stable. At that moment a roar of rage or excitement echoed from behind him, and even under Carl Neilson's hat and above the steady beat of Achilles' hooves, he recognized that voice. Baldwin.

The grassy track ended at the back of the meadow, where it intersected with a narrow bridle path. He had a moment of panic; there were woods in every direction. Lydia had neglected to tell him which way to go. He tried to pull Achilles up a little to give himself time to think. Then engine noise and a quick glance behind him told him that Baldwin was coming as far as he could in a car. A loud blast of the car horn, and the issue was decided. Achilles started, half reared, and took the left fork.

The path then veered sharply to the right; as Achilles rounded the bend at a canter, they were suddenly on top of a file of three novices, whose mounts were moving at a bone-crushing trot. Their riders bounced painfully with a precarious lack of connection to saddle or horse. The one in the rear had lost a stirrup; her back was already eloquent with panicked insecurity when Achilles snorted and barreled past them, crowding the three bored horses over to the verge. A howl of despair told Lucas what had happened; he reined in to make sure that he had not created a disaster and looked back in time to see Baldwin, red-faced and panting, snatch the bay mare with the awkward gait from its fallen rider and mount.

"Lucas," he yelled. "Get off that goddamn horse and come back here. You're under arrest, you bastard."

Without thinking for a moment of the consequences of his actions, Lucas bent over Achilles' arching neck and spoke into the ear that was cocked back to catch the excitement behind them. "Come on, Achilles," he murmured. "Let's move." And he dug his heels with their nonexistent spurs in the gelding's side for an instant. Achilles lowered his head, stretched out his body and broke into a fast, relaxed gallop. Lucas glanced back. The bay mare, resentful of her new and heavier burden, was resisting the invitation to race.

Suddenly up ahead he could see bright sunlight that spoke of the end of the wooded area. He cursed and looked back.

The bay mare was still behind them, although falling farther and farther back with each of Achilles' strides. The bridle path ended at a gravel road that ran off to the right, dividing the woods from farmland; to the left were woods, except for a meadow enclosed in white fencing, which had been carved out of the brush. As they drew closer, Lucas could see that the field held six or eight mares and their foals; he had a choice between the gravel road, which could carry a vehicle searching for them, and the mares. He nudged Achilles to the left and urged him toward the formidable gate. "I hope you jump as well as you run, baby," he said, and held his breath as he felt the horse consider the distance, adopt a deliberate and workmanlike pace, gather himself up, and sail over. "Beautiful, Achilles," said Lucas, patting him on the neck. "Now where?"

The gray continued his more measured stride as Lucas scanned the field. Up ahead there was another gate, leading into woodland. "Where there is a gate, there is a path, Achilles," he said. "Let's go."

They had now gathered an admiring crowd of mares, running inquisitively along with them, drowning out the noises from behind. Then, as Achilles jumped easily over the far gate, Lucas heard an indistinct and angry yell from the far side of the meadow. This time he didn't look back.

The path on the other side of the pasture joined what was evidently the same long string of paths throughout these woods. He must have missed some fork earlier in his journey while he was concentrating on Baldwin. Achilles was continuing on a steady, untiring gallop. "Easy, there," said Lucas soothingly. "No need to do yourself in. We're safe. I think we'll just mosey along here and then cool down."

Achilles turned an ear to listen, caught the tone, and slowed to a canter, then to a disciplined trot and a comfortable walk. The woods were filled with lacy sunshine, filtered through the bare-branched, budding trees, and Lucas found himself wondering whether Lydia Neilson would sell Achilles and how much she might want for him if she did. Surely she had more use for a sturdy pony that the boy could ride than for a restless gray who was over seventeen hands and needed serious exercising. His pleasant reverie was interrupted by the sound of a car driving by. He looked up, startled. Ahead, the path turned sharply to the left; the wood ended in a broad grassy ditch, and beyond it was a two-lane paved road. Lucas dismounted, rather stiffly—he was going to pay for this tomorrow, he knew—and began walking the gray gelding along the path.

It was time to think. Was it possible that the voice he had heard in the background at Homicide had been Baldwin's? Baldwin had meant him to think that Sanders was at Freyfields. Baldwin came out to the house to confront him, not to bring him in. Nobody in his senses would set out alone after someone who was suspected, in that lovely old phrase, of being armed and dangerous. Not even an old colleague. And Baldwin had left everyone else behind when he set out after him. What had he been planning to do? Get him alone, shoot, and claim self-defense? Lucas patted the weapon in his shoulder holster and reflected that he was a fool to be carrying it around. All Baldy needed to do was place it in his dead fingers and fire it once. But why out here, he wondered, and the answer came with a swiftness that horrified him.

They wanted him out of the way because he stood between them and Grainne.

If this were true, then Baldy wouldn't be around anymore, he reckoned. He might have left someone at Lydia Neilson's place for appearances' sake, but the heavy artillery would have pulled out. And that meant he could ride back toward Freyfields, leave Achilles near home to find his own way to the stable, and search for the little park by the river where he had left Tricia's car. "Come on, fella," he said, "we're going back." Achilles tossed his head impatiently and then stood as Lucas threw his stiffening leg over the gelding's back.

This time they followed the main path back. As they neared the area that bordered on the Neilsons' road, Lucas heard the rush of the small river that told him he was near the car. "This is where we part company, Achilles, my friend," he said as he dismounted. He shortened the stirrups, checked the reins, headed him in the direction of home, and gave him a little slap on the rump. Achilles started off at a trot, slowed, and looked back, puzzled; then he shook his head in an equine gesture of dismissal at the follies of mankind and set off again.

In less than five minutes, Lucas broke through the thick brush growing alongside the river and came to the small park. In summer it would be filled with tired motorists and city picnickers; on a Monday in March it was deserted. Tricia's car was waiting. He brushed the twigs off his corduroy pants and got in, anxious to go, very apprehensive of what he would find.

CHAPTER 16

Once past the pretty white-fenced farms, the road skirted an aged shopping mall, crumbling, down-at-heel and discouraged-looking, before heading into the industrialized suburbs. Rob Lucas spun the Jag into the parking lot and headed for the pay phone. With fumbling hands, he dialed his father's number, was reminded by a mechanical voice that his call was long-distance, swore at the seconds lost, and started all over again.

"What's happened?" he asked as soon as he heard Tricia's voice. His words were strangled with worry.

"Happened? Nothing. We had lunch, and we talked, and Grainne's taking a nap. Is something wrong? You sound out of breath."

"Oh, God." He sagged against the wall of the booth in relief. "I was sure they'd found her."

"Well, they haven't. Whoever they are. And I certainly wouldn't have let them in if they had. Have a little faith, Robin. We're very comfortable and cozy. We're going to eat and watch a couple of movies. Nothing to worry about. And, Robin—"

"Mmm?" He barely heard her over the roar of panic subsiding in his head.

"She's awfully nice. If you don't mind my saying so. And very attractive, although she's terribly thin and does need some clothes—"

"You're not taking her shopping, Tricia," he yelled. "And

you're not leaving her alone while you go off, either. She doesn't need clothes. She's not going anywhere."

"Relax, sweetheart. I'm not going to leave her alone. Will you be here for dinner?"

"Better not. I'll call you as soon as I know anything. And—"

"Yes. I'll look after her. Bye-bye." And the click cut him off. As he stepped out of the booth, a woman waiting to use the phone gave him a very curious look.

Rob turned north from King Street, pulled into the network of alleyways behind his apartment building, and left Tricia's car in the cramped parking area beside the rear door. Although only the ground floor contained offices, the structure was not residential, technically. For this reason, certain conventions were observed for the benefit of city inspectors, who would otherwise be forced to acknowledge that the illegal second- and third-floor apartments were not used for warehousing, or as design lofts. The underlit and badly maintained halls, for example. And the absence of a buzzer system. Or security. If you liked space and valued privacy, the arrangement was ideal. Lucas liked it.

As he ran up the broad staircase to the third floor, he was aware of twinges that were going to turn into stiffened legs tomorrow. Terrible to let himself get that far out of shape, he thought cheerfully, pulling out his keys. From now on, everything was going to be different.

It was the light from the open refrigerator door that stopped him in the doorway, catching his attention first.

His kitchen was neatly arranged in the windowless corner to the left of the entrance. The counter that formed the barrier between the kitchen and the rest of the apartment had been knocked over; it was surrounded by broken dishes and glassware. Long, pale splinters caught the light where the screws anchoring it in its place had been wrenched out of the broad floorboards. His filing cabinet lay on its side, its contents scattered across the floor. Every drawer—desk, cabinet, wardrobe—had been dumped. Not the result of a frantic search, he concluded. Just someone amusing himself, that was all. Someone who hated him. Someone who had taken the trouble to break in and had discovered that there was no one in the apartment. He walked over and closed the refrigerator door, and then bent and picked up a wine-glass that had miraculously escaped the carnage.

"Sort of messy, eh?" said a voice behind him.

Lucas jumped and turned around. Framed in the doorway he had left so invitingly open stood two uniformed consta-bles, their faces blank, uninterested. "Yeah. It is," said Lucas casually. "Did you guys do it?"

"Us? Hell no," said the other one. "Not our style. Any-way, we were sent over to bring you in, Lucas. Sorry."

The first man's hand rested on his weapon, already released from the confinement of its holster. Rob spread his arms peacefully in an outward gesture. "It's under my jacket," he said.

John Sanders stretched out his legs and accepted a beer with a sigh of deep relief. The afternoon had been maddening. Cassidy, the chauffeur, had not been amenable to dissection; he was, by turns, hostile, bored, and then irritated by ques-tioning but devoid of incriminating responses. Yes, he had met Neilson's friend Annie, and thought she was a scrawny, stuck-up bitch who could use a few sharp lessons. Which Neilson had given her, he was glad to say. Otherwise he had no opinions. He did what he was told, he said; that's what he was paid for. And no one confessed any of their secrets to him—he was just the chauffeur. Dubinsky insisted he was a clever bastard, clever enough to disguise a relation-ship with Annie; Sanders was not so sure. In the end, a painstaking search had turned up nothing of any interest in Cassidy's apartment at Freyfields.

Lucas had called in from a Toronto number, disproving Dubinsky's theory that he was dead, and had disappeared again. Then Harriet had disappeared. That was the final blow. Harriet's disappearance had been temporary, fortunately, and here he was, in her apartment, surrounded by greasy and sticky cartons of Chinese food, allowing himself to be supplied with plates, glasses, napkins, and other unnecessary amenities.

"Where were you?" he asked. "I've been calling you since four o'clock. Every fifteen minutes."

Harriet sat down beside him, reached into a container of shrimp with acquisitive chopsticks, and grabbed the largest one. "I was drinking soda water with a lecherous architect at the Park Plaza," she said. "About a job. I only meet him in public places. It's safer. Here, have a shrimp, Inspector—they're wonderful."

Sanders heaped rice, shrimp, chicken, pork, and vegetables onto a plate and settled back. He waited a minute for the hot, the sour, and the fish-salty sauces to penetrate the rice and then picked up a fork, took one mouthful of the resulting mixture, and put the fork down again.

"Something wrong?" asked Harriet. "You're not actually upset about that architect, are you? Because—"

John laughed and shook his head. "No. I just feel I shouldn't be here, lounging around, eating shrimp—"

"From soggy cardboard boxes. You're right. I can understood how luxury like this might upset you. But I'm fresh out of dry bread and stale turnips."

"It's your warmth and sympathy I love, Harriet. You must be what they mean by a supportive woman." He shook his head. "It's not that. I'm restless. My body is telling me to rush downtown and work all night, and yet I know damn well there's absolutely nothing happening. Not until we find Lucas again—and his witness. And God knows where he's gone to ground this time. So I might as well be sitting here."

"Have another beer," said Harriet unsympathetically. She put down her chopsticks and walked over to the kitchen. "Anyway, I thought you had more leads than that." Her voice was slightly muffled as she rooted around in the refrigerator. "Who wanted to kill him?"

"Lots of people," said Sanders. "The line forms to the right. He was cheating his business partners. Of course, we don't know who they were, so that's not a helluva lot of help. Someone he injured could have killed him—that girl in his apartment, for example. Lucas said she was bruised and beat-up–looking. Or—"

"Or Lydia," said Harriet, handing him an open bottle.

"Well, yes. Lydia." He paused, concentrating on pouring his beer. "How much do you know about her, Harriet? About her private life, I mean?"

"Only what I told you. She had a lover, poor thing. And I can't say I blame her, considering what Neilson was like."

"Just one lover?"

"What do you mean, just one? I don't know what impression of her you picked up, but she isn't some wild, free spirit who sleeps with everyone she meets. She's actually rather conventional, in spite of the lover."

"You wouldn't expect to find her at an orgy, then?"

"*Lydia?* At an *orgy?*" Harriet stared in disbelief. "You're kidding."

"We have some rather interesting pictures of Lydia," said Sanders. "Not suitable for publication, you might say," he added evasively. "And she has a story, a rather thin story, about being drugged and kidnapped at a huge birthday party Neilson gave for her. The trouble is, no one has even heard of this birthday party. All the people connected with Neilson—office personnel, restaurant employees, the housekeeper, the chauffeur—claim that Lydia never went to any of his parties, ever. The office and restaurant people have never even seen her."

Harriet frowned in concentration. "Where was this alleged party?"

"At La Celestina. Three or four years ago. Nobody there remembers a huge party then. They claim she's never set foot in the place."

"Well, it's not true. She did. But that wasn't an orgy," said Harriet almost primly. "It was a perfectly respectable costume party."

"You were there?"

"Of course I was. We were still friends at that point. Dressed as a clown, fittingly enough. Lydia was something classical, I think. A nymph, maybe." She paused to stretch and scratch her earlobe. "Come to think of it, poor Lydia got smashed, and when the birthday cake and presents came out, no one could find her. Neilson oozed about, apologizing and looking embarrassed. I'd forgotten that. So he couldn't have been whisking her away and— But then, he didn't do his own dirty work, did he?"

"No, I don't suppose he did. Dammit," he added, "I should have asked you about all this before."

"Exactly. Why didn't you?"

He shrugged. "Well, those pictures made it all a bit awkward. And besides, it never occurred to me that you were at the party. Do you remember anything else about it?"

"It was on April Fools' Day. That was why I went as a clown. I remember that. Her birthday was actually on the second." She stared off into the distance. "And I assumed she was drunk because when I went up to wish her happy birthday, she was hanging on to a couple of guys—I thought at first that one of them was the mysterious lover. She could have been drugged, though. She had that vague, spacey look. They sort of elbowed me aside and dragged her off. Out of the dining room somewhere."

"Dragged her off?" said Sanders. "Unwillingly?"

"Hard to tell. But there was something—now I remember. They called her Mrs. Neilson; that was what was strange. Like employees, not friends. And certainly neither one was like a lover. Want some coffee?"

"Just a minute," said Sanders, reaching for the telephone.

"A lot of things were happening at the restaurant in April," he said when Harriet returned with two mugs of coffee. "A few days after that party there was a murder in the alley behind it, and it came in for a lot of scrutiny and bad publicity. That was probably when Neilson upgraded the place. New staff and so on. Would you remember the men who dragged Lydia away if you saw them again?" he asked.

"I'm not sure. Possibly."

"Well, then, my love, prepare yourself for a happy day looking at mug shots tomorrow. Maybe we can find some of Neilson's associates and pals after all."

Matt Baldwin set the telephone receiver down and leaned back in his chair. Patrick Kelleher stood, stiff and uneasy, next to the door; Eric Patterson sprawled gloomily in a chair pushed back against a file cabinet. "He isn't home," said Baldwin. "And he hasn't responded to his call."

"Probably turned the damn thing off," said Patterson. "After all, he's human. Well, if we can't get Sanders to come and talk to him, maybe he'll say something to me."

Baldwin paused a second and then jerked his head in the direction of the interview room. Patterson rose quietly and left.

"Hi, Rob." Patterson's voice was calm. It was always calm. "What are you playing at? If you don't mind my asking. Because you get too cute, and they'll charge you with murder."

"Whose murder?" asked Lucas. They were his first words in two hours.

"Neilson's. And the witness's. I can't do much about Neilson—after all, he's lying on a slab in Grenville Street. Someone killed him. But it would help one whole heap if you'd produce the girl. Everyone's convinced she's under a snowbank somewhere."

"Not much left in the way of snowbanks," said Lucas. "Sorry, Eric. But before I start talking, I have one or two little things I want to say to Inspector Sanders. That's all."

"They can't raise him," said Patterson. "It could be a long wait."

"That's okay. I could use some sleep." And Rob Lucas stretched out in the chair he was seated on and closed his eyes.

John Sanders had stopped, rigid, in the middle of taking off his raincoat. "Lucas is here?" he said. Dubinsky nodded. "Since yesterday?" Ed nodded again. "When did you find out?"

His partner looked at his watch. "One minute and four seconds ago. I called. You had left. They said," he added, drawling his disbelief, "that they couldn't reach you. And it didn't occur to them to try me."

"Christ almighty! More of Baldwin's tricks." He threw his coat over a chair and started for the door. "Sometime he's going to try to get the jump on all of us once too often. Where is he? Lucas, I mean."

Lucas was sitting in the interview room, tousled and unshaven, but remarkably clear-eyed and awake. "Who can hear us?" he asked as soon as Sanders, still white-faced with rage, took his place at the table.

"Hear us? In here? No one. You think I'm wired or something?" He spread open his suit jacket in an impatient gesture of proof. "See?"

"That doesn't prove much," said Lucas, his voice so low that Sanders had to lean forward to pick up what he said.

"But don't strip. I'll take your word for it. I am sorry to make all this fuss," he continued softly, "but you're the only person who was out of town—far out of town—when Neilson was killed and when Jennifer Wilson was killed. I realize that's not a guarantee, but right now I have to trust someone."

"What in hell are you talking about?"

"Let me explain to you what has been happening." And Lucas's quiet, steady voice went on and on, setting out the string of events, enumerating the coincidences, until he came to his reasons for hiding out in the woods.

"If you're so sure of all this, what made you come back?"

"We had to. I think they're convinced they won't be safe until they get rid of her, even though she can only identify them by voice. They have a point. Her identification wouldn't be worth much in a jury trial, but once you know who they are, it'll be easy to find better evidence. Or they may think she saw them. Anyway, we can't spend the rest of our lives hiding. And she knows a fair amount of detail that should help in the investigation. Like, Neilson was expecting delivery of cash—a lot of cash—at the apartment; that's why he let his murderers in. The money must be somewhere, and you might be able to trace it."

"Is she sure of that?"

He nodded. "It was something Neilson said to her. About his pension being delivered that afternoon."

"Where is Miss Hunter now?"

He shook his head. "She's safe."

"For chrissake, Rob, I have to talk to her."

"No. Somebody here, some guy maybe standing out there in the hall right now listening, murdered Neilson. And killed Jennifer Wilson. And injured Grainne."

"Who?"

"I don't know." He looked very young and helpless. "The only person I can think of," he said, lowering his voice even further, "is Baldwin. He got my reports. He was the one who wanted to keep the investigation contained, to run every aspect of it himself. He sent me out to Neilson's place yesterday. It was crazy, the way he was doing things. If you think about it."

Sanders suddenly felt very tired. "Shit," he muttered, jumped up, and threw open the door. "Dubinsky!" he roared.

"No," said Lucas frantically. "Don't tell anyone else. Not yet."

"I can't do anything without help. And if I can't trust Ed, I can't trust anyone. Even myself. You're sure it's someone in the department?"

"Or a friend of someone in the department."

The door opened. "Yeah?"

"Who worked on that case—the one that involved Neilson? You know—the murder of the hooker in the alley behind his restaurant."

"Baldwin and Patterson."

"No. Not just them. Everybody. I want the name of anyone who could possibly have talked to Neilson around the time of the investigation. And when you've got that, get an ID shot of everyone on the list. No matter who they are. And then call Harriet, apologize to her very carefully for me, and take the pictures over to her place. She knows about it. Sort of. Thanks." He turned back to Lucas. "Now, your witness. You can't keep her hidden under a bed somewhere forever. You may think she's safe, but I'd be willing to bet that thirty minutes over coffee with a couple of your pals and a quick look through your file, and I'd find her. She's at an apartment belonging to a friend or relative you trust—right? So I'd check with parents, cousins, aunts, uncles—not really hard to find if you go about things carefully. It's better for us to get there first."

A distant pounding lingered in Grainne's ears. It took her a measurable length of time to orient herself—to the silky covering, the darkened room, the crisp sheets, the dying odor of expensive perfume. The pounding continued, and then she knew that it existed in the real world, not in some dream or nightmarish vision. She had been heavily, dizzily asleep, but fear rapidly cleared her head. She sat up.

Tricia's lazy voice drifted in through the door. "Who is it, Mrs. Henderson?"

"It's a policeman, madam." Mrs. Henderson sounded cool and unperturbed. "He'd like to talk to you."

Grainne drew the warm comforter to her chest like a shield and listened intently. "Ask him to wait outside, please." The lazy voice had developed a sharp edge. She heard the click of narrow heels on the parquet floor. Now the conversation dropped to a distant murmur, and she could no longer distinguish what was going on. Finally, Tricia Lucas's voice rose enough for her to catch the words. "Not a chance. Not without a warrant. Now if you would just step back, I'd like to close the door." There was another pause, during which Grainne heard nothing but faint background noise. Then Tricia Lucas's voice, shaking with anger, rose again. "Mrs. Henderson. Call Thomas and Thomas. Button five." The wall shook as the heavy front door smashed open against the foyer wall.

Grainne was off the bed and half-running toward the door on the far side of the room. It was a bathroom. A bathroom with one door and a skylight, in an apartment that was twenty-four stories above the surface of Lake Ontario. She was trapped. Destined, she thought wryly in spite of her fear, to cower forever in bathrooms. She looked about for some avenue of escape, some place to hide, but this room was not equipped with woman-size shelving. She headed back into the bedroom.

They were almost at the apartment building when the call came. An uncertain, guilt-ridden Rob Lucas, shaved and tidied up, and John Sanders. The call was from Thomas and Thomas, barristers and solicitors to the rich, furious that their client, Mrs. Bertram Lucas, had had her apartment door forced open a few moments ago by a police officer without a warrant.

"Oh, God," said Lucas, turning ash-gray. "You were right. They're after Grainne."

A patrol car, lights flashing, pulled up ahead of them in front of the apartment building. "That's fast," said Sanders to the two constables as they jumped out. "Who sent you?"

"Building security. There's been a break-in on the penthouse floor."

All four men raced for the front door. The concierge flung it open and rushed toward the open door of the elevator. "Oh, hello, Mr. Lucas," he said politely, mindful of all his duties. "But you don't have to worry. It's the Schneidermanns' apartment. I locked the elevators, in case," he added. "And so maybe someone should stay down here by the stairs." Sanders nodded at one of the constables.

When they arrived at the penthouse level, they were met by Tricia Lucas, standing in the open door to her apartment, in silk-embroidered dressing gown and high-heeled bedroom slippers, perfectly made-up, and absolutely furious. Leaning against the wall outside the apartment, was Eric Patterson, smiling in his ironic, self-deprecating way.

"Hi, Rob, old boy," he said. "Inspector. Nice to see you."

"What in hell is going on here?" Sanders glared at Patterson.

"This man forced his way into my apartment, damaging the door and the wall as he went," Tricia snapped, pointing a long, perfect finger in the direction of his chest.

"Acting on information received—" Patterson's voice began its professional drone.

"Without a warrant—"

"From whom?"

"A source," said Patterson. "I got a tip that the witness

we were searching for was in this apartment." He shrugged
his shoulders and smiled. "So I didn't have time to grab a
judge and get a warrant. What else is new? But I couldn't
find her."

"Which is breaking and entering, as far as I'm concerned—"

"Look, I'm sorry about the door, lady. But you were
being damned uncooperative."

"Excuse me, Officers," said the concierge for the fourth
time.

"What now?" Sanders was getting tired of the demanding
little voice.

"I don't know what's going on at the Lucases', but it was
the Schneidermanns' apartment that was broken into." His
voice throbbed with desperation. "And I don't know how,"
he added, "because no one went up to the penthouse this
morning but this man, and the only staircase up to the roof
is monitored all the time, and there was no one on it this
morning. I'll open the door for you, but I'm not going in.
I'm not getting killed."

Before he had finished, the elevator chimed discreetly.
Everyone turned as the ornamented brass doors slid apart
and a red-faced Matt Baldwin stepped out, followed by a
much paler Patrick Kelleher.

"Hello, Matt." Sanders raised a hand in greeting. "What
brings you here this morning?"

"You won't need me, then?" said Patterson.

"Stick around," said Sanders. "I'll be with you in a
minute."

"Do you mind?" said the concierge, his voice rising to
a near shriek. "Anything could be going on in there."
And with a flourish of his keychain, he opened the
Schneidermanns' door. Absolute quiet billowed out of the
apartment. The six men, Sanders and Lucas, Baldwin and
Kelleher, Eric Patterson and the uniformed constable—
followed by Tricia Lucas, who had never seen the inside of

the Schneidermanns' apartment and was not going to miss the chance now, burglar or no burglar—moved with only a faint swish of shoe leather toward the living room.

And there, sitting huddled on the chesterfield, wearing a warm nightgown belonging to Tricia and a wool dressing gown belonging to Rob Lucas, sat Grainne Hunter, staring fixedly at the procession. As soon as Rob came around the corner, she leaped to her feet like a nervous cat and took one step in their direction.

A voice rang out in the enormous room. "Watch it! She has a gun."

Kelleher yanked his weapon out and raised it just as Lucas threw himself at the man's arm on its upward swing. The noise of a shot smashed through the room; Grainne's arms flew to her chest, and she rolled onto the floor. At almost the same moment, Ed Dubinsky stepped in the doorway and grabbed Kelleher's wrist, clutching it in a grip so massive that his fingers splayed helplessly. The weapon fell to the floor with a small clatter. Dubinsky bent down and scooped it up with his other hand. Grainne lay without moving.

Lucas was on his knees beside the fallen girl. As he wrapped his arms around her, she opened her tightly shut eyes, smiled tentatively, and tried to move her arms away from her chest, hampered somewhat by Lucas's ferocious grip. "I hate loud noises," she whispered.

"My God, darling, I thought you were dead," said Lucas.

"No, just getting out of the way. It seemed like a good idea at the time." Her voice faded away to the faintest of whispers and she began to tremble violently.

"What in hell is going on?" asked Patterson. Dubinsky had released his grip, and Patrick Kelleher was rubbing his wrist. "Does she have a gun on her? Who saw it, anyway?"

"I don't know," said Kelleher angrily. "I thought it was Inspector Sanders."

There was silence. Sanders shook his head. "Does she, Lucas?" he asked. "Have a gun in her pocket?"

"My pocket, sir, actually," said Lucas, one arm still holding her firmly by the shoulders while he patted the two roomy pockets of his dressing gown with the other. He shook his head. "Who was it said that Grainne had a gun?" he asked.

An awkward hush fell across the group, separating it into a collection of uneasy individuals. Dubinsky glanced around impatiently and then pulled Sanders over to the door, talking all the while. Matt Baldwin stepped back, his eyes flickering rapidly from person to person, until he allowed his gaze to rest finally on Rob Lucas and Grainne Hunter.

"I want that woman—" he started.

Sanders nodded to his partner, and moved over until he was right next to Baldwin's right ear. "Look, Matt," he whispered, "we have a potentially explosive problem here."

"Explosive?"

"Yeah. One of us is going to have to get Kelleher and Patterson out of here and downtown. Get them to write some sort of reasonable report on this. Otherwise, you know what's going to happen. Jesus, look at this place. Willful damage. There's a hole in that goddamn Persian rug from Kelleher's weapon. Cost a fortune to fix it. Maybe even unlawful discharge of a firearm. And Patterson. Breaking into the apartment next door, all that damage. And the other one can stay and try to straighten things out with Mrs. Lucas there. She looks mad as hell."

As Sanders's voice droned softly on, Baldwin's expression changed. "Good idea," he muttered. "I think I'd better go with Kelleher and Patterson, though. They're my responsibility, after all."

"I suppose they are," said Sanders, as though this was the first time the idea had occurred to him. "Well, I'll stay and tackle the lady."

"What about Lucas and that woman?"

"Don't worry, I'll take care of them."

With an impatient nod, Baldwin summoned up his two problems and stalked out of the apartment. They were followed closely by the constable from the break-and-enter detail, who was not anxious to wait around for any potentially awkward repercussions. Sanders turned quickly to Grainne Hunter. "John Sanders, Miss Hunter. Now, what can you tell us?"

Grainne sat down on the couch again, hunched forward, every muscle taut. "The person who shouted," she whispered, "the one who said, 'She has a gun,' he was one of the men who killed Neilson."

"Who was it?" asked Sanders, looking around. "I wasn't sure."

"I was in the hall," said Dubinsky. "I couldn't tell."

"Neither could I," said Lucas. "I assumed it was Baldwin, but now—I don't know. It could have been any of them. Are you sure, Grainne?"

She nodded. "Positive."

"What about the other one, then?" said Sanders. "You said there were two, didn't you? Did you hear him?"

"This morning? No. And he's hard to miss. He has a really distinctive voice. High-pitched but raspy. Like a tenor with screwed-up vocal cords. Anyway, he's too short to be any of the gang that came in here."

"Shit!" said Dubinsky, who had been listening intently. He grabbed the Schneidermanns' phone. "Get me Collins," he barked into the receiver.

"By the way, what are you doing in here?" asked Sanders. "We were expecting to find you next door."

Splotches of color appeared in Grainne's cheeks. "Oh. Well, when I woke up this morning, I heard Tricia arguing with a policeman. I figured he was looking for me, and so I climbed out of the bedroom window onto the roof, and came around here. They have a Japanese garden," she said, pointing to the floor to ceiling draperies. "I borrowed a rock and smashed a hole in the French window. It's not a very secure system for an expensive apartment," she added. Her tone was censorious.

"It could be worse," said Sanders. "You set off the alarm and collected a lot of police protection."

"And I'm starved," she added plaintively. "I haven't had any breakfast. I didn't like to use their kitchen, somehow."

"Well, take Sergeant Lucas back next door with you and get yourself some breakfast," said Sanders. "We're off."

"Will she be . . ." Rob Lucas's voice trailed off in an unasked question.

"Safe? She should be. Safe as anyone is, anyway. See you later, Rob."

"Are you sure of this?" asked Sanders as they headed for the car.

"Yeah," said Dubinsky. "We just want to get there before they're all finished downtown, that's all. Someone will be there with a warrant."

Eight minutes later they pulled up in front of a boxy, four-story, pale yellow apartment building, surrounded by the grimy detritus of spring. Another gray-suited man slid out of a dark blue Pontiac parked ahead of them and walked back.

"You got it?" asked Dubinsky.

The newcomer patted his jacket pocket.

"Is he back yet?"

He shook his head.

"Give it to me, then. You wait here. We might need you later."

The apartment was on the top floor. The superintendent had looked at the warrant, considered the possibility that they were capable of breaking down the door, and had ridden up with them, grumbling, in the elevator. "I dunno," he said as he unlocked the door. "I could get in real trouble about this, you know. He don't like people going in his apartment. Not even to fix things. I won't be responsible," he added, in final and total rejection of the entire procedure, and left.

It was a low-ceilinged, large-roomed two-bedroom apartment with a rather grubby and old-fashioned kitchen. Buildings like it went up in thousands in the fifties and have remained, squatting in a homely fashion, in areas where it doesn't make financial sense to rip them down and replace them with even homelier structures. The two men looked around, and headed in opposite directions.

Sanders started in the bedroom, moving with an easy rhythm through a large chest of drawers, on the principle of beginning with the easy stuff. Nothing. He opened the closet and looked in jacket pockets; no better luck. Two suitcases stood upright on the shelf above. As he pulled them down, a green tweed hat, narrow of brim and countrified, fell with them. He picked it up with a grin and started for the kitchen. First blood.

A low whistle greeted him as he walked into the room. "You got something?" he asked.

Dubinsky was standing on a chair, his head in a cabinet next to the stove. "Maybe," he said, his voice muffled somewhat. "This ceiling is false. Leads into the kitchen fan, I think." He pushed up one side of the cream-colored, dirty board that formed the ceiling inside the cabinet. There was a thump as something moved. "Here," he said, "take this crap." And he began handing piles of plates down to his partner. "I need some room." Dubinsky raised the board an inch or two and began to slide it over. It moved about five inches and stopped. "Shit," he muttered, and then reached into the opening he had just created. "There it is," he said. "Or at least, there something is." And with infinite delicacy, he pulled and twisted and maneuvered until a small, elegant, dark brown attaché case with gold hinges and clasps dropped down into his hands.

Sanders had it from him before he could blink. "Locked?" he asked.

"It was," said Dubinsky, climbing down. "But it looks like someone already did a number on the lock." He shoved a pile of dirty dishes to one side and set the attaché case down on the counter, pushed in the half-moon-shaped fastenings, and opened it up.

There, lying in piles, each one fastened with a paper wrapper, was about as much neat, clean, sparkling new money as either of them could remember having seen in one place before. "A million?" said Sanders.

"Bit more," said Dubinsky in the confident tones of one who is never wrong. Suddenly he raised a warning hand. "The elevator." In a second he was lounging in the kitchen door, blocking it completely.

Sanders shifted quietly over and leaned back against the counter.

They heard the rattle of a key in the door and then furious footsteps across the living room. A disembodied voice struck Sanders's ears before the face appeared in the doorway. "What in hell do you guys think you're doing?"

"Hi, Eric," said Sanders. His voice was suspiciously mild, even conciliatory. "We needed a word with you. The super let us in."

"So I heard," said Eric Patterson, giving Ed Dubinsky a friendly push into the kitchen. He glanced at their lounging bodies and relaxed. "I must talk to him. He's not supposed to do that." Suddenly his eye fell on the pile of dishes—clean dishes—sitting on the counter beside the stove. One glance at the cupboard, its door discreetly shut again, and his hand darted into his jacket, returning furnished with a cumbersome police-issue revolver. "Move, Ed," he said. Dubinsky shifted over a foot or two, revealing the open attaché case. "I thought so. Come on, move. All the way over beside the Inspector." Patterson edged over to take Dubinsky's place, reaching back with one hand to shut the

lid on the case. Without taking his eyes off his two col-
leagues, he picked up the money and began to back slowly
out of the room. "Sorry, pals. But this is mine."

At the precise moment when the plainclothes officer
grabbed Eric Patterson in an enormous hug from behind,
Dubinsky and Sanders were flinging themselves in opposite
directions down to the floor. Patterson's bullet ricocheted
alarmingly between stove and refrigerator before coming to
its final rest peacefully under the counter. By the time the
two men raised their heads, Patterson's hands were cuffed
behind his back.

"Nicely done," said Sanders.

"We didn't have anything to worry about anyway," said
Dubinsky. "Patterson's a crummy shot. Always was."

They were interrupted by the ping of the elevator and a
light knock on the door. Dubinsky darted by Patterson and
moved swiftly and noiselessly across the living room.

The knock was repeated, louder this time.

"Listen, Patterson, you asshole. I know you're in there. I
saw you go in. You damn well better answer the door."
The voice was odd, hoarse, and high-pitched, as if the
speaker had a cold.

"Glory days," murmured Dubinsky. "A two-for-one." He
opened the door in one swift movement, reached out, and
grabbed the man standing there, first by the hair, then by
his arm. "Hi, Randy," he said. "We wanted to talk to you."

But the thin-faced bookkeeper was, for once, at a loss for
words.

CHAPTER 17

"The nurse is arranging an appointment with Allen Kresnick to look at that arm. Since broken bones aren't really my thing," said the doctor. Grainne sank into an expensive leather chair in the soothing, dark-paneled office. "It would be helpful, of course, if we could send over the original X rays. Where did you say you had it looked after?"

Grainne's eyes widened in panic. "Uh—"

"We didn't, actually," said Lucas. "As a matter of fact, I set it."

Dr. McCaul turned to him in disbelief. "You? When did you take up medicine, Rob?"

"I did a fairly comprehensive course in first aid," he said casually. "As part of my police training. Under the circumstances, it was all that could be done. I doubt if Miss Hunter remembers much about it—she had a high fever at the time."

"And you treated her for that as well."

"Sort of," he said modestly.

"That's quite a course the police department runs. And I suppose you just happened to have plaster around—" Lucas opened his mouth to speak but was cut off. "—in case you felt like doing some sculpture or something." He wrote busily as he spoke. "You're in remarkably good shape in spite of it all, Miss Hunter. You need to take it easy for a while still—eat well, build yourself up. That other problem should clear up by itself. The foot has healed beautifully. I'd like to see you in two weeks; call me if you have any

problems before that. And, Rob," he added, "restrain yourself from amateur surgery, will you?"

"What other problem, my beloved?" said Lucas.

"I'm not your beloved, and it's none of your business,"
said Grainne sharply.

"Yes, you are. I might not be *your* beloved, but you certainly are mine, and I shall cling to you like glue as long as
I possibly can. But I am willing to admit that it's none of
my business," he said humbly. "I'm getting rather arrogant
about your physical well-being, I suppose. I keep trying to
play Pygmalion, and you're nothing at all like Galatea. I
probably wouldn't like you if you were."

Hurt feelings vibrated underneath the inconsequential
talk, and Grainne winced. "Well, I can't discuss it here on
the street, anyway. Really. Take me down there," she said,
pointing to a small pastry shop a few steps below ground
level, "and buy me an espresso—no, a cappuccino—and a
huge pastry, and I'll tell you."

Grainne finished her giant-sized chocolate eclair, pushed
aside her plate, and pulled the cappuccino in its glass cup
closer to her. She began to stir the whipped cream and
chocolate shavings into it with the dedication of an artist
trying to create a smooth, perfect color. She looked up,
opened her mouth, turned pink, and stirred again.

"What is it?" asked Lucas. Vague alarms stirred in his
brain. "You're all right, aren't you? There isn't something
that he told you—"

"What do you mean?" she asked. "Are you afraid I have
AIDS or something? I don't. Neilson was terrified of infec-
tion. He took more precautions than—"

"That was the last thing on my mind," interrupted Lucas,
remembering the contents of Neilson's drawers.

"Anyway, it's less drastic than that. But along the same
lines—"

"Along the same lines?" said Lucas, puzzled. "You mean— No. I would have noticed."

"Don't be stupid," she snapped. "And try to get your mind away from whatever sexually transmitted disease course you once took. Pregnancy, you idiot—that's what we were discussing. I'm over a week late, and the thought had occurred to me that we had spent a lot of time in bed without really giving much consideration to consequences."

He picked up her hand. "Nothing could please me more," he said gravely, "as long as—"

"Well, nothing could please me less right now. I've finally reached the point where I know I can face school next year and really work and—" She paused, and her eyes filled with tears. "Would it really?" she asked. "Is that how you honestly feel? Or are you just being gallant and nice?"

"I was going to add, as long as you were pleased. But yes, that's how I feel—for God's sake, Grainne, I love you. How else would I feel?"

"Well, your Dr. McCaul says he doesn't think I am. He muttered about shock and weight loss and fever and all those things. He recommended I eat more and get healthy and come back in two weeks. Then he'll be able to tell. I think I'll have another pastry."

"Whoa," said Lucas. "We're going out for dinner in a couple of hours."

"Well, all right. I wish I had another piece of respectable clothing to put on," she said, looking down at the overlong skirt she was wearing.

"Don't let Tricia hear you say that, or she'll rush you over to Holt's and buy out the store before you can catch your breath. She's itching to give you something besides a couple of cast-off outfits. I told you my family was dangerous," he said. "Grainne, will you marry me?" he added in a rush. "And don't answer. Not unless it's a yes. Not yet."

She looked doubtfully at him and then returned to the earnest contemplation of her coffee. "Look, Robin, you know you don't mean it. Once you recover from all this shock and everything, you'll see I'm not what you thought I was. I'm a very ordinary sort of person. And I can get very edgy and irritable when I'm working. A couple of weeks of me, and you'll be looking for someone else. Why don't you wait and see how you feel in two or three months?"

Lucas burst into laughter. "You certainly aren't what I thought you were. But people never are, are they? Usually you're presented with some wonderful package, and underneath it you keep getting nasty little flashes of meanness and stupidity. But you, my love, you're hard and bitter on the outside, and then inside every layer gets more fascinating until you're down to the diamond at the core. I may even be down to the real you by now. But I'll wait, if that's what you want. How about until tomorrow?"

"Do you often go in for these flights of poetic fancy?" she asked.

He flushed. "Not that often," he said steadily. "But you won't get rid of me by embarrassing me. I'm determined when I know what I want."

"Damn it all," she said, rubbing her temple with her right hand. "I have to get ready, and I have to think. Robin, I need time to think. I'm so confused. And I must find a place of my own. As soon as I'm feeling a little more agile." She waved her cast in the air. "I can't keep drifting along, living with your stepmother, borrowing her clothes, being pampered, as though nothing mattered anymore."

"I have a nice big apartment," he said. "It's a little untidy at the moment," he admitted. "I haven't put it back together yet. You could help me—I mean, picking out new dishes and things. I hated the old ones anyway. I bought them in one of my to-hell-with-it-all, back-to-the-people moods. And there's room for a piano—even a grand, if you'd like one."

"Stop it, Robin! You're making me dizzy." She smiled to take the sting out of the words. "Take me back to the safety of your wicked stepmother's house. You know," she added, as she stood up, "your wicked stepmother is really quite—"

"I know, I know. Stop making me feel like a louse. She's not nearly as awful as I said. But wait until you meet my father. . . ."

"Is this seat taken?" Harriet's slightly mocking voice cut through Sanders's reverie. He jumped, startled, and half rose as she settled herself into place opposite him. The maître d' snapped her napkin out of the wineglass it was decorating and dropped it onto her lap. "I'll just have some of that," she said, reaching for the bottle of red wine on the table. As her hand moved, prepared to help itself, the horrified man snatched the glass away and disappeared.

"Harriet, you're going to have learn to be civilized if you eat in places like this. That's not a wineglass. You know that. It's a napkin glass," said John. "Here, have some of mine."

Harriet waved the proferred glass away. "I'll wait. Restore my credit with the waiter. Anyway, as you no doubt noticed, that was a white-napkin glass. It's important to be precise. Red-napkin glasses are a different shape." Harriet's face remained solemn, but her green eyes glinted with malicious laughter, making his heart lurch like a lovesick adolescent's. The last few days without her had seemed unbearably long.

He picked up her hand and brushed it lightly with his lips. "You won't believe how much I've missed you, Harriet. I think I got used to having you around all the time. It feels like months."

Harriet's pale cheeks turned pink; she touched his face lightly with one finger and withdrew it hastily. "Then why are we dining here in formal splendor? Instead of eating in some cheerful ethnic haunt? I realize you owe me, John— and I mean, really owe me—for solving your case for you.

How many women could recognize someone after four years from a police photograph? But this!" She waved a hand around. "Or is this a belated apology for abandoning me all week?"

His lips tightened. "For chrissake, Harriet, don't. I apologize. I know I should have called, but it's been hellish over there. And a lot of work. I'm only here because I couldn't stand it anymore."

Harriet brushed aside his complaints with a wave of the hand. "Pay no attention. I'm just bitching. Because I'm starved, and this is the kind of place that serves one minute chunk of meat decorated with two snow peas, a strip of carrot, and a teaspoon of sauce. And I haven't eaten since that Chinese food on Monday. Not properly." As she reached for John's wine, the waiter rushed over with a new glass and filled it. She raised it solemnly. *"Salut,"* she said, and tasted the wine. "This is a spectacular bottle of wine," she admitted. "What's happening?"

"Where do you want me to start? Try this—Rob Lucas invited us to dinner. He pays, his choice of restaurant. That's how it goes. And at the moment we seem to be trapped and helpless—we don't even get menus. They told me to sit here, and a bottle of wine appeared. And then you appeared. And all we need now is a loaf of bread."

"Don't look now," whispered Harriet, "but here it comes." She giggled.

Right after the basket of rolls was insinuated into the middle of the table, a pale young woman with a riot of short curly brown hair and enormous gray eyes walked unsteadily through the tables toward them. Her arm was in a grubby cast, supported and partially hidden by a black silk sling; she was swathed dramatically in more black silk, with a ruffle that started at the bust and fell to the floor on one side. She sat down and smiled uncertainly. "I'm Grainne," she said. "And you must be Harriet, because I know he's Inspector Sanders." She nodded in John's direction. "Rob is back there issuing instructions of some sort. And if I look peculiar, it's because—"

"Don't apologize. You look marvelous," said Harriet. "That's a spectacular dress."

"It's Robin's stepmother's. It's not a very good fit. And I'm sure it's not supposed to trail on the ground like that. Most of my clothes seem to have disappeared somewhere. . . ."

"You didn't seize her clothes as evidence, John, did you? That's going too far."

"We don't do things like that, do we, Rob?"

"Like what?" asked Rob Lucas as he slipped into the fourth chair.

"Like seizing all my clothes as evidence," said Grainne.

"It's a thought," said Lucas. "It would keep you from disappearing again. Much more effective than a subpoena."

The conversation was cut short by the arrival of plates on which were arranged small slices of something, decorated with a dark reddish brown sauce.

"What is it?" asked Grainne, who appeared to be torn between apprehension and curiosity.

"I hope you don't mind. I ordered ahead," said Lucas apologetically. "This way you can get what you want. It should be a partridge galantine with game sauce. Since Grainne likes red wine," he explained, rather obscurely, "and we're celebrating her return to the world. Even if she doesn't have any clothes." He raised his glass with a tentative smile.

Everyone took a hasty gulp of wine, and silence, heavy and uncomfortable, fell across the table. Grainne glanced quickly around, helped herself to a roll, and concentrated her gaze on Sanders. "I don't know about the rest of you," she remarked casually, "but I want to know what's going on. And since Rob is slung out, or suspended—"

"No, no," said Sanders hastily. "On leave, pending an inquiry. That's different."

"Whatever. He claims he knows nothing. You'll have to tell us."

Sanders picked up his wineglass and put it down again. He shrugged. "What the hell. What did you want to know?" he asked, nodding at Grainne.

"What about the policeman?" prompted Harriet.

"Patterson? Nothing. He's been sitting in a cell since Tuesday and hasn't said a bloody word to anyone—except his lawyer. He figures he's laughing as long as he keeps his mouth shut. He knows you didn't see him. That means you can't make a positive ID."

"How does he know?"

"My guess is that you looked straight at him in that apartment and didn't react. That's the only thing he's said so far. To use his words, our evidence isn't worth a pinch of shit and go ahead."

"But the money! You said that Patterson had more than a million dollars belonging to Carl and that would be proof enough," said Grainne, turning accusingly to Rob. "How did Patterson get his hands on it?" she asked curiously. "Carl was so damned suspicious of everyone."

"That was the last million or so that Neilson was able to squeeze out of the company in cash without blowing the whistle on himself," said Sanders. "Randy was supposed to deliver it to him before he left the country for good. And Patterson had it, all right," said Sanders. "And we'll get him. Randy is talking so fast, we need revolving teams to get it all down. He swears he never killed anyone— Patterson shot Neilson and the man at the cabin and wounded you," he added, counting off each one on his fingers. "And killed the Wilson girl. You're lucky the guy really is a lousy shot."

"Randy may not have killed anyone, but the poker was his idea," said Grainne and shuddered.

"Randy West has a basically nasty disposition, I believe," said Lucas, as he reached over to fill everyone's glass. "He was so annoyed at not finding Grainne in my apartment that he made a brave attempt to reduce everything in it to rubble. But he did say he was sorry," added Lucas dryly.

"Are you sure you want to sit here and listen to this?" interrupted Harriet, her voice icy with disapproval.

"No, I'm fine," said Grainne. "That all happened a lifetime ago. Anyway, Randy's probably telling the truth. He wouldn't have touched me if he'd been alone. I think. But why bother killing Carl? Aside from general humanitarian motives—for the good of mankind."

"Partly spite. Mostly to cover their tracks. Patterson seems to have been the mystery half owner of La Celestina," said Sanders. "And before that he was on Neilson's payroll as a troubleshooter. That's why he was helping Neilson with his little marital problem. Which was his big mistake," added Sanders, waving a hand in grave acknowledgment across the table, "since Harriet was able to recognize him from the costume party and give us a crucial link between him and Neilson. Pure luck for us, because Neilson almost never let his respectable or family life mix with his professional life. And that brought us to the question of how Patterson could afford to buy a half interest in the restaurant on his salary."

"Especially since he was paying twelve hundred dollars a month in child support. He used to grouse about that all the time," said Lucas.

"That, too. We've been ploughing through his financial records for days," Sanders added, "and it'll take weeks more."

"So how did he?" said Harriet. "Let me guess. He was an old school chum of Neilson's, who gave the restaurant to him in memory of happier days."

"You're close," said Sanders. "According to Randy, Neilson did give Patterson half the place."

"He did?" asked Grainne, surprised. "That doesn't seem in character—not at all. Not for Carl."

"According to Randy, it was to keep Patterson quiet."

"Blackmail?" said Grainne. "Patterson was blackmailing Carl? I love it. The biter bit. What had he done?"

"It all had to do with some poor prostitute who was beaten to death and dumped in the alley behind the restaurant," said Sanders. "Her pimp was tried for murder but got off—he claimed he was elsewhere at the time, and the jury believed him. The investigation never went any further because the team decided they'd found the murderer but hadn't managed to get a conviction. Now Randy claims that Neilson got overenthusiastic and killed this little hooker at the club one night and then called Patterson for help. Patterson took one look—there was Neilson in an upstairs room with the body of a skinny sixteen-year-old—and saw a gold mine. Randy said the death was probably an accident."

"Accident!" said Harriet in dangerous tones. "How can you accidentally beat a sixteen-year-old girl to death?"

"Randy's words, not mine," said Sanders hastily. "Patterson asked for and got half the operation in return for his help; he cleaned up the room, moved the body, and then steered the investigation away from the restaurant. It worked, too."

"So why kill the goose that lays the golden eggs?" asked Harriet. "Or did he have ambitions to run the restaurant on his own?"

"Not at all," said Sanders. "Patterson was perfectly happy. It was Neilson who was in trouble. Everything else was closing in on him. He had a lot of reasons for wanting to get out of the country. People were getting annoyed at him, and that fire and the inquiry were the last straw. He had been squirreling away money for about a year, as far as we can tell, and moving it into his operations in Florida. And for the last couple of months, he skimmed every penny out of the restaurant that he could. The place was about to fall on its face."

"Leaving Patterson with nothing?" asked Harriet.

Sanders nodded.

"That's neat. How did Patterson find out?"

"Randy told him. Randy also told him about the money in the attaché case. So they reckoned they could get rid of Neilson and split the cash."

"How much?" Grainne asked curiously.

"A million and a half or thereabouts. Neilson had already transferred several million to Miami during the last year."

"Who gets the money?" asked Harriet. "Lydia?"

"She should. It was earned more or less legitimately," said Sanders. "She'll get whatever there is. And it will be a considerable amount, I expect, once she moves all that cash out of its hiding places. She told me the other day that she's going to do what she can to reorganize Carl's businesses on a sounder and more legitimate footing, and once they're going concerns again, she'll sell everything and move farther out into the country. She said that she wanted to get away from all this corruption and evil as soon as possible. By that, I assumed that she meant her husband's corruption and evil."

"By the time she finishes cleaning up all the rot in North-sea/Baltic," said Harriet, "she'll have recovered from the entire episode. I wonder if her nameless friend is anywhere around still?" Discreet black-clad arms swooped down and removed the remains of the tournedos Henri IV, interrupting her train of thought for a moment. "But speaking of money, the thing that really startles me," she added, "is the sweet and *trusting* side to Randy West's nature, letting Patterson get his hands on all that cash." Harriet looked with sad eyes at the basket of rolls that were, at that moment, being whisked away.

"He figured that as Neilson's money man, he would be watched too closely. He couldn't hide it safely. But Patterson—who would suspect Patterson? And no one would have if you hadn't been there," he added, turning to Grainne.

"Cowering in the damned bathroom." She shook her head. "But what about that other guy?" she said, turning to Lucas. "What was his name? Bechstein? Steinway? No—Baldwin. I knew it was a piano. I thought you said he was the one who—"

Lucas reddened. "That's what I thought. It never occurred to me it could be Eric. I mean, every piece of information I had I gave to Baldwin and—"

"And Eric helped himself to it. Nothing easier," said Sanders. "Baldwin wouldn't have noticed if Eric had walked in with a shopping cart and started filling it with confidential documents. And that's one tremendous advantage to all this," he added cheerfully. "Once the inquiry is over, I'll never have to have nightmares about working under Matt Baldwin again. You won't even be able to find the closet he's stashed away in."

A tiny dish of ice cream, chestnuts, and whipped cream was set in front of each person; glasses were snatched away again and replaced. The wine steward arrived with an ice bucket and champagne, which he set up with a flourish beside Rob Lucas. As the steward started to remove the foil from the cork, Lucas addressed a quiet word in his direction. The champagne was deposited rapidly into the ice bucket, and the man melted away.

"Robin, this is obscene," said Grainne, starting to laugh. "Champagne! You're behaving like a—like a—"

"Tycoon? Playboy? Ostentatious rat?"

"Something like that. What is it in aid of? If anything."

"Oh, this is in aid of something," he said, taking a deep breath and looking her hard in the eye. "It certainly is. It's to celebrate our engagement. We are engaged, aren't we?" He stumbled slightly over the words and waved his hand in exasperation.

The muted conversation from the tables in the rest of the room served only to intensify the silence. Grainne turned scarlet. "This isn't fair," she said at last. "It really isn't. I'm so embarrassed." She buried her face in her napkin to cover her confusion. After a moment she raised her head, her eyes strangely bright, and looked over at the calmly waiting Lucas. "Oh, for heaven's sake, all right. We're engaged," she said, in a muffled voice and dropped her napkin back in her lap. But just as her natural pallor and composure were beginning to return, she looked at him again and erupted in laughter. "Is this where you drag out the diamond the size of an apartment building and make me put it on?"

"Oh, no," he said. "Nothing so vulgar." He took the rose from the tiny vase in the center of the table and handed it solemnly to her, and then turned his attention to opening the bottle of champagne.

"I feel as if I've just lived through a Victorian melodrama," said Harriet as they wandered along Bloor Street, vaguely in the direction of her neighborhood. "Did you have any idea he was going to do something that outrageous? And if you did, you might have warned me."

"Well, I asked him yesterday what he was going to do if the disciplinary hearing didn't turn out well. And he said that hearing or no hearing, he was going to quit the force, go to law school, marry Grainne, and be happy. The only problem he could see with his plan was that Grainne persisted in not believing him when he said he wanted to marry her. He said he wasn't sure if this was a ploy to get rid of him or if she really thought he proposed to everyone he met. But he didn't say he was going to stage a public declaration."

"There's a man who's used to having his own way," said Harriet. "Gorgeous or not, he'll be a handful. I would have crawled under the table if someone had done that to me."

"You're not used to standing center stage," said John. "She is. Look how quickly she recovered. Anyway, I suspect she's used to having her own way, too. They're a pair of prima donnas madly in love with each other; they'll get along very well. Don't you envy them all that happiness?"

"Why should I envy them? I'm very happy," said Harriet, leaning her head on his shoulder as they walked along. "Aren't you? Anyway, doesn't the thought of marriage terrify you? It does me. Perhaps I'm too old and too bruised for it."

"No," he said gently. "It doesn't terrify me. Not anymore. After all, it depends on who you're thinking of marrying."

ABOUT THE AUTHOR

MEDORA SALE is the author of three previous novels, *Murder on the Run* (1986), which won the Crime Writers of Canada Arthur Ellis Award for Best First Novel, *Murder in Focus* (1989), and *Murder in a Good Cause* (1990). She received her B.A. in modern languages and her Ph.D. in medieval studies from the University of Toronto. A former teacher who is now a full-time writer, she lives with her husband in downtown Toronto.